ISAAC ASIMOV'S
SF-LITE

**EDITED BY
GARDNER DOZOIS**

ACE BOOKS, NEW YORK

If you purchased this book without a cover you should be aware that this book is stolen property. It was reported as "unsold and destroyed" to the publisher and neither the author nor the publisher has received any payment for this "stripped book."

This book is an Ace original edition,
and has never been previously published.

ISAAC ASIMOV'S SF LITE

An Ace Book / published by arrangement with
Bantam Doubleday Dell Direct, Inc.

PRINTING HISTORY
Ace edition / March 1993

All rights reserved.
Copyright © 1993 by Bantam Doubleday Dell Direct, Inc.
Cover art by Gary Freeman.
This book may not be reproduced in whole or in part,
by mimeograph or any other means, without permission.
For information address: The Berkley Publishing Group,
200 Madison Avenue, New York, NY 10016.

ISBN: 0-441-37389-5

Ace Books are published by The Berkley Publishing Group,
200 Madison Avenue, New York, NY 10016.
The name "ACE" and the "A" logo
are trademarks belonging to Charter Communications, Inc.

PRINTED IN THE UNITED STATES OF AMERICA

10 9 8 7 6 5 4 3 2 1

GALACTIC GIGGLES!
HYPERDRIVE HILARITY!
WARP SPEED WIT!

ISAAC ASIMOV roasts the literary scene in "The Critic on the Hearth." (Medium rare, please.)

HOWARD WALDROP pumps up the volume at a radical class reunion in "Do Ya, Do Ya, Wanna Dance?" (You say you want a revolution?)

SHARON N. FARBER confesses a close encounter of the Elvis kind in "Space Aliens Saved My Marriage." (Inquiring minds want to know.)

TERRY BISSON reveals how only you can prevent forest fires in "Bears Discover Fire." (Don't call them Smokey.)

AND MUCH MORE . . .

*Isaac Asimov's
SF Lite*

Books in this series from Ace

ISAAC ASIMOV'S ALIENS edited by Gardner Dozois
ISAAC ASIMOV'S MARS edited by Gardner Dozois
ISAAC ASIMOV'S FANTASY! edited
by Shawna McCarthy
ISAAC ASIMOV'S ROBOTS edited by Gardner Dozois
and Sheila Williams
ISAAC ASIMOV'S EARTH edited by Gardner Dozois
and Sheila Williams
ISAAC ASIMOV'S SF LITE edited by Gardner Dozois

Grateful acknowledgment is made to the following for permission to use their copyrighted material:

"The Critic on the Hearth" by Isaac Asimov, copyright © 1992 by Dell Magazines, reprinted by permission of the author;

"Perpetuity Blues" by Neal Barrett, Jr., copyright © 1987 by Davis Publications, Inc., reprinted by permission of the author;

"Bears Discover Fire" by Terry Bisson, copyright © 1990 by Davis Publications, Inc., reprinted by permission of the author;

"The Sorceress in Spite of Herself" by Pat Cadigan, copyright © 1982 by Davis Publications, Inc., reprinted by permission of the author;

"Nine Tenths of the Law" by Susan Casper, copyright © 1991 by Davis Publications, Inc., reprinted by permission of the author;

"The Front Page" by Ronald Anthony Cross, copyright © 1989 by Davis Publications, Inc., reprinted by permission of the author;

"Body Man" by Avram Davidson, copyright © 1986 by Davis Publications, Inc., reprinted by permission of the agent, Richard D. Grant;

"Pickman's Modem" by Lawrence Watt-Evans, copyright © 1991 by Davis Publications, Inc., reprinted by permission of the Scott Meredith Literary Agency;

"Space Aliens Saved My Marriage" by Sharon N. Farber, copyright © 1990 by Davis Publications, Inc., reprinted by permission of the author;

"The Hemstitch Notebooks" by John M. Ford, copyright © 1989 by John M. Ford, reprinted by permission of the agent, Valerie Smith;

"The Faithful Companion at Forty" by Karen Joy Fowler, copyright © 1987 by Davis Publications, Inc., reprinted by permission of the author;

"Blunderbore" by Esther M. Friesner, copyright © 1990 by Davis Publications, Inc., reprinted by permission of the author;

"Stable Strategies for Middle Management" by Eileen Gunn, copyright © 1988 by Davis Publications, Inc., reprinted by permission of the author;

"Something Rich and Strange" by R. A. Lafferty, copyright © 1986 by R. A. Lafferty, reprinted by permission of the Virginia Kidd Literary Agency;

"The Day the Invaders Came" by O. Niemand, copyright © 1984 by Davis Publications, Inc., reprinted by permission of the author;

"Do Ya, Do Ya, Wanna Dance?" by Howard Waldrop, copyright © 1988 by Davis Publications, Inc., reprinted by permission of the author;

"Jesse Revenged" by Don Webb, copyright © 1986 by Davis Publications, Inc., reprinted by permission of the author;

"Ado" by Connie Willis, copyright © 1987 by Davis Publications, Inc., reprinted by permission of the author.

All stories previously appeared in *Asimov's Science Fiction* magazine, published by Dell Magazines.

ACKNOWLEDGMENTS

The editor would like to thank the following people for their help and support:

Shawna McCarthy and Kathleen Moloney, who purchased some of this material; Sheila Williams, who has labored behind the scenes on *Asimov's* for many years and who played a part in the decision-making process involved in the buying of some of these stories; Susan Casper, who helped me with much of the word-crunching and lent me the use of her computer; Ian Randal Strock, Scott L. Towner, and Adam Stern, who did much of the other thankless scut work involved in preparing the manuscript; Constance Scarborough, who cleared the permissions; Cynthia Manson, who set up this deal; and especially to my own editor on this project, Susan Allison.

CONTENTS

THE SORCERESS IN SPITE OF HERSELF
Pat Cadigan — 1

ADO
Connie Willis — 16

PERPETUITY BLUES
Neal Barrett, Jr. — 26

BLUNDERBORE
Esther M. Friesner — 61

THE FRONT PAGE
Ronald Anthony Cross — 72

STABLE STRATEGIES FOR MIDDLE MANAGEMENT
Eileen Gunn — 86

THE FAITHFUL COMPANION AT FORTY
Karen Joy Fowler — 101

SOMETHING RICH AND STRANGE
R. A. Lafferty — 112

JESSE REVENGED
Don Webb — 128

THE CRITIC ON THE HEARTH
Isaac Asimov — 135

THE DAY THE INVADERS CAME
O. Niemand — 146

NINE TENTHS OF THE LAW
Susan Casper — 153

THE HEMSTITCH NOTEBOOKS
John M. Ford — 161

PICKMAN'S MODEM
Lawrence Watt-Evans — 170

BODY MAN
Avram Davidson — 178

SPACE ALIENS SAVED MY MARRIAGE
Sharon N. Farber — 183

DO YA, DO YA, WANNA DANCE?
Howard Waldrop   194

BEARS DISCOVER FIRE
Terry Bisson   229

SF-LITE

THE SORCERESS IN SPITE OF HERSELF

Pat Cadigan

"The Sorceress in Spite of Herself" was purchased by Kathleen Moloney during her brief tenure as editor, and appeared in the December 1982 issue of Asimov's, *with an illustration by Janet Aulisio. Cadigan has gone on to be a mainstay of* Asimov's *since then, under two subsequent editors. Many of her stories have appeared on major award ballots, and one of them, "Pretty Boy Crossover," an* Asimov's *story, has recently appeared on several critics' lists as being among the best science fiction stories of the 1980s. Born in Schenectady, New York, Cadigan now lives in Overland Park, Kansas. She made her first professional sale in 1980. She was the co-editor, along with husband Arnie Fenner, of* Shayol, *perhaps the best of the semiprozines of the late '70s; it was honored with a World Fantasy Award in the "Special Achievement, Non-Professional" category in 1981. She has also served as Chairman of the Nebula Award Jury and as a World Fantasy Award judge. Her short work has been assembled in the landmark collection* Patterns. *Her first novel,* Mindplayers, *was released in 1987 to excellent critical response, and her second novel,* Synners, *appeared in 1991 to even better response. She has just turned in a new novel called* Fools.

"Oh, damn it, *please* be here," she muttered for the millionth time, yanking open the top drawer of her bureau and pawing through the mess of lingerie inside. Her frantic fingers brushed a small green box and she flicked the lid open with her thumb. It was empty. She stared at it for several seconds, trying to remember what had been in it originally—the silver leaf brooch or the butterfly pin? She shook her head, putting the box on the cluttered dresser top. It was an old box, and she probably hadn't put any jewelry in it for ages. She continued searching the drawer.

"Lou?"

She jumped, making a small shriek and inadvertently tossing several pairs of panties into the air. In the mirror she saw Tony standing in the doorway of the bedroom, looking amused. She hoped he couldn't see the stricken expression in her own reflection at that distance. If she could get through the evening without his finding out, maybe she could get to a jeweler tomorrow and buy replacements. It would put her in hock up to her ears, which was as good a level as any, considering, but since they had separate bank accounts, it wouldn't be hard to conceal the expenditure from him. She'd done that often enough in the past.

"I realize turning thirty is traumatic," he said with gentle sarcasm, "but if you don't put a move on, we're going to be unforgivably late for your birthday dinner. They'll give our reservations away."

"Oh, yeah. Right." She looked down at the open drawer and then at the scatter of items on the bureau top. There was no use in continuing her search. This was the fourth time she'd ransacked the dresser, and if they weren't there the first three times, they weren't about to appear now. Besides, if she delayed any longer, Tony was going to be suspicious. She pushed the drawer closed, plucked her purse out of the mess on the bureau, and forced a bright smile as she turned around. "Well, then, let's go."

Tony shook his head. "Aren't you forgetting something?"

A cold knot gathered in Lou's stomach. "Ah, am I?"

Tony tapped his left earlobe. "I thought you wanted to show off tonight."

"Oh. Well." She shrugged, trying to look natural. "You know, I was reading the paper and there was this news story about a woman who was wearing some ruby earrings and a guy walked right up to her on the street and just ripped them right out of her ears. Tore her earlobes to shreds. She had to go to the hospital and everything." Lou shuddered. "It kind of scared me, you know? I mean, I'm thinking about not even taking a purse tonight."

She could tell he didn't buy the explanation by the stunned look on his face. "Oh, Lou, you didn't—"

"They're safe, honest, Tone, I put them away—"

"—didn't *really* lose them—"

"—in the box where I always—"

"—*please* tell me you didn't lose the diamond earrings that cost me half a year's savings—"

"—for Chrissakes, they're in the drawer now. Let's go! We're going to be *late!*"

They stared across the room at each other in the sudden silence.

"Oh, God, Lou," Tony said finally.

Lou burst into tears. That was a dead giveaway. She knew it as soon as she did it, but she couldn't control herself. She was a crier under pressure, and she could no more break herself of that than she could break herself of losing things. Sobbing as much over her lack of control as with sorrow for Tony's discovery of the loss, she groped her way to the bed and sat down.

Tony stood helplessly in the doorway for a few moments and then went to her. "Lou, Lou, Lou," he chanted, pulling her into his arms. The comforting sound he was trying to put into his voice was not quite there. She sobbed harder.

"Come on, now," he said after a minute. "Pull yourself together, and I'll help you look for them."

"It's no use, Tony," she wept, pushing him away. She went to the bureau and slid a tangle of necklaces off a box of tissues.

Before taking one, she felt around the inside of the box, but it contained nothing but tissues. "They're gone for good. I looked everywhere and they're not in the house."

"Did you ever take them off at work?"

She wagged her head from side to side. "I never wore them to work. Diamonds in the office would be a little much." She blew her nose.

"Are you *sure?*"

"Yes, I'm *sure!*" she snapped. "I'm not a complete feeb, you know!"

Tony stood up and folded his arms. "Don't get mad at *me. I'm* not the one who lost your earrings."

"No? I'm not so sure about that." She lifted her head, her tears drying up almost instantly. "You're always cleaning things up and putting things away where I can't find them. Maybe you saw my earrings lying around and decided to put them in a safe place. Only it's so safe that it's even safe from me!"

Tony's face hardened. "Look you, you can't just leave diamond earrings *lying around.* And someone's got to pick up the clutter around here. If I didn't, we'd be ass-deep in junk and you know it!"

Lou's shoulder's slumped and she leaned on the bureau. "Oh, God, Tony. My *earrings.*"

He took a deep breath. "When did you see them last?"

"I don't know," she said sadly, staring at the floor.

"Try to remember. Did you wear them last weekend?"

"I don't know."

"Well, when was the last time you wore them that you *can* remember?"

She made a pained face. "I think I wore them to the company dinner. In fact, I *know* I did, because Jack Waverly said something about them."

"Okay. Then what? After we came home, what did you do?"

"How should I know? That was a week and a half ago."

"Think."

THE SORCERESS IN SPITE OF HERSELF

"I must have put them where I always put them—on top of the bureau. In my jewelry box."

He got up and looked at the jumble of necklaces, pins, and other earrings in the shallow open box. "Are you sure they're not in there hiding under something?"

"I looked a million times, Tone."

"Goddamit, I don't see how you can find anything in that mess." He snatched the box off the bureau and upended it over the bed.

"Jesus, Tony, now you've made a bigger mess."

He spread the jewelry around, combing through it with his fingers. She stood and watched, waiting for him to give up. It was a scene they had replayed over and over through six months of marriage, with car keys, house keys, wallets, rings, eyeglasses, and a multitude of other things, usually hers, being the objects of the search. Long ago he had learned not to give her anything of his to hold, not even for a moment, because she would make it disappear. That was her special talent, making things disappear. Mostly they were small but important items, though she had, in the past, worked miracles with a ten-pound bag of charcoal briquets, a twenty-five-pound frozen turkey and once, in an unparalleled feat of dematerialization, a full barrel of trash. She insisted even to herself that the barrel had been stolen on collection day. If that indeed had been the case, however, someone had stolen the trash in it as well, because Tony had discovered the loss before the collection truck arrived.

Now Tony picked up the jewelry box and shook it vigorously over the bed again to dislodge anything that might have been jammed in there. Lou shook her head. He knew as well as she did that the box was empty. He dropped it on the bed and threw up his hands.

"How do you *do* it?"

She stared at his incredulous face, feeling like a monster.

"How do you make things disappear like that? Tell me. Tell me and I'll die a happy man!"

"Oh, Tony—"

"No, come on, now, Lou. How do you do it? Don't you have *any* idea?"

She brushed past him and began to gather up the scattered jewelry on the bed, dumping it back into the box by the handful. "Magic."

Tony slapped the bureau with his hand. "Well, goddamit, why didn't you just say so? Magic. That's great. Better than I thought. If you were just careless or disorganized, I'm not sure what I'd do. I mean, here you are, a woman with a Master's degree in Business Administration who spends her days keeping the largest manufacturing firm in the state rolling along turning out widgets, gidgets, and gadgets but who can't keep track of her possessions from one moment to the next—that would be too absurd to believe. But *magic*. Now *there's* an explanation that's not only rational, but full of potential for profit! We could both quit our jobs and tour the country with our own magic act. Louise Belmont performing prestidigitation and sleights-of-hand before your very eyes, aided by her faithful husband Tony. We'll play everywhere—Vegas, the Borscht circuit, who knows? Maybe even a command performance for the Queen in London! Your Majesty, where did you say you remember seeing the Crown Jewels last?"

Lou straightened up slowly, holding the box tight against her stomach so she wouldn't fling it in her husband's face. "That's no way to talk to a woman with a curse on her."

Tony exploded with laughter. She ignored him and set the box on the bureau. Then she sat down on the edge of the bed and watched him coldly until he wound down.

"Oh, God," he said, grabbing a tissue. "If this weren't so serious, it really would be funny." He dabbed at his eyes and laughed a little more.

Lou's mouth was an angry line. "Funny to *you*. I'm the one with the curse."

Tony's smile faded away. "You don't actually believe that—"

"I don't know what else it could be." She looked away from him. "I've tried everything to keep from losing stuff—making lists, memory courses—I even went to a fancy, high-priced psychiatrist for some industrial-strength analysis. You know what he told me? I tend to lose things. What an analysis. I knew that already." She wiped her light brown hair away from her forehead. "The only explanation left is magic. Sorcery. I'm an inadvertent sorceress. Somehow I put spells on things and make them go away."

Tony bent and squinted into her face. "Lou."

"What."

"Look at me."

She raised her eyes to meet his.

"Now I want you to look me square in the face and say all that again without laughing."

She turned away. "Lay off, Tone."

"I mean it, Lou. If you actually believe all that garbage you just said, you've got a bigger problem than just losing things. Not only am I going to have to lock up everything of value, but I'll have to have you deprogrammed as well."

"I'm not crazy."

"Oh, no?"

Lou sat up sharply, bouncing a little on the mattress. "I'll prove it. Give me something."

Tony rolled his eyes. "Sweetheart—"

"I'm not kidding. Give me something."

"For God's sake—"

"Give me something."

He picked up one of her necklaces from the bureau.

"Not that. Something of yours. Something important to you. Something you don't want to do without."

After a moment of thought, he began pulling off his wedding ring.

"Oh, thanks a lot, *pal.*"

He held the ring up. "Something important to me."

Lou's eyes narrowed. "You're putting me in a bad spot, Tone. If it disappears, it's gone forever. You'll never see it again. But if it doesn't, that'll say more about you than it does about me. All of it bad."

"It's important to me," he insisted. "And you can't make things disappear by magic. You're just careless."

"I am not." She took the ring from him. It was a simple white-gold band, just like her own, with their initials and the date of their wedding engraved on the inside. "Now. Observe." He groaned as she reached down and pulled her blazer pocket inside out. "An ordinary pocket, perfectly intact, no holes in it—"

"Lou, you're getting silly—"

"Perfectly intact, no holes in it." She pushed the lining back down again. "Now. I'm going to drop the ring into this pocket." She did so and held the pocket open. "Look. Look down inside and make sure the ring is still there."

Tony sighed.

"Do it or you'll never believe me."

He looked and nodded. "I see it."

"Fine." She folded her hands on her knees. "Now we wait."

"For what?"

"For the ring to disappear. I think it takes me a little longer with precious metals than with ordinary objects." She tilted her head thoughtfully. "I must have a lot of trouble vanishing precious gems. You gave me those earrings three months ago at least."

"Lou, this is insane."

She arched her eyebrows at him. "Is it?"

"Yes, it is. There's no such thing as real magic. And if there were, you wouldn't be able to perform it by accident. Magic requires a lot of ritual."

"If there's no such thing, how would you know that?"

"I've read about magic, just like anyone else has. Including you, it would seem. Except I never heard you mention any of this stuff before." He frowned at her suspiciously. "Did you ever fool around with witchcraft?"

"I don't know anything about witchcraft. That's probably part of my problem. If I did study up on it, maybe I could find out what I was doing or saying and stop it." Lou wet her lips. "I never said anything before because it sounds as crazy

THE SORCERESS IN SPITE OF HERSELF

to me as it does to you. For a long time I never considered such a thing. But all my life I've been a loser. Literally. I don't know how I got through school. I had to pull all-nighters constantly to do papers. If I didn't, I'd have too much time in which to lose them. I wrote my Master's thesis in a week and even then I lost it three times. If I hadn't kept copies with all my friends, I'd probably still be trying to write it." She gave a small laugh. "When I went to work, I really had to learn how to think fast. I used the multiple copy device from college, but even so, an awful lot of important contracts were, ah, lost in the mail. The day I got a secretary was the best day of my life. I just dumped everything with her and called for things as I needed them. Now I've got a whole battalion of assistants, and I do just fine. Except with the office supplies. I've taken to buying my own at a stationery store. It's expensive, but it's easier than trying to explain how I can go through all those paper clips, rubber bands, manila envelopes, and pens so quickly."

Tony stared at her, his mouth partially open.

"If that doesn't sound like magic to you, then what in hell would you call it?" she asked plaintively. He didn't answer. "You can look in my pocket now. I'm sure your ring is gone."

He looked. She kept her face averted as he stood bent over her pocket, transfixed. He made her stand up and patted her down the way cops frisked suspects on television. He felt around on the bed and on the floor underneath, crawling back and forth, digging his fingers into the nap. He took off her shoes and shook them out, peered into her mouth, ran his fingers through her hair.

"Satisfied?" she asked when he finally plumped down on the bed, holding his ringless left hand up in front of his face.

"I don't believe it," he murmured, "but I believe it."

"Wonderful. Now let's go celebrate my thirtieth birthday. Thirty years of losses probably totaling in the hundreds of thousands, including a hundred-dollar wedding ring and a pair of earrings worth over two grand." She laughed bitterly. "Happy birthday to me."

It was a quiet ride to the restaurant.

"Maybe it's swearing," Tony said to her suddenly over their third cocktail.

She nearly spat her daiquiri out onto the table. "Maybe *what's* swearing?"

"Your vanishing act. Your making things disappear."

At the next table, a man glanced up from his menu at them and then looked down again. Lou speared a fried mushroom from the appetizer dish and chewed it sullenly. "What are you talking about?"

Tony leaned over the table, blinking at her. He'd been drinking Black Russians, and she couldn't really blame him. "You said it was magic, a curse on you, right? Maybe it is. Literally. Maybe every time you curse, you lose something." He tried to stab a mushroom for himself, missed, and tried again.

"That's the dumbest thing I ever heard."

Tony switched his attention from mushrooms to black olives with success. "Listen to that," he said to the olive on the end of the plastic pick he was holding. "She tells me there's a magic curse on her, and when I make a suggestion as to what's causing it, she says it's dumb." He popped the olive into his mouth and gave her a dirty look.

"Before you put all that alcohol in your system, you thought it was all pretty dumb."

"Of course it's dumb." Tony took a sip of his Black Russian. "I'm drunk. And well I should be. Today my wife disposed of a pair of diamond earrings and my wedding ring. Right now everything else sounds reasonable."

Lou sighed, rested her elbow on the table, and plunked her chin in her hand. "All right. But just what made you come up with the idea that my swearing would make things disappear?"

"I made the association. Curse—cursing—swearing. Simple as that."

THE SORCERESS IN SPITE OF HERSELF

"There's only one thing wrong with that theory, bright guy. I didn't curse when your ring disappeared."

Tony's chin lifted abruptly. "Yes, you did. You said 'hell.' "

"I didn't." Lou frowned. "Did I?"

"Yep. You said something about how if your losing things wasn't magic, what the hell was it? Or something like that." He looked around for the waitress and signalled for two more drinks.

"I guess I did." Lou rubbed the side of her face. "I don't really remember. I'm a little toasted myself. Wish the food would come."

"We're lucky you didn't say, 'Wish the *goddam* food would come.' God knows what you'd lose now."

"It still doesn't work, Tone."

"And why not?"

"Because I must have cursed hundreds of times during the three months I had the earrings."

"Regular little potty-mouth, aren't you? So?"

"Well, I didn't lose them till tonight, *dear,*" she said with exaggerated patience. "Do you see what I mean?"

"Ah." He nodded, grimacing at the appetizer plate. *"Ah."* He pointed a finger at her. "But maybe conditions weren't right."

"Conditions?"

The waitress came and set down two more glasses, picking up the empty ones. "It shouldn't be much longer," she told them. "Chicken Cordon Bleu takes a little time to do right." Neither of them paid any attention to her.

"Remember what you said when you did the magic act in the bedroom?" Tony asked. "How I had to give you something I really cared about?"

The waitress gave Lou a strange look before she walked away.

"I cared about my earrings," Lou said huffily. "They weren't just trinkets, for Chr—"

Tony put up his hand. "Restrain yourself. I may not have this right, but let's not take any chances, okay?"

Lou looked up at the ceiling. When she looked down, she found the man at the next table was staring at her again. She wrinkled her nose at him. "Okay, okay. But I still cared about my earrings."

"Sure. In a distracted way. Tonight, though, you really wanted to wear them. So you went looking for them and as soon as you did, you started worrying because you know you always lose things. The pressure was building up, you probably said something like 'hell,' and—" He popped his cheek with his finger. "Gone without a trace. Just like my ring, which was as important to you as it was to me."

Lou sat perfectly still. "I said, 'damn it.' "

Tony's eyes widened. "Oh. You did?"

She nodded.

"Uh-huh." He tapped his fingers on the table. "You know, I still didn't quite believe it. I mean, I was just talking. One absurdity's as good as another absurdity. Now I'm getting nervous." He took a large drink from his glass. "And sober. But not for long, I hope."

Lou sipped at her own drink without tasting it. "That isn't going to help me figure out how to beat this thing."

Tony shrugged. "Try watching your mouth?"

"It would be better if I could find a way to get un-cursed. I don't want to be a sorceress. I've been making things disappear all my life, ever since I was a little girl—"

"Sneaking little curses under your breath, no doubt."

"No. *No.*" Lou rapped her knuckles on the table. "Now that I do know. I was a very clean little kid. The worst thing I ever said was 'Oh, my God.' "

"Which is technically swearing."

"It *is?*"

"Taking You-Know-Who's name in vain. That's swearing. Cursing."

"Oh, G—great."

Tony brightened. "Hey. Maybe we can figure a way to bring things back."

"What?"

"Yeah. Now that we've figured out how you're losing things, maybe we can dope out some way you can reverse the spell and find them again."

The waitress came with their meals, setting the plates down in front of them slowly, in case there was any more interesting talk about magic acts in the bedroom. When there wasn't, she left. Lou picked up her knife and fork and began sawing at her chicken.

"I don't think so," she said. "Tonight was the first time I'd done anything like I did with your ring. I was always too terrified that it would work. Which it did. It took me thirty years to get to that point. I'll probably be sixty before I stumble over a reversing spell. And I don't think there is one."

"There has to be," Tony said around a mouthful of red snapper. "Magic is symmetrical. Yin and yang, all that."

"You're talking about the magic you've come across in books. Popular culture stuff and covens in California. What we're dealing with is magic that works. That stuff doesn't."

Tony dragged his head from side to side. "If it works one way, it's got to work the other. Even magic—real magic—must have laws, just like nature. Hell, you're even governed by one of them. Action: swear. Reaction: disappearance."

The light buzz Lou had been feeling was beginning to wear off as her stomach filled. "All right. That sounds reasonable, about as reasonable as it can sound, considering. H—heck."

Tony winced. "That was close."

"I thought there had to be *conditions*."

"Don't tempt fate."

"This is peachy," she said sourly. "I can spend my life either losing things or sounding like Little Mary Sunshine. What the—What is this, anyway? I didn't ask to be a sorceress."

"Relax." Tony patted her hand clumsily. "Cheer up. I helped you find out why you always lost things. I bet I can help you find them again." Much to her dismay, he signalled for another drink.

• • •

By the time they were ready to leave, Tony was nearly in a stupor. She managed to get him to walk from the restaurant to where the car was parked but there was no question of his driving. "Thanks a lot, Tone," she muttered as she buckled him into the passenger seat. "My birthday and *you* get bombed. Thanks a *bundle*."

His eyes opened to slits and he smiled at her sleepily. "You're welcome. Happy birthday." Then he was out again, really out. She slammed the car door and stalked around to the driver's side, not very steady herself. She hated driving when she'd had even just one drink, but she'd always been able to hold her alcohol better than Tony. Still, she couldn't remember the last time she'd seen him so drunk.

Not that she wouldn't have liked to be smashed herself, she thought, keeping to an even twenty-five miles per hour all the way home. She had more reason for it than Tony did certainly. She glanced at his limp form, drooping like a rag in the shoulder harness, and felt a little surge of anger. Here she was, an unwilling sorceress in the middle of a modern American city with a power that could do her absolutely no good at all, and when she needed his help, what did he do? Got drunk and passed out.

She clamped her lips together. Don't say it, she told herself. Don't say it or you're sure to vanish the house keys, because in a few more blocks they're what you're going to want most.

She maintained control, not even allowing a sigh to escape her until she drove the car into the garage attached to their house. If Tony had been not indisposed, he would have insisted on backing the car in so he could just drive out the next day, but she wasn't about to attempt such a thing. Tony could just back out of the driveway for a change. It wouldn't kill him.

She got out of the car and went to unlock the door to the kitchen, fumbling with the keys in the dark. She flipped the garage light switch and found to her great annoyance the bulb was burned out. Now she'd have to practically carry Tony

THE SORCERESS IN SPITE OF HERSELF

inside in the dark. Sighing, she unlocked the door and began feeling her way around to Tony's side of the car.

"Tony? Tony, we're home." She heard a faint answering moan. He was going to be righteously sick in the morning. "Tony, wake up so I can get you in—" Her foot hit something hard with an alarming clatter and she lost her balance, falling sideways onto the hood of the car. "Oh, god*damm*it!" she yelled, struggling to push herself upright.

Then she froze, leaning on the car, realizing what she had said.

"Tony! *Tony!*" She pushed herself around the front of the car, banging her knee on the bumper. "Tony, I said it! I slipped and said 'goddam', Tony, quick, wake up, we've got to find out what I lost this time. The house keys—"

She yanked the car door open. The flash of the dome light hurt her eyes, and for several seconds she could only stand blinking at the empty front seat.

"Oh, darn," she said miserably. "Oh, goshdarn it all to blazes."

The front seat stayed empty.

ADO

Connie Willis

"Ado" was purchased by Gardner Dozois, and appeared in the January 1988 issue of Asimov's, *with an illustration by Laura Lakey. It is one of a long sequence of memorable stories by Connie Willis that have appeared in* Asimov's *under four different editors over the last decade, since her first* Asimov's *sale to George Scithers—stories that have made her one of the most popular writers that* Asimov's *has ever published, and a mainstay of the magazine. In 1982 she won two Nebula Awards, one for her superb novelette "Fire Watch," and one for her poignant short story "A Letter from the Clearys" (both* Asimov's *stories); a few months later, "Fire Watch" went on to win her a Hugo Award as well. In 1989, her powerful novella "The Last of the Winnebagoes" (another* Asimov's *story) won both the Nebula and the Hugo, and she won another Nebula last year for her novelette "At the Rialto." Her books include the novels* Water Witch *and* Light Raid, *written in collaboration with Cynthia Felice,* Fire Watch, *a collection of her short fiction, and the outstanding* Lincoln's Dreams, *her first solo novel. Just released is a major new solo novel,* Doomsday Book, *and a new collection is coming up. Willis lives in Greeley, Colorado, with her family.*

In the story that follows, she delivers a stinging, razor-edged satire about the future of education—one that is, alas, all too likely to come true. . . .

The Monday before spring break I told my English lit class we were going to do Shakespeare. The weather in Colorado is usually wretched this time of year. We get all the snow the ski resorts needed in December, use up our scheduled snow days, and end up going an extra week in June. The forecast on the *Today* show hadn't predicted any snow 'til Saturday, but with luck it would arrive sooner.

My announcement generated a lot of excitement. Paula dived for her corder and rewound it to make sure she'd gotten my every word, Edwin Sumner looked smug, and Delilah snatched up her books and stomped out, slamming the door so hard it woke Rick up. I passed out the release/refusal slips and told them they had to have them back in by Wednesday. I gave one to Sharon to give Delilah. "Shakespeare is considered one of our greatest writers, possibly *the* greatest," I said for the benefit of Paula's corder. "On Wednesday I will be talking about Shakespeare's life, and on Thursday and Friday we will be reading his work."

Wendy raised her hand. "Are we going to read all the plays?"

I sometimes wonder where Wendy has been the last few years—certainly not in this school, possibly not in this universe. "What we're studying hasn't been decided yet," I said. "The principal and I are meeting tomorrow."

"It had better be one of the tragedies," Edwin said darkly.

By lunch the news was all over school. "Good luck," Greg Jefferson the biology teacher said in the teachers' lounge. "I just got done doing evolution."

"Is it really that time of year again?" Karen Miller said. She teaches American lit across the hall. "I'm not even up to the Civil War yet."

"It's that time of year again," I said. "Can you take my class during your free period tomorrow? I've got to meet with Harrows."

"I can take them all morning. Just have your kids come into my room tomorrow. We're doing 'Thanatopsis.' Another thirty kids won't matter."

" 'Thanatopsis'?" I said, impressed. "The whole thing?"

"All but lines ten and sixty-eight. It's a terrible poem, you know. I don't think anybody understands it well enough to protest. And I'm not telling anybody what the title means."

"Cheer up," Greg said. "Maybe we'll have a blizzard."

Tuesday was clear, with a forecast of temps in the sixties. Delilah was outside the school when I got there, wearing a red Seniors Against Devil Worship in the Schools T-shirt and shorts. She was carrying a picket sign that said, "Shakespeare is Satan's Spokesman." Shakespeare and Satan were both misspelled.

"We're not starting Shakespeare till tomorrow," I told her. "There's no reason for you not to be in class. Ms. Miller is teaching 'Thanatopsis.' "

"Not lines ten and sixty-eight, she's not. Besides, Bryant was a Theist, which is the same thing as a Satanist." She handed me her refusal slip and a fat manila envelope. "Our protests are in there." She lowered her voice. "What does the word 'thanatopsis' really mean?"

"It's an Indian word. It means, 'One who uses her religion to ditch class and get a tan.' "

I went inside, got Shakespeare out of the vault in the library and went into the office. Ms. Harrows already had the Shakespeare file and her box of Kleenex out. "Do you have to do this?" she said, blowing her nose.

"As long as Edwin Sumner's in my class, I do. His mother's head of the President's Task Force on Lack of Familiarity with the Classics." I added Delilah's list of protests to the stack and sat down at the computer.

"Well, it may be easier than we think," she said. "There have been a lot of suits since last year, which takes care of *Macbeth, The Tempest, Midsummer Night's Dream, The Winter's Tale,* and *Richard III.*"

"Delilah's been a busy girl," I said. I fed in the unexpurgated disk and the excise and reformat programs. "I don't remember there being any witchcraft in *Richard III.*"

She sneezed and grabbed for another Kleenex. "There's not. That was a slander suit. Filed by his great-great-grand-something. He claims there's no conclusive proof that Richard III killed the little princes. It doesn't matter anyway. The Royal Society for the Restoration of Divine Right of Kings has an injunction against all the history plays. What's the weather supposed to be like?"

"Terrible," I said. "Warm and sunny." I called up the catalog and deleted *Henry IV, Parts I and II,* and the rest of her list. *"Taming of the Shrew?"*

"Angry Women's Alliance. Also *Merry Wives of Windsor, Romeo and Juliet,* and *Love's Labour's Lost."*

"Othello? Never mind. I know that one. *Merchant of Venice?* The Anti-Defamation League?"

"No. American Bar Association. And Morticians International. They object to the use of the word 'casket' in Act III." She blew her nose.

It took us first and second period to deal with the plays and most of the third to finish the sonnets. "I've got a class fourth period and then lunch duty," I said. "We'll have to finish up the rest of them this afternoon."

"Is there anything left for this afternoon?" Ms. Harrows asked.

"As You Like It and *Hamlet,"* I said. "Good heavens, how did they miss *Hamlet?"*

"Are you sure about *As You Like It?"* Ms. Harrows said, leafing through her stack. "I thought somebody'd filed a restraining order against it."

"Probably the Mothers Against Transvestites," I said. "Rosalind dresses up like a man in Act II."

"No, here it is. The Sierra Club. 'Destructive attitudes toward the environment.' " She looked up. "What destructive attitudes?"

"Orlando carves Rosalind's name on a tree." I leaned back in my chair so I could see out the window. The sun was still shining maliciously down. "I guess we go with *Hamlet*. This should make Edwin and his mother happy."

"We've still got the line-by-lines to go," Ms. Harrows said. "I think my throat is getting sore."

I got Karen to take my afternoon classes. It was sophomore lit and we'd been doing Beatrix Potter—all she had to do was pass out a worksheet on *Squirrel Nutkin*. I had outside lunch duty. It was so hot I had to take my jacket off. The College Students for Christ were marching around the school carrying picket signs that said, "Shakespeare was a Secular Humanist."

Delilah was lying on the front steps, reeking of suntan oil. She waved her "Shakespeare is Satan's Spokesman" sign languidly at me. " 'Ye have sinned a great sin,' " she quoted. " 'Blot me, I pray thee, out of thy book which thou has written.' Exodus Chapter 32, Verse 30."

"First Corinthians 13:3," I said. " 'Though I give my body to be burned and have not charity, it profiteth me nothing.' "

"I called the doctor," Ms. Harrows said. She was standing by the window looking out at the blazing sun. "He thinks I might have pneumonia."

I sat down at the computer and fed in *Hamlet*. "Look on the bright side. At least we've got the E and R programs. We don't have to do it by hand the way we used to."

She sat down behind the stack. "How shall we do this? By group or by line?"

"We might as well take it from the top."

"Line one. 'Who's there?' the National Coalition Against Contractions."

"Let's do it by group," I said.

"All right. We'll get the big ones out of the way first. The Commission on Poison Prevention feels the 'graphic depiction of poisoning in the murder of Hamlet's father may lead to copycat crimes.' They cite a case in New Jersey where a sixteen-year-old poured Drano in his father's ear after reading the play. Just a minute. Let me get a Kleenex. The Literature Liberation Front objects to the phrases, 'Frailty, thy name is woman,' and 'O, most pernicious woman,' the 'What a piece of work is man' speech, and the queen."

"The whole queen?"

She checked her notes. "Yes. All lines, references, and allusions." She felt under her jaw, first one side, then the other. "I think my glands are swollen. Would that go along with pneumonia?"

Greg Jefferson came in, carrying a grocery sack. "I thought you could use some combat rations. How's it going?"

"We lost the queen," I said. "Next?"

"The National Cutlery Council objects to the depiction of swords as deadly weapons. 'Swords don't kill people. People kill people.' The Copenhagen Chamber of Commerce objects to the line, 'Something is rotten in the state of Denmark.' Students Against Suicide, the International Federation of Florists, and the Red Cross object to Ophelia's drowning."

Greg was setting out the bottles of cough syrup and cold tablets on the desk. He handed me a bottle of valium. "The International Federation of Florists?" he said.

"She fell in picking flowers," I said. "What was the weather like out there?"

"Just like summer," he said. "Delilah's using an aluminum sun reflector."

"Ass," Ms. Harrows said.

"Beg pardon?" Greg said.

"ASS, the Association of Summer Sunbathers objects to the line, 'I am too much i' the sun,' " Ms. Harrows said, and took a swig from the bottle of cough syrup.

We were only half-finished by the time school let out. The Nuns' Network objected to the line, "Get thee to a nunnery," Fat and Proud of It wanted the passage beginning, "Oh, that this too too solid flesh should melt," removed, and we didn't even get to Delilah's list, which was eight pages long.

"What play are we going to do?" Wendy asked me on my way out.

"*Hamlet*," I said.

"*Hamlet?*" she said. "Is that the one about the guy whose uncle murders the king and then the queen marries the uncle?"

"Not anymore," I said.

Delilah was waiting for me outside. " 'Many of them brought their books together and burned them,' " she quoted. "Acts 19:19."

" 'Look not upon me, because I am black, because the sun hath looked upon me,' " I said.

It was overcast Wednesday but still warm. The Veterans for a Clean America and the Subliminal Seduction Sentinels were picnicking on the lawn. Delilah had on a halter top. "That thing you said yesterday about the sun turning people black, what was that from?"

"The *Bible*," I said. "Song of Solomon. Chapter one, verse six."

"Oh," she said, relieved. "That's not in the Bible anymore. We threw it out."

Ms. Harrows had left a note for me. She was at the doctor's. I was supposed to meet with her third period.

"Do we get to start today?" Wendy asked.

"If everybody remembered to bring in their slips. I'm going to lecture on Shakespeare's life," I said. "You don't know what the forecast for today is, do you?"

"Yeah, it's supposed to be great."

I had her collect the refusal slips while I went over my notes. Last year Delilah's sister Jezebel had filed a grievance halfway through the lecture for "trying to preach promiscuity, birth control, and abortion by saying Anne Hathaway got pregnant before she got married." Promiscuity, abortion, pregnant, and before had all been misspelled.

Everybody had remembered their slips. I sent the refusals to the library and started to lecture.

"Shakespeare—" I said. Paula's corder clicked on. "William Shakespeare was born on April 23, 1564, in Stratford-on-Avon."

Rick, who hadn't raised his hand all year or even given any indication that he was sentient, raised his hand. "Do you intend to give equal time to the Baconian theory?" he said. "Bacon was not born on April 23, 1564. He was born on January 22, 1561."

Ms. Harrows wasn't back from the doctor's by third period, so I started on Delilah's list. She objected to forty-three references to spirits, ghosts, and related matters, twenty-one obscene words (obscene misspelled), and seventy-eight others that she thought might be, such as pajock and cockles.

Ms. Harrows came in as I was finishing the list and threw her briefcase down. "Stress-induced!" she said. "I have pneumonia, and he says my symptoms are stress-induced!"

"Is it still cloudy out?"

"It is seventy-two degrees out. Where are we?"

"Morticians International," I said. "Again. 'Death presented as universal and inevitable.' " I peered at the paper. "That doesn't sound right."

Ms. Harrows took the paper away from me. "That's their 'Thanatopsis' protest. They had their national convention last week. They filed a whole set at once, and I haven't had a chance to sort through them." She rummaged around in her stack. "Here's the one on *Hamlet*. 'Negative portrayal of interment preparation personnel—' "

"The gravedigger."

" '—And inaccurate representation of burial regulations. Neither a hermetically-sealed coffin nor a vault appear in the scene.' "

We worked until five o'clock. The Society for the Advancement of Philosophy considered the line, "There are more things in heaven and earth, Horatio, than are dreamt of in your philosophy," a slur on their profession. The Actors' Guild challenged Hamlet's hiring of non-union employees, and the Drapery Defense League objected to Polonius being stabbed while hiding behind a curtain. "The clear implication of the scene is that the arras is dangerous," they had written in their brief. "Draperies don't kill people. People kill people."

Ms. Harrows put the paper down on top of the stack and took a swig of cough syrup. "And that's it. Anything left?"

"I think so," I said, punching *reformat* and scanning the screen. "Yes, a couple of things. How about, 'There is a willow grows aslant a brook/That shows his hoar leaves in the glassy stream.' "

"You'll never get away with 'hoar,' " Ms. Harrows said.

Thursday I got to school at seven-thirty to print out thirty copies of *Hamlet* for my class. It had turned colder and even cloudier in the night. Delilah was wearing a parka and mittens. Her face was a deep scarlet, and her nose had begun to peel.

" 'Hath the Lord as great delight in burnt offerings as in obeying the voice of the Lord?' " I asked. "First Samuel 15:22." I patted her on the shoulder.

"Yeow," she said.

I passed out *Hamlet* and assigned Wendy and Rick to read the parts of Hamlet and Horatio.

" 'The air bites shrewdly; it is very cold,' " Wendy read.

"Where are we?" Rick said. I pointed out the place to him. "Oh. 'It is a nipping and an eager air.' "

" 'What hour now?' " Wendy read.

" 'I think it lacks of twelve.' "

Wendy turned her paper over and looked at the back. "That's it?" she said. "That's all there is to *Hamlet?* I thought his uncle killed his father and then the ghost told him his mother was in on it and he said 'To be or not to be' and Ophelia killed herself and stuff." She turned the paper back over. "This can't be the whole play."

"It better not be the whole play," Delilah said. She came in, carrying her picket sign. "There'd better not be any ghosts in it. Or cockles."

"Did you need some Solarcaine, Delilah?" I asked her.

"I *need* a Magic Marker," she said with dignity.

I got her one out of the desk. She left, walking a little stiffly, as if it hurt to move.

"You can't just take parts of the play out because somebody doesn't like them," Wendy said. "If you do, the play doesn't make any sense. I bet if Shakespeare were here, he wouldn't let you just take things out—"

"Assuming Shakespeare wrote it," Rick said. "If you take every other letter in line two except the first three and the last six, they spell 'pig,' which is obviously a code word for Bacon."

"Snow day!" Ms. Harrows said over the intercom. Everybody raced to the windows. "We will have early dismissal today at 9:30."

I looked at the clock. It was 9:28.

"The Over-Protective Parents Organization has filed the following protest: 'It is now snowing, and as the forecast predicts more snow, and as snow can result in slippery streets, poor visibility, bus accidents, frostbite, and avalanches, we demand that school be closed today and tomorrow so as not to endanger our children.' Buses will leave at 9:35. Have a nice spring break!"

"The snow isn't even sticking on the ground," Wendy said. "Now we'll never get to do Shakespeare."

Delilah was out in the hall, on her knees next to her picket sign, crossing out the word "man" in "Spokesman."

"The Feminists for a Fair Language are here," she said disgustedly. "They've got a court order." She wrote "person" above the crossed-out "man." "A court order! Can you believe that? I mean, what's happening to our right to freedom of speech?"

"You misspelled 'person,'" I said.

PERPETUITY BLUES

Neal Barrett, Jr.

"Perpetuity Blues" was purchased by Gardner Dozois, and appeared in the May 1987 issue of Asimov's, *with an illustration by Laura Lakey. Barrett became one of the magazine's most popular writers in the last half of the '80s, and gained wide critical acclaim with a string of pungent, funny, and unclassifiably weird stories like "Ginny Sweethips' Flying Circus," "Stairs," "Highbrow," "Trading Post," "Class of '61" . . . and particularly the story that follows, which has become an underground cult classic, and may well be one of the funniest stories we've ever read.*

Born in San Antonio, Texas, Neal Barrett, Jr. grew up in Oklahoma City, Oklahoma, spent several years in Austin, hobnobbing with the likes of Lewis Shiner and Howard Waldrop, and now makes his home with his family in Fort Worth, Texas. He made his first sale in 1959, and has been a full-time freelancer for the past twelve years. His books include Stress Pattern, Karma Corps, *the four-volume* Aldair *series, the critically acclaimed novel* Through Darkest America, *and its sequel,* Dawn's Uncertain Light. *His most recent book is a* very *strange new novel,* The Hereafter Gang.

On Maggie's seventh birthday she found the courage to ask Mother what had happened to her father.

"Your father disappeared under strange circumstances," said Mother.

"Sorghumdances?" said Maggie.

"Circumstances," said Mother, who had taught remedial English before marriage and was taking a stab at it again. "Circumstances: a condition or fact attending an event or having some bearing upon it."

"I see," said Maggie. She didn't, but knew it wasn't safe to ask twice. What happened was Daddy got up after supper one night and put on his cardigan with the patches on the sleeves and walked to the 7-Eleven for catfood and bread. Eight months later he hadn't shown up or called or written a card. Strange circumstances didn't seem like a satisfactory answer.

Mother died Thursday afternoon. Maggie found her watching reruns of "Rawhide" and "Bonanza." Maggie left South Houston and went to live with Aunt Grace and Uncle Ned in Marble Creek.

"There's no telling who he might of met at that store," said Aunt Grace. "Your father wasn't right after the service. I expect he got turned in Berlin. Sent him back and planted him deep in Montgomery Wards as a mole. That's how they do it. You wait and lead an ordinary life. You might be anyone at all. Your control phones up one day and says 'the water runs deep in Lake Lagoda' and that's it. Whatever you're doing you just get right up and do their bidding. Either that or he run off with that slut in appliance. I got a look at her when your uncle went down to buy the Lawnboy at the End-of-Summer Sale. Your mother married beneath her. I don't say I didn't do the same. The women in our family got no sense at all when it comes to men. We come from good stock but that doesn't put money in the bank. Your grandfather Jack worked directly with the man who invented the volleyball net they use all over the world in tournament play. Of course he never got the credit he deserved. This family's rubbed elbows with greatness more than once but you wouldn't know it. Don't listen to your Uncle Ned's stories. And for Christ's sake don't ever sit on his lap."

Maggie found life entirely different in a small town. There were new customs to learn. Jimmy Gerder and two other fourth graders took her down to the river after school and tried to make her take off her pants. Maggie didn't want to and ran home. After that she ran home every day.

Uncle Ned told her stories. Maggie learned why it wasn't a good idea to sit on his lap. "There was this paleontologist," said Uncle Ned, "he went out hunting dinosaur eggs and he found some. There was this student come along with him. It was this girl with nice tits is who it was. So this paleontologist says, 'be careful now, don't drop 'em, these old eggs are real friable.' And the girl says, 'hey that's great, let's fry the little fuckers.' " Uncle Ned nearly fell out of his chair.

Maggie didn't understand her uncle's stories. They all sounded alike and they were all about scientists and girls. Ned ran the hardware store on Main. He played dominoes on Saturdays with Dr. Harlow Pierce who also ran Pierce's Drugs. On Sundays he watched girls' gymnastics on TV. When someone named Tanya did a flip he got a funny look in his eyes. Aunt Grace would get Maggie and take her out in the car for a drive.

Maggie found a stack of magazines in the garage behind a can of kerosene. There were pictures of naked girls doing things she couldn't imagine. There were men in some of the pictures and she guessed they were scientists, too.

Aunt Grace and Uncle Ned were dirt poor but they gave a party for Maggie's eighth birthday. Maggie was supposed to pass out invitations at school but she threw them all away. Everyone knew Jimmy Gerder chased her home and knew why. She was afraid Aunt Grace would find out. Uncle Ned gave her a Philips screwdriver in a simulated leather case you could clip in your pocket like a pen. Aunt Grace gave her a paperback history of the KGB.

Maggie loved the freedom children enjoy in small towns. She knew everyone on Main who ran the stores, the people on the streets and the people who came in from the country Saturday nights. She knew Dr. Pierce kept a bottle in his office and another behind the tire in his trunk. She knew Mrs. Betty Keen Littler, the coach's wife, drove to Austin every Wednesday to take ceramics and came back whonkered with her shoes on the wrong feet. She knew about Oral Blue, who drank wine and acted funny and thought he came from outer space. Oral was her favorite person to watch. He drove a falling-down pickup and lived in a trailer by the river. He came into town twice a week to fix toasters and wire lamps. No one knew his last name. Flip Gator who ran Flip Gator's Exxon tagged him Oral Blue. Which fit because Oral's old '68 pickup was three shades of Sears' exterior paint for fine homes. Sky Blue for the body. Royal blue for fenders. An indeterminate blue for the hood. Oral wore blue shirts and trousers. Blue Nikes with the toes cut out and blue socks.

"Don't get near him," said Aunt Grace. "He might of been turned. And for Christ's sake don't ever sit in his lap."

Maggie kept an eye on Oral when she could. On Tuesdays and Thursdays she'd run home fast with Jimmy Gerder on her heels and duck up the alley to the square. Then she'd sit and watch Oral stagger around trying to pinpoint his truck. Oral was something to see. He was skinny as a rail and had a head too big for his body. Like a tennis ball stabbed with a pencil. Hair white as down and chalk skin and pink eyes. A mouth like a wide open zipper. He wore a frayed straw hat painted pickup-fender blue to protect him from the harsh Texas sun. Uncle Ned said Oral was a pure-bred genetic albino greaser freak and an aberration of nature. Maggie looked it up. She didn't believe anything Uncle Ned told her.

Ten days after Maggie was eleven Dr. Pierce didn't show up for dominoes and Ned went and found him in his store. He took one look and ran out in the street and threw up. The medical examiner from San Antone said Pierce had sat on the floor and opened forty-two-hundred pharmaceutical-type products, mixed them in a five-gallon jug and drunk most of it down. Which accounted for the internal explosions and extreme discoloration of the skin.

Maggie had never heard about suicide before. She imagined you just caught something and died or got old. Uncle Ned began to drink a lot more after Dr. Pierce was gone. "Death is one of your alternate lifestyles worth considering," he told Maggie. "Give it some thought."

Uncle Ned became unpleasant to be around. He mostly watched girls' field hockey or Eastern Bloc track and field events. Maggie was filling out in certain spots. Ned noticed her during commercials and grabbed out at what he could. Aunt Grace gave him hell when she caught him. Sometimes he didn't know who he was. He'd grab and get Grace, and she'd pick up something and knock him senseless.

Maggie stayed out of the house whenever she could. School was out and she liked to pack a lunch and walk down through the trees at the edge of town to the Colorado. She liked to wander over limestone hills where every rock you picked up was the shell of something tiny that had lived. The sun fierce-bright and the heat so heavy you could see it. She took a jar of ice water and a peanut butter sandwich and climbed up past the heady smell of green salt-cedar to the deep shade of big live oaks and native pecans. The trees here were awesome, tall and heavy-leafed, trunks thick as columns in a bad Bible movie. She would come upon the ridge above the river through a tangle of ropy vine, sneak quietly to the edge and look over and catch half a hundred turtles like green clots of moss on a sunken log. Moccasins crossed the river, flat heads just above the water leaving shallow wakes behind. She would eat in the shade and think how it would be if Daddy were there. How much he liked the dry rattle of locusts in the summer, the sounds that things made in the wild. He could tell her what bird was across the river. She knew a crow when she heard it, that a cardinal was red. Where was he? she wondered. She didn't believe he'd been a mole at Montgomery Wards. Aunt Grace was wrong about that. Why didn't he come back? He might leave Mother and she wouldn't much blame him if he did. But he wouldn't go off and leave *her*.

"I don't want you to be dead," she said aloud. "I can think of a lot of people who it's okay if they're dead, but not you."

She dropped pieces of sandwich into the olive-colored water. Fish came up and sucked them down. When the sun cut the river half in shadow she started back. There was a road through the woods, no more than ruts for tires but faster than over the hills. Walking along thinking, watching grasshoppers bounce on ahead and show the way. The sound came up behind her and she turned and saw the pickup teeter over the rise in odd dispersions of blue, the paint so flat it ate the sun in one bite. Oral blinked through bug spatters, strained over the wheel so his nose pressed flat against the glass. The pickup a primary disaster, and Oral mooning clown-faced, pink-eyed, smiling like a zipper, and maybe right behind some cut-rate circus with a pickled snake in a jar. He spotted Maggie and pumped the truck dead; caliche dust caught up and passed them both by.

"Well now, what have we got here?" said Oral. "It looks like a picnic and I flat missed it good. Not the first time, I'll tell you. I smell peanut butter I'm not mistaken. You want to get in here and ride?"

"What for?" said Maggie.

"Then don't. Good afternoon. Nice talking to you."

"All right. I will." Maggie opened the door and got in. She couldn't say why, it just seemed like the right thing to do.

"I've seen you in town," said Oral.

"I've seen you too."

"There's a lot more to life than you dream of stuck on this out of the way planet I'll tell you that. There's plenty of things to see. I doubt you've got the head for it all. Far places and distant climes. Exotic modes of travel and different ways of doing brownies."

"I've been over to Waco and Forth Worth."

"That's a start."

"You just say you're a space person, don't you," said Maggie, wondering where she'd gotten the courage to say that. "You're not really are you?"

"Not any more I'm not," said Oral. "My ship disintegrated completely over The Great Salt Lake. I was attacked by Mormon terrorists almost at once. Spent some time in Denver door-to-door. Realized I wasn't cut out for sales. Sometime later hooked up with a tent preacher in Bloomington, Indiana. Toured the tri-state area, where I did a little healing with a simple device concealed upon my person. Couldn't get new batteries and that was that. I was taken in by nuns outside of Reading,

Pennsylvania, and treated well, though I was forced to mow lawns for some time. Later I was robbed and beaten severely by high-school girls in Chattanooga where I offered to change a tire. I have always relied on the kindness of strangers. Learned you can rely on 'em to kick you in the ass." Oral picked up a paper sack shaped like a bottle and took a drink. "What's your daddy do? If I'm not mistaken, he sells nails."

"That's not my daddy, that's my uncle. My father disappeared under strange circumstances."

"That happens. More often than you might imagine. There are documented cases. Things I could tell you you wouldn't believe. Look it up. Planes of existence we can't see or not a lot. People lost and floating about in interdimensional yogurt."

"You think my father's somewhere like that?"

"I don't know. I could ask."

"Thank you very much."

"I got this shirt from a fellow selling stuff off a truck. Pierre Cardin irregular is what it is. Dirt cheap and nothing irregular about it I can see. Whole stack of 'em there by your feet."

"They're all blue."

"Well, I know that."

"Where are we going now?"

"My place. Show you my interstellar vehicle and break open some cookies. You scared to be with me?"

"Not a lot."

"You might well ask why I make no effort to deny my strange origin or odd affiliation. I find it's easier to hide out in the open. You say you're from outer space, people tend to leave you alone. I've lived in cities and I like the country better. Not so many bad rays from people's heads. To say nothing of the dogshit in the streets. What do *you* think? You have any opinion on that? People in small towns are more tolerant of the rare and slightly defective. They all got a cousin counting his toes. I can fix nearly anything there is. Toasters. TVs. Microwave ovens. Everything except that goddamn ship. If Radio Shack had decent parts at all I'd be out of here and gone."

Oral parked the truck under the low-hanging branches of a big native pecan. The roots ground deep in the rigid earth, squeezed rocks to the surface like broken dishes. The tree offered shade to the small aluminum trailer, which was round as a bullet. Oral had backed it off the road some time before. The tires were gone, tossed off in the brush. The trailer sat on rocks. Oral ushered Maggie in. Found Oreos in a Folger's coffee can, Sprite in a mini-fridge. A generator hacked out back. The trailer smelled of wine and bananas and 3-In-One oil. There was a hotplate and a cot. Blue shirts and trousers and socks.

"It's not much," said Oral. "I don't plan to stay here any longer than I have to."

"It's very cozy," said Maggie, who'd been taught to always say something nice. The trailer curved in from the door to a baked plastic window up front. The floor and the walls and the roof were explosions of colored wire and gutted home computers. Blue lights stuttered here and there.

"What's all this supposed to be?" said Maggie.

"Funky, huh?" Oral showed rapid eye movement. "No wonder they think I'm crazy. The conquest of space isn't as easy as the layman might imagine. I figure on bringing in a seat from out of the truck. Bolt it right there. Need something to seal up the door. Inner tubes and prudent vulcanizing ought to do it. You know about the alarming lack of air out in space?"

"I think we had it in school."

"Well, it's true. You doing all right at that place?"

The question took Maggie by surprise. "At school you mean? Sort of. Okay I guess."

"Uh-huh." Oral hummed and puttered about. Stepped on a blue light and popped it like a bug. Found a tangle of wire from a purple Princess phone and cut it free. Got needle-nose pliers and twisted a little agate in to fit. "Wear this," he told Maggie. "Hang it round your waist and let the black dohicky kind of dangle over your personal private things."

"Well, I never!" Maggie didn't care for such talk.

"All right, don't. Run home all your life."

"You've been spying on me."

"You want a banana? Some ice cream? I like to crumble Oreos over the top."

"I think I better start on home."

"Go right up the draw and down the hill. Shortcut. Stick to the path. Tonight's a good night to view the summer constellations. Mickey's in the Sombrero. The Guppy's on the rise."

"I'll be sure and look."

When Maggie was twelve, Aunt Grace went to Galveston on a trip. The occasion was a distant cousin's demise. Uncle Ned went along. Which seemed peculiar to Maggie since they wouldn't *eat* together, and seldom spoke.

"We can't afford it, God knows," said Aunt Grace. "But Albert was a dear. Fought the Red menace in West Texas all his life. Fell off a shrimper and drowned, but how do we know for sure? *They'd* make it look accidental."

She left Maggie a list of things to eat. Peanut butter and Campbell's soup. Which was mostly what she got when they were home. Aunt Grace said meat and green vegetables tended to give young girls diarrhea and get their periods out of whack.

"Stay out of the ham and don't thaw anything in the fridge. Here's two dollars that's for emergencies and not to spend. Call Mrs. Ketcher you get sick. Lock the doors. Come straight home from school and don't look at the cable."

"I'm scared to stay alone," said Maggie.

"Don't be a fraidy cat. God'll look after you if you're good."

"Don't tell anyone we're gone," said Uncle Ned. "Some greaser'll break in and steal us blind."

"For God's sake, Ned, don't tell her *that*."

Uncle Ned tried to slip a paper box in the back seat. Maggie saw him do it. When they both went in to check the house she stole a look. The carton was full of potato chips and Fritos, Cheetos and chocolate chip cookies. There was a cooler she hadn't seen iced down with Dr Pepper and frozen Snickers and Baby Ruths. There were never any chips or candy bars around the house. Aunt Grace said they couldn't afford trash. But all this stuff was in the car. Maggie didn't figure they'd be bringing any back. When the car was out of sight she went straight to the garage and punched an ice pick hole in the kerosene can that hid Uncle Ned's stash of magazines. She did it on a rust spot so Ned'd never notice. Then she went out back and turned over flat rocks and gathered half a pickle jar of fat brown Texas roaches that had moved up from Houston for their health. Upstairs she emptied the jar where Aunt Grace kept her underwear and hose. Downstairs again she got the ice pick and opened the freezer door and poked a hole in one of the coils. In case the roasts and chickens and Uncle Ned's venison sausage had trouble thawing out she left the door open wide to summer heat.

"There," said Maggie, "y'all go fuck yourselves good." She didn't know what it meant but it seemed to work fine for everyone else.

When Maggie was thirteen, Jimmy Gerder nearly caught her. By now she knew exactly what he wanted and ran faster. But Jimmy had been going out for track. He had the proper shoes and it was only a matter of time. Purely by chance she came across Oral's gimmick in the closet. The little black stone he'd twisted on seemed to dance like the Sony when a station was off the air. Why not, she thought, it can't hurt. Next morning she slipped it on under her dress. It felt funny and kinda nice, bouncing on her personal private things. Jimmy Gerder caught her in an alley. Six good buddies had come to watch. Jimmy wore his track outfit with a seven on the back. A Marble Creek Sidewinder rattler on the front. He was a tall and knobby boy with runny white-trash eyes and bad teeth. Maggie backed against a wall papered with county commissioner flyers. Jimmy came at her in a fifty meter stance. His mouth moved funny; a peculiar glaze appeared. A strange invisible force picked him up and slammed him flat against the far alley wall. Maggie hadn't touched him. But something certainly had. Onlookers got away fast and spread the word. Maggie wasn't much of an easy lay. Jimmy Gerder suffered a semi-mild concussion, damage to several vertebrae and ribs.

She hadn't seen Oral in over a year. On the streets sometime, but not at the extraterrestrial aluminum trailer by the river.

"I wanted to thank you," she said. "I don't get chased any more. How in the world did you do that?"

"What took you so long to try it out? Don't tell me. I got feelings too."

Nothing seemed to have changed. There were more gutted personal home computers and blue lights, or maybe the same ones in different order.

"You wouldn't believe what happened to me," said Oral. He brought out Oreos and Sprites. "Got the ship clear out of the atmosphere and hit this time warp or something. Nearly got eat by Vikings. Worse than the Mormons. Fixed up the ship and flipped it out again. Ended up in Medieval Europe. Medicis and monks, all kinds of shit. Joined someone's army in Naples. Got caught and picked olives for a duke. Look at my face. They got diseases you never heard of there."

"Oh my," said Maggie. His face didn't look too good. The bad albino skin had holes like a Baby Swiss.

"I taught 'em a thing or two," said Oral, blinking one pink eye and then the other. "Simple magic tricks. Mr. Wizard stuff. Those babies'll believe anything. Ended up owning half of Southern Italy. Olive oil and real estate. Not a bad life if you can tolerate the smell. Man could make a mint selling Soft 'n Pretty and Sure."

"I'm glad you're back safe," said Maggie. She liked Oral a lot, and didn't much care what he made up or didn't. "What are you going to do now?"

"What can I do? Try to get this mother off the ground. I'm thinking of bringing Radio Shack to task in federal court. I feel I have a case."

Maggie listened to the wind in the trees. "Do you really think you can do it, Oral? You think you can make it work again?"

"Sure I can. Or maybe not. You know what gets to me most on this world? Blue. We got reds and yellows and greens up the ass. But no blue. You got blues all over." Oral put aside his Sprite and found a bottle in a sack. "You hear from your daddy yet?"

"Not a thing. I'm afraid he's gone."

"Don't count him out. Stuck in interstellar tofu most likely. Many documented cases."

"Daddy hates tofu. Says it looks like someone threw up and tried again."

"He's got a point."

"What's it like where you come from, Oral. I mean where you lived before."

"You said you been to Fort Worth."

"Once when I was little."

"It doesn't look like that at all. Except out past Eighth Avenue by the tracks. Looks a little like that on a good day."

Maggie did fine in school after Jimmy Gerder left her alone. He cocked his head funny and walked with a limp. His folks finally sent him to Spokane to study forest conservation. By the time she reached sixteen Maggie began to make friends. She was surprised to be chosen for the Sidewinderettes, the third finest pep squad in the state. She joined the Drama Club and started writing plays of her own. She was filling out nicely and gave Uncle Ned a wide berth.

They were still dirt poor, but Uncle Ned and Aunt Grace attended several funerals a year. Two cousins died in Orlando not far from Disneyland, a car mishap in which both were killed outright. A nephew was mutilated beyond recognition in San Francisco, victim of a tuna-canning machine gone berserk. A new family tragedy could be expected around April, and again in late October when the weather got nice. Maggie was no longer taken in. She knew people died year round. They died in places like Cincinnati and Topeka where no one wanted to go. What Aunt Grace and Uncle Ned were doing was having fun. There wasn't much question about that. Maggie didn't like it but there was nothing she could do about it, either.

When Maggie was eighteen her play "Blue Sun Rising" was chosen for the senior drama presentation. It was a rousing success. Drama critic Harcourt Playce from San Angelo, Texas, told Maggie she showed promise as a writer. He gave her his personal card and the name of a Broadway theatrical producer in New York. The play was about a man who was searching for the true meaning of life on a world "very much like our own," as the program put it. There was no night at all on this world. A blue sun was always in the sky. Maggie wanted to ask Oral but was sure the principal wouldn't let him in.

Aunt Grace died a week after graduation. Maggie found her watching reruns of "M.A.S.H." She secretly wrote a specialist in Dallas. Told him what had happened to her mother and Aunt Grace. The specialist answered in time and said there might be genetic dysfunction. They were making great strides in the field. He advised her to avoid any shows in syndication.

Life with Uncle Ned wasn't easy. With Aunt Grace gone he no longer practiced restraint of any kind. Liquor came out of the nail bin at the store, and found its way to the kitchen. Girl and scientist magazines were displayed quite openly with *National Geographic*. Maggie began to jump when she heard a sound. There was a good chance Uncle Ned was there. Standing still too long was a mistake.

"You're going to have to stop that," said Maggie. "I mean it, Uncle Ned. I won't put up with it at all."

"You ought to get into gymnastics," said Uncle Ned. "I could work with you. Fix up bars and stuff out back. I know a lot more about it than you might think."

Maggie looked at Uncle Ned as if she were seeing him for the first time. His gaze was focused somewhere south of Houston. There seemed to be an electrical short in his face. His skin was the color of chuck roast hit with a hammer.

"I'm going to go," said Maggie. "I'm getting out of here."

"On what?" said Uncle Ned.

"I don't care on what, I'm just going. You try to stop me you'll wish you hadn't."

"You haven't got busfare to the bathroom."

"Then I'll walk."

"You do and you'll get raped and thrown in a ditch."

"I can get that first part here. I'll worry about the ditch when I come to it."

"Don't expect any help from me. I haven't got two dimes to rub together."

"You will," said Maggie. "Some cousin'll get himself hacked up in a sawmill in Las Vegas."

"Now that's plain ignorant," said Uncle Ned. "Especially for a high-school graduate. There isn't a lot of timber in Nevada. That's something you ought to know."

"Goodbye, Uncle Ned."

It took maybe nine minutes to pack. She took "Blue Sun Rising" and a number two pencil. Left her Sidewinderette pep jacket and took a sensible cloth coat. It was the tail end of summer in Texas, but New York looked cold on "Cagney and Lacey." She searched for something to steal. There were pawn shops all over New York. People stole for a living and sold the loot to buy scag and pot and ludes and whatever they could find to shoot up. There was no reason you couldn't buy food just as well. In the back of her aunt's closet she found a plastic beaded purse with eight dollars and thirty cents. Two sticks of Dentyne gum. Downstairs, Uncle Ned was watching the French National Girls' Field Hockey Finals. Maggie was stopped at the front door.

"It was me poured kerosene on your magazines," she said. "I thawed all the meat out too."

"I know it," said Uncle Ned. He didn't turn around. A girl named Nicole blocked a goal.

Hitchhiking was a frightening experience. She felt alone and vulnerable on the interstate. Oral's protective device was fastened securely about her waist. But what if it didn't work? What if she'd used it up with Jimmy Gerder? A man who sold prosthetic devices picked her up almost at once. His name was Sebert Lewis and he offered to send her to modeling school in Lubbock. He had helped several girls begin promising careers. Many were now in national magazines.

When Sebert stopped for gas, Maggie got out and ran. There were trucks everywhere. A chrome-black eighteen-wheeler city. They towered over Maggie on every side. In a moment she was lost. Some of the trucks were silent. Others rumbled deep and blinked red and yellow lights. There was no one about. She spotted a cafe through the dark. The drivers were likely all inside. It seemed like the middle of the night. French fries reached her on a light diesel breeze.

"I don't know what to do next!" she said aloud, determined not to cry. A big red truck stood by itself. A nice chrome bulldog on the front. It wouldn't hurt to rest and maybe hide from Sebert Lewis. She wrapped her coat around her and used her suitcase for a pillow. In a moment she was asleep. Only a short time later, a face looked directly into hers.

"Oh, Lord," said Maggie, "don't you dare do whatever it is you're thinking."

"Little lady, I'm not thinking on anything at all," the man said.

"Well all right then. If you mean it."

He was big, about as big a man as Maggie had ever seen. Dark brown eyes nearly lost in a face like a kindly pie. "You better be glad I'm a bug on maintenance," he said. "If I'd of took off you lyin' there under the tire I'd a squashed you flatter'n a dog on the road to Amarillo. You got a name, have you?"

"I'm Maggie McKenna from Marble Creek."

"You running away?"

"I'm going to New York City to write plays."

"You got folks back home?"

"My mother's dead and my father disappeared under strange circumstances. I'm a highschool graduate and a member of the Sidewinderettes. They don't take just everybody wants to get in. If you're thinking about calling Uncle Ned you just forget it."

"Not my place to say what you ought to do. I'm Billy C. Mace. How'd you get to here?"

"A man named Sebert Lewis picked me up. Said he'd put me through modeling school in Lubbock."

"Lord Jesus!" said Billy Mace. "Come on, get in. Nothing's going to happen to you now."

Riding in the cab of an eighteen-wheeler wasn't anything at all like a '72 Ford. You towered over the road and could see everything for miles. Cars got out of the way. Billy talked to other truckers on the road. His CB handle was Boomer Billy. He let Maggie talk to Black Buddy and Queen Louise and Stoker Fish. The truck seemed invulnerable. Nothing could possibly reach her. The road hummed miles below. There was even a place to sleep behind the driver. Billy guessed she was hungry, and before they left the stop he got cheeseburgers and onion rings to go. Billy kept plenty of Fritos and Hershey bars with almonds in the truck, and had Dr Peppers iced in a cooler. Maggie went to sleep listening to Waylon Jennings tapes. When she woke it was morning. Billy said they'd be in Tulsa in a minute.

"I've never been out of the state," said Maggie. "And here I am already in Oklahoma."

Billy pulled into a truck stop for breakfast. And then to another for lunch. He measured the distance in meals. "Two-hundred miles to lunch," he'd tell Maggie, or "a hundred-seventy to supper."

Maggie read him "Blue Sun Rising" while he drove.

"I don't know a lot about plays," said Billy when she was through, "but I don't see how that sucker can miss. That third act's a doozie."

"It needs a little work."

"Not as I see it it don't. You might want to rein in the Earth Mother symbolism a little, but that's just a layman's suggestion."

"You may be right," said Maggie.

She already knew Billy was well read. There was a shelf of books over the bunk. All the writers' names were John. John Gunther. John Milton. John D. McDonald.

"John's my daddy's name, God rest him," said Billy. "A man named John tells you something you can take it for a fact."

She told him about Uncle Ned and Aunt Grace. She didn't mention Oral Blue as they had not discussed the possibilities of extraterrestrial life. Billy was livid about her experience with Sebert Lewis.

"Lord Jesus himself was looking after you," he said. "No offense meant, but a girl pretty as you is just road bait, Maggie.

That modeling studio thing is likely a front. I expect this Sebert's a Red agent and into hard astrology on the side. Probably under deep cover for some time. I imagine there's a network of such places spread right across the country. Sebert and his cohorts cruise the roads for candidates like yourself. Couple of days in a little room and you're hopeless on drugs, ready to do unspeakable acts of every kind. There's a possibility of dogs. You wake up in bed with some greaser with a beard gets military aid from this godless administration. That's where your tax dollar goes. I don't want to scare you but you come real close to a bad end."

"I guess I don't know much do I?" said Maggie. "I feel awful dumb."

"You learn quick enough when you drive the big rigs. There's things go on you wouldn't believe. The Russians got the news media eatin' out of their hands. I could give you names you'd recognize at once if I was to say 'em. There are biological agents in everything you eat. Those lines and numbers they got on the back of everything you buy? What that is is a code. If you're not in the KGB or the Catholic Church you can't read it. Don't eat anything that's got three sixes. That's the sign of the beast. I wish to God I had control of my appetite. I can feel things jabbing away inside. White bread and tomatoes are pretty safe. And food isn't the only way they got you. TV's likely the worst. I can't *tell* you the danger of watching the tube."

"I already know about that," said Maggie.

Billy Mace had it all arranged. As good as any travel agent could do. He left her with a Choctaw driver named Henry Black Bear in St. Louis. Henry took her to Muncie, Indiana. Gave her over to a skeletal black man named Quincy Pride. Quincy's CB handle was "Ghost." He taught her the names of every Blues singer who had lived in New Orleans at any time. He played their tapes in order of appearance. At Pittsburgh she transferred to Tony D. Velotta, a handsome Italian with curly hair. Maggie thought he was the image of John Travolta.

And then very early in the morning, she woke to the bright sun in her eyes and crawled down from the bunk and Tony pointed and said, "Hey, there it is, kid. We're here."

Maggie could scarcely believe her eyes. The skyline exploded like needles in the sun. A lonely saxophone wailed offstage. She could see the trees blossom in Central Park. Smell the hotdogs cooking at the zoo. They were still in New Jersey, but they were close.

"Lordy," said Maggie, "it looks near as real as a movie."

As they sliced through upper Manhattan, Tony pointed out the sights. Not that there was an awful lot to see. He tried to explain the Bronx and Brooklyn and Queens, drawing a map with his finger on the dash. Maggie was thoroughly confused, and too excited to really care.

"So what are you going to do now? Where you going to stay?"

"I don't know," said Maggie. "I guess I'll find a hotel or something."

"How much money you got, you don't mind me asking?"

"Eight dollars and thirty cents. Now I know that's not a lot. I may have to look for work. It could take some time before I get my play produced."

"Holy Mother," said Tony. "You'd better stay with us."

"Now I couldn't do that. I'll be just fine."

"Right. For six, maybe eight minutes, tops."

The Velottas lived in Brooklyn. It might as well have been Mars as far as Maggie was concerned. There were eight people in the family. Tony and his wife Carla and little Tony who was two. Tony's father and mother, two younger brothers and a sister. They took in Maggie at once. They said she talked funny. They loved her. Carla gave her dresses. There was always plenty to eat. The Velottas had never heard of peanut butter. Maggie ate things called manicotti and veal piccata. Carla made spaghetti that didn't come out of a can. Nothing was like it was at Aunt Grace's and Uncle Ned's. The family was constantly in motion. Talking and running from one end of the house to the other.

Everyone yelled at each other and laughed. Maggie tasted wine for the first time. She'd never seen a wine bottle out of a paper sack. Everyone worked in the Velotta family bakery. Maggie helped out, carrying trays of pastry to the oven.

Tony stayed a week and went back on the road. Maggie talked to Carla one evening after little Tony was in bed.

"I've got to go see my producer," she said. "You all have been wonderful to me but I can't live off you forever. The sooner I get 'Blue Sun Rising' on Broadway the better."

"Yeah, right," said Carla. She looked patient and resigned. The whole family conferred on directions. An intricate map was drawn. Likely locations of muggers and addicts were marked with an 'x.'

"Don't talk to *anyone*," said Tony's mother. She crossed herself and gave Maggie a medal. "Especially don't talk to blacks and Puerto Ricans. Or Jews or people with slanty eyes or turbans. No turbans! Avoid men with Nazi haircuts and blue eyes. *Anyone* with blue eyes."

"Watch out for men in business suits and ties," said Papa Velotta. "They carry little black cases. Like women's purses only flat. There's supposed to be business inside but there's not. It's dope is what it is. Everybody knows what's going on."

"Don't talk to anyone on skates with orange hair," said Carla.

"A Baptist with funny eyes will give you a pamphlet," said Papa. "Don't take it. Watch out for white socks."

"I'll try to remember everything," said Maggie.

"I'll light a candle," said Mama Velotta.

Maggie called Marty Wilde, the Broadway producer. Wilde said she had a nice voice and he liked to encourage regional talent. He would see her at three that afternoon.

"What's the name of this play?" he wanted to know.

" 'Blue Sun Rising,' " said Maggie.

"Jesus, I like it. You don't have an agent or anything do you?"

"I just got in town," said Maggie.

"Good. I like to work with people direct."

PERPETUITY BLUES

• • •

Her first impression was right. Manhattan was as real as any cop show she'd ever seen. It was all there. The sounds, the smells, the people of many lands. There was a picture show on nearly every block. Everything was the same, everything was different. The city changed before her eyes. A man lying in the street. A kid tying celery to a cat. A woman dressed like a magazine cover, getting out of a cab. She watched the woman a long time. Maybe she'll come to see my play, Maggie thought. She looks like a woman who'd see a play.

Marty Wilde had a small office in a tall building. The building was nice outside. Inside, the halls were narrow. There was bathroom tile on the floors. A girl with carrot hair said Mr. Wilde would see her, and knocked on the wall. Marty came out at once.

"Maggie McKenna from Marble Creek, Texas," he said. "That's who you are. Maggie McKenna who wrote 'Blue Sun Rising.' Hey, get in here right now."

Marty ushered her in and offered a chair. The office was bigger than a closet and had faded brown pictures on the wall. Maggie realized these were Broadway greats, people she would likely meet later. There was very little light. The window looked out on a window. Black men in *Kung Fu* suits kicked at the air. There were piles of plays in the room. Plays spilling over tables and chairs and onto the floor. This sight left Maggie depressed. If there were that many plays in New York, they might never get around to "Blue Sun Rising."

Marty Wilde took her play and set it aside. He perched on the edge of his desk. "So tell me about Maggie McKenna. I can read an author like a page. I can see your play right on your face. A character sits down stage right. The phone rings. I can see that."

"That's amazing," said Maggie. Marty Wilde seemed worn to a nub. A turkey neck stuck out of his shirt. His eyes slept in little hammocks. "There's not much to tell about me. I think my play's good, Mr. Wilde. If it needs any changes I'm willing to do the work."

"Every play needs work. You take your Neil Simon or your Chekhov. A hit doesn't jump out of the typewriter and hop up on the stage."

"No, I guess not."

"You better believe it. Who's this guy give you my name?"

"Harcourt Playce, he works on the San Angelo paper."

"Short little man with a club foot. Wears a Mexican peso on a chain. Sure I remember."

This didn't sound like Mr. Playce but Maggie didn't want to interrupt.

"You say you haven't got an agent."

"No, sir, I sure don't."

"Let's cut the sir stuff, Maggie. I'm older than you in years but there's a spirit of youth pervades the stage. You're a very pretty girl. How you fixed for cash?"

"Not real good right now."

"My point exactly. Here's what I suggest. It's just an idea I'm throwing out. I take in a few writers on this scholarship thing which is hey, my way of paying Lady Broadway back in a small way. You stay at my place, we work together. I got a friend can give you good photo work. He's affiliated with a national modeling chain. All semi-tasteful stuff. You'd know his name the minute I said it."

"You want to take my picture?"

"Just an idea. Let's get you settled in."

"This sounds a lot like girls and scientists, Mr. Wilde. I don't see what it has to do with my play."

Marty came off the desk. "I want you to be comfortable with this."

"I'm not very comfortable right now."

"So let's talk. Tell me what you're feeling."

"You just talk from over there."

"You remind me a lot of Debra Winger. In a very classical sense."

"You remind me of someone, too."

"Jesus, what a sweet kid you are. We won't try to push it. Just let it happen." He took a step closer. A strange invisible force picked him up and hurled him against the wall. Pictures of near-greats shattered. Some crucial fault gave way in the stacks of plays. Acts and scenes spilled over Marty on the floor.

"I think you broke something," said Marty. "Where'd you learn that hold? You're awful quick."

The girl with carrot hair came in.

"Call somebody," said Marty. "Get me on the couch."

"I don't think we can work together," said Maggie. "I'm real displeased with your behavior."

"I can see you don't know shit about the theatre," said Marty. "You can't just waltz in here and expect to see your name in lights."

"You ought to be in jail. If you try to get in touch with me, I'll press charges."

Carla said she could stay as long as she wanted. There wasn't any reason to go look for another place.

"I've got to try it on my own," said Maggie. "I believe in my play. I don't believe everyone on Broadway's like Marty Wilde."

Carla could see that she was determined. "It's not easy to get work. Tony thinks a lot of you, Maggie. We all do. You're family."

"Oh, Carla." Maggie threw her arms around her. "You're the very best family I ever had."

Carla persuaded her to wait for the Sunday *Times*. Mama Velotta filled her up with food. "Eat now. You won't get a chance to later."

The room was on East 21st over an all-night Chinese restaurant. Maggie shared it with three girls named Jeannie, Eva, and Sherry. They all three worked for an insurance company. Maggie got a waitress job nights at the restaurant downstairs. There was just enough money to eat and pay the rent. She slept a few hours after work and took the play around days. No one wanted to see her. They asked her to mail copies and get an agent. Maggie cut down her meals to one a day, which allowed her to make a new copy of "Blue Sun Rising" every week. She even started a new play, using Sherry's portable Smith Corona and the backs of paper placemats from the job. The play was "Diesel and Roses," a psychological drama set in a truckstop cafe. Billy Mace was in it, and so was Henry Black Bear and Quincy Pride and Tony Velotta. Carla called. There was a postal money order from Marble Creek for $175 and a note.

"It's not good news," said Carla.

"Read it," said Maggie.

" 'Dying. Come home. Uncle Ned.' "

"Oh, Lord."

"I'm real sorry, honey."

"It's okay. We weren't close."

The thing to do was take the money and eat and make some copies of "Blue Sun Rising." And forget about Uncle Ned. Maggie couldn't do it. Even Uncle Ned deserved to have family put him in the ground. "I'll be back," she told New York, and made arrangements to meet Carla and get the money.

The first thing she noticed was things had changed in the year she'd been away. Instead of the '72 Ford, there was a late model Buick with a boat hitch on the back. Poking out of the garage was a Ranger fishing boat, an 18-footer with a big Merc outboard on the stern.

"You better be dead or dying," said Maggie.

The living room looked like Sears and Western Auto had exploded. There was a brand new Sony, and a VCR, and hit tapes like *Gymnasts in Chains*. The kitchen was a wildlife preserve. Maggie stood at the door but wouldn't go in. Things moved around under plates. There were cartons of Hershey bars and chips. Canned Danish hams and foreign mustards. All over the house there were things still in boxes. Uncle Ned had dug tunnels through empty bottles and dirty books. There were new Hawaiian shirts. Hush Puppies in several different styles. A man appeared in one of the tunnels.

"I'm Dr. Kraftt, I guess you're Maggie."

PERPETUITY BLUES

"Is he really dying? What's wrong with him?"

"Take your pick. The man's got everything. A person can't live like that and expect their organs to behave."

Maggie went upstairs. Uncle Ned looked dead already. There were green oxygen tanks and plastic tubes.

"I'm real glad you came. This is nice."

"Uncle Ned, where'd you get all this *stuff?*"

"That all you got to say? You don't want to hear how I am?"

"I can see how you are."

"You're entitled to bad feelings. I deserve whatever you want to dish out. I want to settle things up before I go to damnation and meet your aunt. Your father had an employee stock plan at Montgomery Wards. Left your mother well off and that woman was too cheap to spend it. We got the money when she died and you came to us. We sort of took these little vacations. Nothing big."

"Oh Lord."

"I guess we wronged you some."

"I guess I grew up on peanut butter and Campbell's soup is what happened."

"I've got a lot to answer for. There are certain character flaws."

"That's no big news to me."

"I can see a lot clearer from the unique position I got at the moment. Poised between one plane of being and the next. When your aunt died weakness began to thrive. I didn't mean to buy so much stuff."

"I don't suppose there's anything left."

"Not to speak of I wouldn't think. All that junk out there's on credit. It'll have to go back. The bank's got the house. There's forty-nine dollars in a Maxwell House can in the closet. I want you to have it."

"I'll take it."

"I wish you and me'd been closer. I hope you'll give me a kiss."

"I'd rather eat a toad," said Maggie.

• • •

Maggie saw Jimmie Gerder at the funeral. He still had a limp and kept his distance. She walked along the river to see Oral. It was fall, or as close as fall gets in that end of Texas. Dry leaves rattled and the Colorado was low. The log where she used to watch turtles was aground, trailing tangles of fishing line. The water was the color of chocolate milk and the turtles were gone. Oral was gone too. Brush had sprung up under the big native pecan. The place looked empty without the multi-blue pickup and the extraterrestrial trailer. Maggie wondered if he'd gotten things to work or just left. She asked around town, and no one seemed to remember seeing him go. After a Coke and a bacon and tomato at the cafe she figured she had enough to get back to New York if she sold a couple of things before Sears learned Uncle Ned was dead. Put that with her forty-nine-dollar inheritance and she could do it. There was fifteen dollars left from the ticket. Even dying, Uncle Ned had remembered to pay for only one way.

Winter in New York was bad. The Chinese restaurant became an outlet for video tapes. Sherry and Jeannie and Eva helped all they could. They carried Maggie on the rent and ran copies of "Blue Sun Rising" down at the insurance company. The Velottas tried to help, but Maggie wouldn't have it. She got part-time work at a pizza place on East 52nd. After work she walked bone-tired to the theatre district and looked at the lights. She read the names on the posters and watched people get out of cabs. There was a cold wet drizzle every night, but Maggie didn't mind. The streets reflected the magic and made it better. When the first snow fell she sewed a blanket in her coat. The coat smelled like anchovies and Sherry said she looked like a Chinese pilot. "For God's sake, baby, let me loan you a coat."

"I can manage," said Maggie, "you've done enough."

She could no longer afford subways or buses so she walked every day from her room. She lost weight and coughed most of the time. The owner asked her to leave. He said customers didn't like people coughing on their pizza. She didn't tell the girls she'd lost her job. They'd want to give her money. She looked, but there weren't any jobs to be had. Especially for girls who looked like bag ladies and sounded like Camille. She kept going out every day and coming back at night. Hunger wasn't a problem. She felt too sick to eat. One night she simply didn't go home. "What's the point? What's the use pretending? No one wants to look at 'Blue Sun Rising.' I can't get a job. I can't do anything at all."

The snow began to fall in slow motion, flakes the size of lemons. Broadway looked like a big Christmas tree someone had tossed out and forgot to take the lights.

"Look at the blues," said Maggie. "Oral liked the blues so much."

A man selling food gave her a pretzel and some mustard. The pretzel came up at once. A coughing fit hit her. She couldn't stop. First nighters hurried quickly by. Maggie pulled her coat up close and looked in the steamy windows of Times Square. Radios and German bayonets were half-off. There was a pre-Christmas sale on marital aids. She could still taste the mustard and the pretzel. A black man in sunglasses approached.

"You hurtin' bad, mama. You need something, I can maybe get it."

"No thank you," said Maggie.

I can't just stand here, she thought. I've got to do something. She couldn't feel her feet. Lights were jumping about. There was a paper box in the alley. The thing to do was to sit down and try to figure things out. She thought of a good line for "Diesel and Roses" and then forgot it. A cat looked in and sniffed; there were anchovies somewhere about. Maggie dreamed of daddy when he took her to the zoo. She dreamed of Oral under a tree and riding high with Billy Mace. The cab was toasty warm and Billy had burgers from McDonald's. She dreamed she heard applause. The cat started chewing on her coat. Oh Lord, I love New York, thought Maggie. If I can make it here, I can make it anywhere . . .

• • •

Carla looked ethereal, computer-enhanced.

"I guess I'm dying," said Maggie. "I'm sorry to get you out in this weather."

"Oh baby," said Carla, "hang on. Just hang on, Maggie."

Everything was fuzzy. The tubes hurt her nose. The walls were dark and needed painting. Sherry and Eva and Jeannie were there and all the Velottas. They bobbed about like balloons. Everyone had rings around their eyes.

"I want you to have 'Blue Sun Rising,' " said Maggie. "All of you. Equal shares. I've been thinking about off-Broadway lately. That might not be so hard. Don't see a man named Marty Wilde."

"All right, Maggie."

"She's going," someone said.

"Goodbye, Daddy. Goodbye, Oral," said Maggie.

The room looked nice. There was a big window with sun coming in. The doctor leaned down close. He smelled like good cologne. He smiled at Maggie and wrote something and left. A nice-looking man got up from a chair and stood by the bed.

"Hello. You feeling like something to drink? You want anything just ask."

"I'd like a Dr Pepper if you have one."

"You got it."

The man left and Maggie tried to stay awake. When she opened her eyes again it was late afternoon. The man was still there. A nurse came in and propped her up. The man brought her a fresh Dr Pepper.

"You look a lot like Tony," said Maggie. He did. The same crispy hair and dark eyes. A nice black suit and a gray tie. Maybe a couple of years older. "You know Tony and Carla?"

"They ask about you every day. You can see them real soon. Everybody's been pretty worried about you."

"I guess I 'bout died."

"Yeah, I guess you did."

"This place looks awful expensive. I don't want the Velottas or anyone spending a bundle on me."

"They won't. No problem."

"Hey, I know a swell place like this isn't *free*."

"We'll talk about it. Don't worry." The man smiled at Maggie and went away.

Maggie slept and got her appetite back and wondered where she was. The next afternoon the man was back. He helped her in a wheelchair and rolled her down the hall to a glassed-in room full of plants. There were cars outside in a circular drive. A fountain turned off for the winter. A snow-covered lawn and a dark line of trees. Far in the distance, pale blue hills against a cold and leaden sky. Men in sunglasses and overcoats walked around in the snow.

"I guess you're going to tell me where I am sometime," said Maggie. "I guess you're going to tell me who you are and what I'm doing in this place I can't afford."

"I'm Johnny Lucata," the man said. "Call me Johnny, Maggie. And this house belongs to a friend."

"He must be a friend of yours, then. I don't remember any friends with a house like this."

"You don't know him. But he's a friend of yours too." He seemed to hesitate. He straightened his tie. "Look, I got things to tell you. Things you need to know. You want we can talk when you feel a little better."

"I feel okay right now."

"Maybe. Only this is kinda nutsy stuff, you know? I don't want to put you back in bed or nothing."

"Mr. Lucata, whatever it is, I think I'll feel a lot better when I know what's going on."

"Right. Why not? So what do you know about olives?"

"What?"

"Olives. They got olives over in Italy. There's a place where the toe's kicking Sicily in the face. Calabria. Something like a state, only different. The man lives here, he's got a lot of the olive oil business in Calabria. Been in his family maybe four, five hundred years. You sure you want to do this now?"

"I'm sure, Mr. Lucata."

"Okay. There's this city called Reggio di Calabria right on the water. You can look and see Sicily real good. A couple of miles out of town is this castle. Been there forever, only now it's a place for monks. So what happens is a couple of months back this monk's digging around and finds this parchment in a box. It's real old and the monk reads it. What he sees shakes him up real bad. He's not going to go to the head monk because Catholics got this thing about stuff that even *starts* to get weird. But he's a monk, right? He can't just toss this thing away. He's got a sister knows a guy who's family to the man who lives here. So the box gets to Reggio and then it gets to him." Johnny Lucata looked at Maggie. "Here's the part I said gets spooky. What this parchment says, Maggie, is that the old duke who started up the family left all the olive business to *you*."

Maggie looked blank. "Now that doesn't make sense at all, Mr. Lucata."

"Yeah, tell me. It's the straight stuff. The experts been over it. I got a copy I can show you. It's all in Latin, but you can read the part that says Maggie McKenna of Marble Creek, Texas. We got the word out and we been looking all over trying to find you. But your uncle died and you came back to New York. We didn't know where to take it after that. Then someone in Tony's family mentions your name and it gets to us. The thing is now, the man lives here, he doesn't know what to make of all this, and he don't want to think about it a lot. He sure don't want to ask some cardinal or the Pqpe. What he *wants* to do is make it right for *you*, Maggie. This duke is his ancestor and he figures it's a matter of honor. I mean, he doesn't see you ought to get it *all*, but you ought to be in for a couple of points. He wants me to tell you he'd like to work it where you get maybe three, four mill a year out of this. He thinks that's fair and he knows you're pressed for cash."

Maggie sat up straight. "Are you by any chance talking about dollars? Three or four million *dollars?*"

"Five. I think we ought to say five. He kind of left that up to me. Don't worry about the taxes. We'll work a little off-tackle

Panama reverse through a Liechtenstein bank. You'll get the bread through a Daffy Duck Christmas Club account."

"I just can't hardly believe this, Mr. Lucata. It's like a dream or something. No one even knew I was going to *be* back then. Why, there wasn't even a *Texas!*"

"You got it."

"This castle. There's just these monks living there now?"

"Palazzo Azzuro. Means blue palace. I been there, it's nice. Painted blue all over. Inside and out. Every kind of blue you ever saw."

"*Blue?* Oh my goodness!"

"You okay?"

"Oral," said Maggie, "Oh Oral, you're the finest and dearest friend I ever had!"

When she was feeling like getting up and around, Johnny Lucata helped her find a relatively modest apartment off Fifth Avenue. Five mill or not, Maggie had been poor too long to start tossing money around. She did make sure there were always Dr Peppers and Baby Ruths in the fridge. And steaks and fresh fruit and nearly everything but Chinese food and pizza. Carla helped her find Bloomingdale's and Saks. Maggie picked out a new cloth coat. She sent nice perfume to Jeannie and Sherry and Eva, and paid them back triple what they'd spent to help her out. She gave presents to the Velottas and had everyone over for dinner. Johnny Lucata dropped by a lot. Just to see how she was doing. Sometimes he came in a cab. Sometimes he came in a black car with tinted windows and men wearing black suits and shades. He took her out to dinner and walks in the park. Sometimes Maggie made coffee, and they talked into the night. She read him "Blue Sun Rising" and he liked it.

"You don't have to say that, just because it's me."

"I mean it. I go to plays all the time. It's *real,* Maggie. You don't have to wonder what everybody's thinking, they just say it. I want you to talk to Whitney Hess."

"Whitney Hess the producer? Do you know him?"

"Yeah, sure I know him."

"I don't want to do that, Johnny. I don't want to get help from somebody just because he's a friend of yours. That's not right. I want 'Blue Sun Rising' to stand on its own."

"Are you kidding?" said Johnny. "Whitney Hess wouldn't buy a bad play from his dying mother. Besides, I want five points of this up front. You're not going to cut *me* out of a winner."

Tony and Carla and Tony's brothers and his sister and Mama and Papa Velotta dressed up for opening night. Johnny Lucata sent a limo to pick them up, and another to get Jeannie and Sherry and Eva. Tony got out the word, and the truckers found Billy Mace and Henry Black Bear and Quincy Pride. They all had seventh row center seats.

Maggie thought sure she was dreaming. Her name up in lights at the Shubert Theatre. Ladies in furs and jewels dressed up for opening night. Spotlights and TV cameras and people she'd only seen in the movies. She stayed outside for a long time. Standing in the very same spot where she'd thrown up pretzels in the street. Not far from the alley where she'd curled up in a box and nearly died. You just never know, she told herself. You just don't.

There was no need to wait for the reviews. After the first act, Whitney Hess said they had a smash on their hands. After the third act curtain, even Maggie believed it was true. The audience came to its feet and shouted, "author! author!" and someone told Maggie they meant *her*.

Johnny hurried her out of the Shubert by the side door. He wouldn't say where they were going. A black car was by the curb around the corner. There were men in overcoats and shades.

"I want you to meet somebody," said Johnny, and opened the rear door. "This is Maggie McKenna," he said. "Maggie, I'd like you to meet my father."

Maggie caught the proper respect in his voice. She looked inside and saw an old man sitting in the corner. He was lost in a black suit, a man no more substantial than a cut-rate chicken in a sack.

"That was a nice play," he said. "I like it a lot. I like plays with a story you can't guess what's going to happen all the time. There's nothing on the television but dirt. The Reds got people in the business. They built this place in Chelyabinsk looks just like Twentieth Century Fox. Writers, directors, the works. They teach 'em how to do stuff rots out your head then they send them over here. This is a great country. You keep writing nice plays."

"Thank you," said Maggie, "I'm very glad you liked it."

"Here. A little present from me. Your big night. You remember where you got it."

"I'm very grateful," said Maggie. "For everything." She leaned in and kissed him on the cheek.

"That's very nice. You're a nice girl. She's a nice girl, Johnny."

Johnny took her back inside, and on the way home after the big party Whitney Hess gave at the Plaza, Maggie opened her present. It was a pendant shaped like an olive. Pale emeralds formed the olive and a ruby sat on top for the pimento.

"It's just lovely," said Maggie.

"The old man's got a lot of class."

"Why didn't you tell me that was your father's house, Johnny? I kinda guessed later but I didn't know for sure."

"Wasn't the right time."

"And it's the right time now?"

"Yeah, I guess it is."

"Whitney Hess wants to go into rehearsal on 'Diesel and Roses' next month. I'm going to ask Billy Mace and Henry Black Bear and Quincy Pride to come on as technical advisors. There's not a thing for them to do, but I'd like to have them around."

"That's nice. It's a good idea."

"Whitney says everyone wants the movie rights to 'Blue Sun Rising.' Which means we'll get a picture deal up front for 'Diesel and Roses.' Oh Lordy, I can't believe all this is really happening. Everything in my life's been either awful or as good as it can be."

"It's going to stay good now, Maggie." He leaned over and kissed her quickly. Maggie stared at the tinted glass.

"You've never done *that* before."

"Well, I have now."

Maggie wondered what was happening inside. She felt funny all over. She was dizzy from the kiss. She liked Johnny a lot but she'd never liked him quite like this. She wanted him to kiss her again and again, but not *now*. Not wearing Oral's protective device, which she'd worn since her very first day in New York. It was something she'd never thought about before. What if you really *wanted* someone to do something to you? Would the wire and the black stone know that it wasn't Jimmy Gerder or Marty Wilde? She certainly couldn't take the chance of finding out.

The phone was ringing when they got to her apartment.

"You're famous," said Johnny. "That'll go on all night."

"No, it won't," said Maggie, "just take it off the hook. I can be famous tomorrow. Tonight I just want to be me."

Johnny had a funny look in his eyes. She was sure he was going to kiss her right then. "Just wait right there," she said. "Don't go away. Get me a Dr Pepper and open yourself a beer." She hurried into the bedroom and shut the door. Raised up her skirt and slipped the little wire off her waist. Her heart was beating fast. "I hope you know what you're doing, Maggie McKenna."

Johnny gave a decidedly angry shout from the other room. Another man yelled. Something fell to the floor.

"Good heavens, what's that?" said Maggie. She rushed into the room. Johnny had a young man backed against the wall, threatening him with a fist. The man wore a patched cardigan sweater and khaki pants. He was trying to hit Johnny with a sack.

"Who the hell are *you*," said Johnny, "what are you doing in here!"

"Oh my God," said Maggie. She stopped in her tracks, then ran past Johnny and threw her arms around the other man's neck. "Oh Daddy, I *knew* you wouldn't leave me! I knew you'd come back!"

"Maggie? Is that you? Why, you're all grown up! Say, what a looker you are. Where am I? How's your mother?"

"We'll talk about that. Just sit down and rest." She could hardly see through her tears. "I'll explain," she told Johnny. "At least I'll give it a try. Oh, Oral, I hope you're wherever it is you want to be. Johnny, get Daddy a Dr Pepper." She gave him the sack. "Put this in the kitchen and you come right back."

"It's just catfood and bread," said Daddy. "I think that fella there took me wrong."

"Everything's all right now."

"Maggie, I feel like I've been floating around in yogurt. Forever or maybe an hour and a half. It's hard to say. I don't know. I'm greatly confused for the moment. I *ought* to be more than five years older'n you."

"It happens. There are documented cases. Just sit down and rest. There's plenty of time to talk." Johnny came back with a Dr Pepper. She gave it to her father and led Johnny to the kitchen.

"I don't get it," said Johnny.

"You got all that business with the monks, you can learn to handle this. Just hold me a minute, all right? And do what you did in the car."

Johnny kissed her a very long time. Maggie was sure she was going to faint.

"I'm a real serious guy," said Johnny. "I'm not just playing around. I got very strong emotions."

"I like you a lot," said Maggie. "I'm not sure I could love a man in your line of work."

"I'm in olives. I got a nice family business."

"You've got a family in overcoats and shades, Johnny Lucata."

"Okay, so we'll work something out."

"I guess maybe we will. I keep forgetting I'm in olive oil too. Maybe you better kiss me again. Johnny there's *so* much I want us to do. I want to show you Marble Creek. I want to show you green turtles on a log and the Sidewinderettes doing a halftime double-snake whip. I want to see every single shade of blue in that castle and I've got a simply *great* idea for a play. Oh, Johnny, Daddy's back and you're here and I've got about everything there *is*. New York is such a knocked-out crazy wonderful town!"

BLUNDERBORE

Esther M. Friesner

"Blunderbore" was purchased by Gardner Dozois, and appeared in the September 1990 issue of Asimov's, *with an illustration by George Thompson. Friesner's first sale was to* Asimov's, *under George Scithers in 1982, and she's made several sales here subsequently under Gardner Dozois (we also have several new stories by her in inventory). In the years since 1982, she's become one of the most prolific of modern fantasists, with thirteen novels in print, and has established herself as one of the funniest writers to enter the field in some while. Her many novels include* Mustapha and His Wise Dog, Elf Defense, Druid's Blood, Sphinxes Wild, Here Be Demons, Demon Blues, Hooray for Hellywood, Broadway Banshee, Ragnarok and Roll, *and* The Water King's Daughter. *She's reported to be at work on her first hard science fiction novel. She lives with her family in Madison, Connecticut.*

In the hilarious story that follows, she takes us along on a very modern woman's very modern date in modern Manhattan with a very old-style bachelor . . .

"Jack? *That* pipsqueak? What do you *think* I did with the spunkless little blowhard?" Another dart flew from the huge hand, landed with surprising accuracy dead center on the distant target. A long gob of spittle, no less precisely aimed, whizzed from between massive teeth gappy and yellow enough to pass for a jaundiced Stonehenge.

The lady shuddered as the giant's expectoration splatted *perfecto* right between her well-shined shoes. Not a driblet landed on their newly Vaselined black patent leather, but sometimes the *thought* is more than enough.

"I can't for the life of me imagine," she managed to reply. As a feeble jest she suggested, "Ground his bones to make your bread?"

The giant roared, a sound that might have been laughter or a bout with sinusitis. His nose was humped and sickled, red with many draughts of Guinness and lousy with pock-marks. Black hairs bristled angrily from the nostrils, hinting at hibernating porcupines.

"Grind his bones to make my bread? *There's* a good 'un!" He reached for another dart. The barkeep made haste to assure his client of a constant supply. "How'd the weensy manling live to juggle all them cowpats about killing me if I'd done *that*, eh?" The giant's lips pursed, the lower resembling a saddle of mutton, the upper two hams. "Oversight, that. I never thought he'd want it noised 'round how I used him. Writing it all up, though, telling it twisty, making out as he'd done for *me*—Well, I learned much of men from that, I did. Grind his bones. . . ." He grinned. "Not his bones. 'Tis nut bread I fancy."

The barkeep refilled the giant's mug and leaned across the counter to inquire softly, deferentially of the lady whether she would like another Bombay gin? She shook her head. Her lips were dry, her throat drier. The proper business suit that was her chrysalis of choice remained pressed, immaculate, entire, unsplit, though this was Saturday night and by rights she should be swinging by nyloned knees from the ceiling fixtures along about this hour.

The giant drained his measure and launched his dart. It split the first, just like Robin Hood's arrow always splintered those arrogant shafts of his unworthy rivals if they dared hog the bullseye before he shot. The legendary arrows were wood; the actual darts were steel. The metal let out a high, terrified shriek as it was so cavalierly violated from feathered wazoo to razored tip.

"But enough about me," said the giant. He shifted his weight on the bar. No stool would hold him, and he wasn't about to stand after a hard day's labor. The wood complained much, but only buckled a little. Bare feet with toes like hairy pattypan squashes swung back and forth, drumming the mahogany. "How'd a nice girl like *you* come to run a personal ad, then?"

The lady took a deep breath. Her left hand began to wrench at the rings on her right. "It was my roommate's idea," she began. The rush of red murder she sent bubbling over a vision of her roommate's face left her giddy. How could she speak coherently when every second sentence to come to mind was *the bitch dies?*

Carthago delenda esse.

Two hours ago she had been afflicted merely with the usual crawful of first-meeting jitters, the nausea and palpitations often prequel to lucky at love. Then the giant walked in. He knew her at once (his telephone voice gave no warning, its quaint accent, seductive pitch and timbre conspiring only to make her silly with lust, inspiring her to heights of self-descriptive facility that left her thoroughly, instantly identifiable among thousands). She could not evade him by pretending to be someone else, or via the more practical shrieks of the bar's other patrons as they fled wildly out of the place beneath the fuzzy arbors of his armpits.

She had tried, though. He caught her.

Trapped, she had spent the time since in imagining all the most agonizing, crippling, humiliating ways one might dispose of a roommate who gave bad advice and did not clean the kitchen sufficiently well to make up for it. She supposed she might turn her over to the giant. There *was* that. First, however, present survival.

"You see," she went on, "I've been involved with someone for a very long time. His name's Ian. We had a—an understanding. A completely open twoness based on mutual respect and noninterference. But he needed personal space, room for growth, emotional evolution."

"Oh, ar?" the giant commented politely.

She sighed. "Well, he's gone now, you see. To find himself.

And I have to get on with maximizing my own life experience. That's why the ad. It's rather hard to go back to ordinary dating when a long-term relationship ends, don't you agree?"

The giant's brows slipped down into the trenches of his forehead. "Bashed his skull in, did they?" he asked.

"?" she answered. It was really the best she could do, and not too paltry, under the circumstances.

"Trolls. Else renegade knights. One tump of the mace upside your goodman's temple-bone, and you're left to dance the widow's bransle. Too bad, too bad. Likely they raped you after, it's only their way, but still—" His eyebrows now slumped back like eels amorously exhausted. "Did hope as you'd be a virgin. I likes virgins."

"Will you excuse me?" she said, slipping gracefully from the barstool. "I have to go powder my nose." As an out it was retro, and sexist, and shameful in the extreme, but all she asked was that it save her skin long enough for her to get some use out of her thirty-five session contract at the Tropitan Salon.

In the ladies' room was a stall, and in the stall was a toilet, and over the toilet was a window, and *out* the window she did go, as fast as ever she could slink. There were runs in her Dior pantyhose and wrinkles in her Anne Klein linen suit, raw scrapes striping the sides of her Maud Frizon patent heels (one of which landed in the toilet) and four scales gouged out of her genuine alligator belt, but she emerged alive enough to pitch headfirst into the alley outside. In the alley was a dumpster, and in the dumpster were a lot of empty liquor cartons and dud lottery tickets and some really ripe muddled fruit-leavings. This she added to her roommate's account of payments due as she huddled in the taxi, plucked lemon rinds from her hair, and cursed all the way home.

And cursed louder, with renewed gusto, when her roommate told her that *she* didn't have to sit there and listen to *this* crap. *She* hadn't told her to stick the fateful ad in the New York *Review*. *She* thought the *Village Voice* was quite good enough, thank you, and just see where pretensions can leave you, stuck in some downtown bar with a creature out of myth and Jungian archetype whose toenails want cleaning.

The roommate quit. She packed. She left and moved in with her boyfriend who played the saxophone and really *understood* the *ausgleibnicht Kunstfertseichnet* of Michael J. Fox movies.

The lady was left with vengeance placed on Hold eternal, and a full month's New York rent to pay in heart's blood.

There was also a message on her answering machine. It was from *him.* Why not?

She changed her telephone number. She changed the locks on her doors. She acquired a new roommate by means of utmost discretion. She made a serious commitment to oat bran and never, never more used the weather or the time of the month as excuses for neglecting her morning jog. She became a whole person, relentless mistress of a whole mind in a whole body. Giants never happened to holistic people. Could be it was attributable to all that fiber. Her wholeness was astonishingly complete, given the strain a middle-management position could put on one's full immersion in the universe. Nothing daunted, she immersed.

He was waiting for her one Friday evening as she came out of her office building on Third Avenue. The air smelled of April and perambulating hot dog wagons. He brought flowers and a dead sheep.

"Sorry I was I got too personal with asking you things," he said, tendering her the bouquet. She took it gingerly, only because if you counted the attaché case clutched tightly in her other hand, it left her no possibility of accepting the sheep.

Apparently he saw it that way, too, for he disposed of the beastie casually, in three bites, head first, fleece and all, just as if it were an afterthought instead of over a hundred pounds of mutton. Wiping lanolin from his chin, he said, "Find it in your heart, could you, to let me buy you a drink, and no hard feelings?"

What could she do? See if he'd take "Just Say No" for an answer? A poor gamble. Run away? Not with the lights and rush hour traffic against her. Scream for help? Her supervisor might be watching. He was everywhere, paranoia justified, like a February flu. He was always looking for excuses to shunt her career into corporate sandpits.

She smiled at the giant. "Why not?" she said. If only to discover how he'd found her. Magic? Sorcery? God's vengeance on her (so Mama would maintain) for the Pill?

No magic was at work, beyond the ordinary levels present in the city, nor any intervention even marginally divine. He reminded her that she herself had told him where she worked when first they'd spoken over the phone. It was a beginner's mistake. Give nothing away. She sipped her drink (*this* bar, too, had turned into a wasteland when they entered) and asked him to pass the bran-nuts.

When guided off the subject of giant-killers, he turned out to be a pleasant enough companion, or at any rate no worse than her mother's idea of a good catch. She wasn't getting any younger, *ipse dixit* Mama. Well, neither was *he*. Three hundred years old, and then some sum he chose not to mention. He had never felt better in his life. He ate right. He took responsibility for his place in the ecoverse. The American climate agreed with him. He loved New York.

She had had worse Friday evenings.

There was *CATS* on Saturday and a gallery opening Sunday morning after brunch at the Plaza. A hansom cab was waiting to convey her all the way home from the office on Monday afternoon. Her bedroom blazed lunatic with flowers. There were no more ovine incidents.

He supported Public Television. He preferred Ebert to Siskel, and had no use under God's great sky for Pauline Kael, unless his sourdough recipe needed an extra shot of calcium some time. He had season tickets to the opera, though he only went for Verdi and *Peter Grimes*. Wagner upset him. Fafnir and the frost giants, you know.

She sympathized. Prejudice was so *fifties*.

He didn't like zydeco, but for her sake he tried to understand it. While Springsteen left him cold, Steeleye Span was all right, and Clam Chower, and any old Joni Mitchell. He couldn't dance at *all*. He subscribed to *The New Yorker*, though only for the cartoons. Desconstructionist criticism gave him the quinsy. He couldn't find shoes that both fit him and made a fashion statement. He wore the poorly tanned skins of those few Central Park carriage horses in their declining years that he had been able to purchase. He had absolutely no taste in neckties.

He insisted that she pick all the restaurants they patronized, and relied on her judgment when it came to ordering the wine.

He was just *filthy* with money, all liquid assets, mostly gold and priceless gems that he had come by in the course of his European career. He didn't really get her joke about how he'd staged unfriendly takeovers of dragon-guarded hoards, but he laughed anyway. He offered to show her the skull of the last dragon he'd killed. That had been on Orkney, and the puny size of the Worm had been what decided him to move across the sea to a fresher, more vital world. A man likes a challenge. Things were better in the Catskills.

His voice in person slowly acquired the beguilement of that same voice over the phone. At her gentle prodding, Hoffritz provided the proper tools for him to trim toenails and nose bristles. He was never late for a date. He let her pay the tab on occasion, without turning it into a favor or patronage. Three hundred years and then some could give a man a certain high octane pick-up rate in mastering the social graces, if he so wished. For her sake, he so wished, and he wasn't shy about letting her know as much. Vulnerability did not terrify him.

And she knew that he needed her.

The first time they made love, she had her qualms. She was haunted by the old chestnut about how the size of a man's nose may give the inquisitive some hint as to the relative proportion of an analogously shaped nether organ. The giant's *nose* was—well—gigantic, *voyons!* A sight too *much* so to leave the lady entirely comfortable in her mind.

Still, needs must. She wanted to. She felt a certain obligation, though through no deed or word of his. His few good-night kisses were not taken from her as if by right of conquest, or even secured as reparation for his having bought her dinner. He never treated her like a feedbag whore. All the marks of tenderness that passed between them were granted on her initiative alone. One kiss from him dewed fully half her face, left her skin atingle with moisture and mint residue from his hastily munched rolls of Breath-Savers. It was an unusual and exhilarating experience. Perverse curiosity needled her on to further experimental delvings.

Were she honest with herself, she would have admitted too that, since Ian, she was hornier than hell.

He was not so eager to accept her offer as she had imagined. "What's wrong?" she demanded. Angry gooseflesh rose beneath the peach satin of her lace-trimmed teddy. The dressing room at Victoria's Secret had been *much* warmer. Chills and rejection coupled together to nettle her deeply.

The giant's jowls drooped, laden with rue. "Ar, it's not *you*, dearie. Sweet as fresh plums you be, and welcome as spring. All as you've done for me up to this—" he fingered the charming regimental-stripe tie she'd had custom made for him at Brooks Brothers "—that's been more'n I ever hoped for. I be content wi' that."

She crossed her arms, being unable to cross her legs. There was nothing in the room for her to sit on. Furniture had been displaced by futons, in deference to accommodating his needs. "You don't find me attractive!" she accused.

He tried to convince her otherwise, but she knew lies when she heard them. She'd lunched with enough salesfolk for that. By bullying and pouting and sniveling dangerously near the precipice of tears, she cudgeled out the truth.

"I ain't—I ain't so much—I don't got too big a—I has me lackings." He showed her proof.

Well, yes, he was right. What he said was *true*. If you were comparing him to other *giants*, that is.

She forced herself to look very solemn. She told him that size was not everything, but love conquers all. If he could lie, so could she.

They were very happy together.

Three weeks later, while she was at work, Ian called. "I've found myself," he told her. "I was right there, all along. I'm a better person now. I'm sensitive to a woman's needs. I can give you the support you want *and* the space you require. I'm ready to nurture. We can complete each other. I'm not afraid of commitment. Isn't that swell?"

"Drop dead," she said.

"But I *need* you."

Well, and what harm was there in meeting him for a drink after work, after all was said and done, after what they'd once meant to each other? She couldn't show herself to be afraid of seeing him again. They could talk about old times, catharsis over cocktails and a mouth-watering assortment of high-fiber, low-cholesterol veggies. She could handle that. She was strong. She was capable.

She was a fool for blonds with black eyebrows.

The giant's brows were black enough to satisfy, but as for *hair*, blond or otherwise, his pate gleamed smooth as a crystal goblet. Some things a woman doesn't miss until someone else points out that she does not have them. This holds as true for textured pantyhose as for men. In the bar with Ian, she found herself recalling how she used to run her fingers through his golden curls. Said fingers began to drum an antsy anthem on the sides of her lowball glass. Odd pulsings disturbed her body's chosen serenity. She really should be getting home.

"I like what you've done with the place," Ian said, kicking off his shoes, tossing his tie onto the futon. "So tell me about your new roommate."

"She minds her own business," she said. "She doesn't ask questions, she doesn't get ideas." She brought the drinks from the living room, even though he knew where everything was kept and had offered to do it. The giant's mug was in the liquor cabinet now. Ian might *not* mistake it for an oversized, spoutless martini pitcher. Few of those had BLUNDERBORE handpainted around their circumference, or an etched pattern of grinning skulls. *Damn* few.

Ian was essentially naked when she returned. A sheet counts for little in the strategies of such impromptu dalliances. He took his drink and raised it in her honor. "To your health," he said. He sipped while she stripped and slipped between the sheets beside him. He paused. A thought had touched him.

"Speaking of which. . . ." He made a pointed inquiry into her social life since last they'd shared bedlinens.

Her eyes narrowed, her mouth screwed itself into a tight little macadamia nut of pique. "I've only seen one other man since you ran out. I'm still seeing him." She laced barbs to this last sentence but he remained unstung.

"And, uh, how well do you know him? I mean, what was he doing before he met *you?* Personal habits? Companions? Lifestyle of choice? *You* know."

"He killed dragons. He ground men's bones to make his bread. He never read any Garrison Keillor."

"*Men's* bones?" Ian's lovesome brows rose a moiety. "Um, did he ever give you any particular reason for, that is, in a manner of speaking, such exclusive tastes?"

"Put up," she told him, "or shut up. In fact, shut up whether you put up or no."

Ian steepled his fingers. "We are very hostile," he said, and *tsk'd* audibly.

"Blunderbore doesn't think so," she shot back. "Blunderbore isn't intimidated by a strong woman."

"Blunderbore?" Ian echoed. The steeple toppled. *"Blunderbore?"*

"It's a perfectly good name for a giant," she said, folding her arms.

Somewhere beyond the bedroom door—the apartment door, to be exact—a key jiggled in a lock.

"Your roommate?" Ian whispered.

"SURPRISE, ME DARLING!"

Oh, it was *very* sad, very sad indeed. A giant is like other men, only with a bigger heart to break. No vows had been uttered, and Blunderbore agreed in principle about mature adult persons in a modern relationship needing their own space, but *still*—

Temper, temper.

The bread was warm from the oven. "Have a piece, love. I'll butter it for you."

BLUNDERBORE

"I'm not that peckish now," said Blunderbore. He leaned his face on one hand and gazed morosely at the steaming slab, very white where it was not yellow with melting butter. "Like to clog me arteries sommat fierce, that be. Take it away."

"Tsk. You're just being difficult. You've eaten butter by the hogshead before this. And after all my trouble, following that silly old family recipe of yours. No appreciation. None whatsoever."

"Ar, all right, all right, cease yer cackling." The giant raised the slice to his lips and bit. He chewed. "Gritty," he said.

"You don't like my cooking." Ian pouted.

"Na, then, I never did say—It's *my* fault,'tis, for not having a more careful eye at the handmill. I'll see to it as I grind 'em finer next time. Oh, it's as grand a baking as ever I've tasted, lad, and that's taking in some three hundred years. Don't take on so, there's me dearie. Come, sit you down on old Blunderbore's knee and tell us how them wicked, wicked futures traders has treated our Ian today."

Ian dimpled and dropped the sulks. Obediently he climbed the giant's knee.

Blunderbore smiled indulgently at his manling. Maybe this one would last. In a certain light, the lad looked just like Jack.

Maybe *this* one wouldn't kiss and tell.

THE FRONT PAGE

Ronald Anthony Cross

"The Front Page" was purchased by Gardner Dozois, and appeared in the November 1988 issue of Asimov's, *with an illustration by Robert Shore. Cross made his first sale to* Asimov's *under Shawna McCarthy in 1983, and has since sold a number of other stories to the magazine, including another odd adventure of Eddie Zuckos, the intrepid hero of "The Front Page." He is also a frequent contributor to* The Magazine of Fantasy and Science Fiction, *and has sold to* Universe, New Worlds, Orbit, Pulphouse, Weird Tales, Far Frontiers, In the Fields of Fire, New Pathways, The Berkley Showcase, *and elsewhere. His only novel to date,* Prisoners of Paradise, *appeared in 1988, and he has his first collection coming up from* Pulphouse's Author's Choice Monthly *series. He lives in Santa Monica, California.*

Here he treats us to a wild and gonzo look at what reporters for supermarket tabloids really have to go through in order to come up with those bizarre headlines you goggle at while waiting in the checkout line. . . .

The door was unlocked, open a crack, but I could see the chains, many chains. And her little glittering eyes. Too bright.

"How can I be sure you're not one of *them?*"

I had no idea who "them" was. "I told you I was one of *us*, and I showed you this I.D." I flashed my *National Revealer* press I.D. card again. "It's the real thing," I said. I ought to know, I

THE FRONT PAGE 73

had worked hard enough to earn it.

"They have many secret superhuman powers," she said. "They could use them easily enough to get a press card." But she sounded a little unsure.

"No they couldn't," I insisted. "No one, but *no* one, could get one of these except a genuine reporter for the *Rev*, as we reporters call it."

"Well . . ." she said coquettishly, and one chain came off.

"But wait a minute," she said. "I know. Who's Liz's secret heartthrob? You should know *that* if you work for the *Revealer*."

My mind spun dizzily. Who was Liz, anyway? I had a vague picture of some overweight, aging movie star who was never very attractive to start with. The publication I worked for had at least one article about her in each issue. Her amazing love life. The food she ate. The shoes she wore. Etc. For some reason I could never get a handle on, she seemed to be just about the most interesting human being in the world to everyone but me.

"I love her," Bernie (that's my boss) had confessed. "I've always loved her. Ever since she was an innocent little seventeen-year-old who loved horses." (Who loved *horses?!?*)

My one respite from the agony of being subjected to a plethora of horrendously trivial assignments was that I had never been assigned to do surveillance on the stars.

"I don't know," I pleaded, "listen, I just write it. I don't read it—okay? Get out your last issue. Page three. 'Lightning Strikes Statue' is the title, by Eddie Zuckos. That's me, see?" I showed her the card again.

"Oh yes, I remember that one. The statue came to life momentarily and walked a few steps across the lawn. You had photos of the footprints."

I nodded yes. A chain came off. I nodded again. Another chain came off. Now I had the key—I just kept nodding and saying "yes" until all the chains were off and I was in the house.

"By the way, who *are* 'they'?" I said.

"Oh, you know!" she said coyly.

Okay. I won't describe the inside of her house. Why should I? It was so full of furniture and lamps and grotesque statues, and little glass figures of every creature under the sun, and paintings of cats made out of copper or tinfoil or whatever, and Jesus Christ over and over: so many paintings and statues of Christ that it was a veritable army, except that it was an army of skinny naked guys being whipped, tortured, and crucified. I won't describe the inside of her house because it was too complex for my consciousness to register. I'd have to live there for a couple of weeks, and each day maybe inventory another corner until I had it all down on paper.

"All right," I said, in my let's-get-down-to-business tone. I was so sick of these Mickey Mouse assignments. When would I ever get on to something *big?*

"Name. Date of birth." I went through the list of personal data.

"Now what exactly was it you wanted to report?"

She turned her head and lowered her eyelids and looked at me slyly, from an odd sideways angle, like a bird.

"*You* know," she said.

"I have to ask these questions," I said, "it's important that I get your exact answers. In your own words. You see? At the *Revealer* we make every possible effort to get the truth, see?"

Really, I knew what it was. I was just hoping we'd got it wrong.

"Well, Eddie," she said, "I vomit rocks."

"You vomit rocks," I repeated, trying to keep the disgust out of my voice.

"Not just any rocks. Some of them are in the shape of Our Lord and Savior Jesus Christ. Some of them look a little like Liz. In profile. That's what Harriet sez. Harriet's my next-door neighbor and she's a big, big fan. Of Liz, not of me, of course. 'Why, that looks just *like* her,' she sez. And I sez, 'Who, Harriet?' and Harriet sez, 'My *God*, Edna, can't you *see* it, it's just as plain as the nose on your face. It looks just like the queen.' Harriet always calls her 'the queen,' you see. I always said, 'Harriet, she's not the queen. That's a different

Elizabeth,' but Harriet always sez, 'She's the queen to me, Edna. Liz'll always be the queen to me.' "

Chattering all the while, Edna led me through the jungle of grotesque bric-a-brac into her bedroom. I was totally lost before we were halfway there.

"Doesn't look like Jesus to *me*," I said, holding the oddly shaped little stone in the palm of my hand. Starting to get interested. "Looks like that guy in the Bruce Lee movie. What's his name? Big mean guy with a beard."

"Does *not* look mean," she said, snatching it out of my hands. "He *is* a movie star, though," she said, getting interested herself.

"Sure," I said. "I can't think of his name." (Who could?) "Great big guy with a beard." A vague picture of a tall, bearded guy with Bruce Lee's foot stuck in his face flitted through my mind's eye.

"Let me get a couple of shots." I started to check out the camera, which was in its case, slung around my neck.

"I thought you were supposed to have someone following you around with a camera, taking all the photos for you."

Sure, that'll be the day.

"He's sick," I said. "And since I'm pretty good at it myself . . ."

"Jack of many trades," she was saying scornfully, when my beeper went off, saving me from the "master of none" part.

"Emergency. Can I use your phone?"

She led me back into the living room, where, sure enough, there was a phone hidden amidst all the bric-a-brac.

"Vomiting *stones?*" Bernie shouted in a shocked voice. "Oh yeah, I forgot. Forget about that. Get the hell over to Fletcher Valley. Can you get there by sundown? Get there, okay? This is important, Eddie. Handle with care, do you dig? Don't fuck it up, or it's your last big assignment as well as your first. Dig? Jesus Christ, vomiting stones, *what* vomiting stones?"

"You're the one gave me the lead," I shouted back into the empty phone. Bernie had already hung up. What was the address he'd given me? 537 Grove Avenue or Grove Street, Fletcher Valley? That had better be it.

A disappointed Mrs. Edna Fosbert let me out of the house every bit as reluctantly as she had let me in.

"Are you sure you can't tell me what it's all about?"

"Secret," I said. "My lips are sealed. But you can read all about it in the next *Rev*. Besides," I said, hoping I was lying, "cheer up, I'll be back to finish up your story."

It was just turning dark when I pulled past the narrow drive leading off the road from the mailbox marked Ms. T. T. Jones 537 Grove Avenue. I breathed a sigh of relief. So far, so good. As Bernie had taken pains to point out to me, this was my first big one. And only because I was the only *Rev* reporter close enough to get here on time. I had better not . . . , etc.

So I drove past and pulled up and parked off the side of the road and hurried up the rustic driveway on foot, sly reporter-style.

The door flew open before I could knock on it.

"Hurry!" she said. "He'll be here soon."

I stood there momentarily stunned, mouth open. It was just too weird to see her here in this rustic environment, standing in the doorway dressed in red silk panties and brassiere, sort of bulging out of everything.

"Well for gawdssake will you hurry up and git *in* here? You spose to be used to this kind of stuff by now, ain't you? Like a doctor or somethin'?"

"Yeah, right," I mumbled, following her as she led me quickly through the front room and straight into her bedroom.

"You can hide in the closet there, and just leave the door open a little, see? He'll be here just any *minute* now. See here, that's his mark." She tilted her head back and showed me two little puckered sores on her neck.

She shivered dramatically and squealed—"Ow, I jess love it!" And smiled. "Quick, get *in* there."

Inside the closet, I set up my camera. Checked it out twice. I would have to use the flash. Great, right? I wished to hell they'd give me one of those cameras with the super film you can use with hardly any light at all, but fat chance.

I was checking out my camera for the third time when I heard a loud fizzy sound like steak sizzling on a barbecue, and I peeked out just in time to see smoke pouring in through the open bedroom window.

"Thet you, Count? Don't you jest come in here thet way without askin' or nothin'. I'm half nakid."

Gradually the smoke took on the shape of a skinny little dark-haired guy, his hair plastered back and greased down flat as a pancake, wearing a tux.

"I like you zat way, princess."

"I don't know why you must insist on callin' me a princess when I must hev told you a million times thet I am only a simple farmer lady. Tina T. Jones, thet's me, is all."

The little guy just practically swooped on her. But she pushed him away from her, playfully.

"You will always be zee princess to me," he said in his phony accent.

Now I could get a pretty good look at him in the moonlight flooding in the open window, and I was amazed at how ugly he was. His nose was too big, his lips were flabby and sort of protruding like he was always on the verge of sucking something, and his eyes were tiny. He was one of those tiny teeny little guys who always look like they're going to break into tears any minute. But he sure wasn't shy. He snatched excitedly at her red brassiere, but she coyly slapped his hand away.

"Honestly," she said, "I don't see what it is you *see* in me. I'm jest a simple farmer lady. Not like some glamor queen you see in the *National Revealer* or nuthin'." She leered knowingly in my direction.

Shit! I figured it better be now or never. So what the hell, I just kicked open the door, and popped the flash. The room lit up.

The little guy actually *hissed*, and held his arm up in front of his eyes in a dramatic pose.

Then the light faded.

"Jesus Christ!" he said in plain English. "Did you just take my picture, with a flash bulb? What the fuck are you, the village idiot?"

Suddenly it dawned on me. Shit, what was I doing? I dropped the camera like a rock, it bounced on my chest, luckily I still had it in the case, and I held my hands up in front of me, forming a cross with my index fingers. "Whooo," I said, inadvertently trying to add a music score. "Whooo, it's the *sign of the cross*."

The count stopped advancing; for a moment he looked puzzled. Then he said, "You're *kidding*."

Suddenly he slapped me in the arm hard enough to spin me around, bounce me off the wall and down on the floor.

"Sanctimonious religious prig!" he shouted in a mean tone of voice. "What the hell do I care about your WASP sensibilities?"

"Ow, damn it, you really hit hard for such a little guy," I groaned.

"Hit hard? Hit *hard?* I'm a *vampire*, you dunce. Get up and I'll show you hit hard!"

All this time Tina was pulling at his elbow. "Don't hurt him, honey. Don't break his camera, okay? I'll *never* git on the cover."

"Get out of my way, you dumb bimbo." He shoved her aside.

"Dumb *bimbo?* You said you loved me. You told me I was your princess. Now I'm just a dumb bimbo. Oh, God. You men! You all are just brute animals. You don't care . . . you don't . . ." She threw herself down on the bed and started weeping hysterically.

The count grabbed hold of my wrist and snapped me up onto my feet like I was a whip and he was cracking it. He grabbed hold of my throat with his other hand, then turned back toward the bed.

"Stop it, will you? Stop that crying. Listen, you *are* still my princess, of course. I just . . . lost control, is all. This was . . . I mean, Zis was a crazy idea, princess. In zee first place, everyone knows you can't take a photo of a vampire."

"I didn't know that," I choked, genuinely surprised.

"Shut up, idiot," the count said, clamping down a little extra on the throat.

"Ztop crying, my zweet. Et weel all be . . ."

"I thought you really loved me," Tina bawled.

"I do. I do!"

"Listen," I choked, barely able to get it out. "If you kill me she's going to be issed-pay."

"Then it's going to be ater-lay for oo-yay. Where she can't ee-say," he hissed, dragging me toward the front door.

"Is thet pig Latin? Are you men talkin' pig Latin around me? Damn you," Tina shouted, sitting up on the bed. "Don't you *dare*."

"Listen, my princess, we are not speaking the . . . how you zay . . . Latin pig talk. But we have to go outside for a moment or two, and . . . well, we have some important things to zettle."

"You men!" Tina said disgustedly. "Well, hurry right back here, Count, because we've got some important things to settle, too, right here between us. And there won't be no more don't-you-know-*what* till they're settled, neither."

I tried to cry out, but he had found just the right amount of pressure to shut me down, and was just dragging me out of the door when my beeper went off again.

"Vot is dat?" he said.

I pointed at my open mouth, and gasped like a fish out of water.

"For gawdssake, will you let go of his throat so the man can answer you?" Tina said.

"All right. All right." He let go.

"Emergency beeper," I said. "Quick, where's your phone?"

I slammed down the receiver. *I can't believe it*, I thought. *Twice in the same day. Me. Eddie Zuckos.*

Tina and the count were staring at me expectantly.

"Flying saucers are invading earth," I said. "They've just set down in a farmer's cornfield a few miles from here. Wilmer Everett?"

"Why, I know him," Tina said, "jest straight up Grove Avenue, take a left on Grove Place, but don't y'all get confused and head on out Grove Lane, ya hear? Anyhow, ya jest go right out Grove Place about half a mile, till ya come to thet great big oak tree, only ya won't be able ta see it, it bein' the pitch black dark middle of the night'n all. But if ya *could* see it, ya jest . . ."

"Oh for Godssake, will you shut up!" the count shouted.

Tina began to weep and mumble about men again, as if that little jerk had anything to do with *men*.

"Sorry," I said in my sincerest tone of voice, "but this is a real Class A emergency here. We can only thank God that farmer had a copy of the *National Revealer* with the emergency number on the cover. He got through to us, and we've got to get through to him."

I put out my hand to the count. "I guess we'll just have to put aside our differences for now, so that I can continue the *Revealer's* policy of bringing the truth to the people.—The sometimes very weird truth," I added.

Tina now had new tears in her eyes. "Thet's *beautiful*," she said.

The next thing I knew, I was in the old Ford, racing up Grove this and down Grove that, with Tina shooting out a steady stream of complex, almost baroque, directions.

"Ya see that old shack over to the right? Course not. How *could* you see it, it bein' dark as sin 'n all? But if ya *could*, you wouldn't have wanted to turn *there*, that bein' about three blocks too soon—hey, slow down, y'all just missed the turn you wanted while I was busy explainin'!" We backed up.

"Wish I hed time ta change inta somethin' nice and do somethin' with this hair." She looked coyly at the count, who ignored her.

"Cue," I said. "Cue."

THE FRONT PAGE 81

"Ze hair looks great," the count grumbled. "This had better be for real, Eddie."

I slammed on the brakes, and the car skidded to a halt, swerving sideways. I locked my glance into his. "Are you questioning the honesty of the *National Revealer?*" I said between gritted teeth.

"Will you men stop squabbling like little boys and get on with it? Of course nobody's questioning the *Revealer*, it bein' the only paper in town prints the whole total weird truth without any regard for its reputation. You can't *get* more honest then thet, can you? Now will you for gawdssake stop squabbling and drive?"

I drove. I had given up trying to ditch the count and Tina, who was now wearing some kind of huge pink puffs for slippers and a fluorescent pink bathrobe, and who looked as if she belonged in a flying saucer anyway.

"What flying saucer?" the old man said, in a slow, mechanical-sounding voice. "You must have created a mistake. Beings from another planet many universes away here have arrived only never.—Not even," he added, just to be sure.

"Well, sorry to have bothered you, old timer. Must have been a crank call. Hard to imagine someone would do that to the *National Rev*, but sorry to have . . ."

"Ix-nay with the ong-wray umber-nay," the count said. "You idiot, can't you tell he's been ossessed-pay?"

"Ossessed-pay?" I mumbled. That was a hard one.

"Being," the farmer said, "ossessed-pay is no part of this vocabulary. Elucidate, please?"

"Possessed!" the count shouted. "Ucking-fay *ossess*ed-pay, get it? Po*sess*ed!" He was positively shrieking with rage.

"Possessed," the old man said. "No, not! Neither controlled nor dominated am I. Not even now by beings from outer space who are not now here.—Even!" he added.

The count shoved the old man aside and rushed into the house. "Where are they? What's going on here?"

"Be careful, honey," Tina said. "He's an old man."

"Be careful, sure," the count grumbled, wandering into the kitchen. "Be especially careful with the body of a host. Sure, that's one of the vampire ten commandments, right?"

The old farmer followed us into the living room: "Do *not*, if I may advise, search out back in the cornfield for little men kneeling down controlling this flesh form with a remote control device. Find them there you will not," the old man suggested helpfully.

And sure enough, that's where we found them. Ugly little green buggers, giggling, one of them apparently controlling the poor old farmer from a device that looked suspiciously like a super-advanced TV remote control. A Sony, probably. The rest of them appeared to be busy constructing a larger machine, unlike anything I'd ever seen before. When they saw us they suddenly shouted "Oh oh! oh oh!" over and over again. Sounded sort of like a chorus of frogs.

"My Gawd, they're ugly," Tina whispered in awe. She ought to know, having a love affair with the count and all.

Pop. Pop. Pop. I lit up the scene with my flash. I had them. I had them now.

They dropped the control, and jumped up, hands over eyes, and stumbled about mumbling, "Hurt. Hurt. Bad light! Too much. Bad bad bad. Now no more good behavior here. No more fun guys! Control everybody on Earth all the time. Hurt you bad and much of it."

The old farmer stumbled and then shook his head. "What the . . ." he said. "Whew, thought I was a *Martian* or somethin' there fer a minute."

Then he looked out into the field at the little men and their machine, and past them at the saucer.

"What the . . . ? You little basterds wrecked half a my cornfield, did you? Think it's just about time to kick me some butt round here."

He started rolling up his sleeves.

Now all the little green men were holding up their little green fists and backing off in a group. Muttering "Fight fight fight, kill kill kill."

"Why, my Gawd," Tina whispered, "they're all stark stitch *nakid*."

The count furled his cape and hissed dramatically. Then he rushed into the field, shouting, "These humans are *my* cattle, and no little green noseballs are taking them away from me!"

The little green men broke and ran for the saucer, all the time yelling "Oh oh! oh oh!" They barely made it, and they slammed the hatch just in front of the count's rather large nose—if "slammed" can be used to describe a process whereby a lot of oddly shaped pieces of some kind of weird shiny silver metal fit themselves together like a crossword puzzle.

And soon we were standing there watching a small glowing light shoot across the sky and blink out.

"Romantic, ain't it?" Tina sighed.

Still hissing and fuming in maniacal rage, the count was prancing about tearing the hell out of their strange machine. Finally, having trampled it to bits, breathing hard, but still looking pissed, he turned back to me. "And now, my friend, you and I have some usiness-bay to tend-ay to."

"Oh, I don't think so, Count," I said. "I think we'll both have to postpone it for some other time."

"And what makes you think *that*, my little human?"

Little—*me?* I was damn near as big as him.

"Well," I said, "see that light around the edges of those mountains over there? Guess what *that* means? I've got a busy day ahead of me; and as for you, well, you do know what they say about vampires and the sun, don't you?"

"Shit," he hissed, and threw his cloak over his head. "I just *hate* the sun!"

Tina put her arm around his shoulder and gave me a look of tender disgust. "Ah never will figure out why he makes such a big fuss over a little sunlight."

"Oh yeah," he mumbled from under his cloak, "try a little skin cancer sometime, princess, see how you like that."

"Oh, thet's not really true," Tina said, leading him back toward the house, "thet's just one of those scare stories the mainstream press is always printin' to up their newspaper sales.

Can't trust none of 'em. 'Cept the *Revealer*, thet is." She turned and smiled at me.

I looked at my watch. Yawned. No rest for the wicked. "Come on," I said, "give you a ride. Gotta get this story off prontissimo."

"Just hold yer horses there a minute, sonny," the old man cut in, "How 'bout givin' me a hint 'bout just what am I supposed to do with all *thet*." He pointed to the broken parts of the alien machinery.

"Well, you probably should call the Army," I said.

"And what will they do with it?"

"Probably label it 'top secret,' then hide it away somewhere where no one can find it, and then forget about it."

"Figures," he said, and turned wearily back toward his house. But then he grunted and turned back around, cupped his hand over his beardcovered mouth, and whispered in my ear, "What *is* he, anyway, sonny, a pansy or somethin'? Never did see a man so upset over a little sunlight."

All the way back, the count huddled under his cloak, mumbling to himself.

"You all stop back agin sometime," Tina said, when I dropped them off. "Sometime when we're better company, a little later on in the evening. He's probly jest gonna spend the whole rest of the day mumblin' to hisself in the closet."

A few days later I picked up a copy of this week's *Rev*, shaking with anticipation, and just froze in disbelief at what I saw on the cover.

I charged to the nearest phonebooth and fairly threw the poor guy who was using it out into the street.

"Will you calm down, Eddie," Bernie said. "It's right there on page three. 'Vampire Saves Earth From Flying Saucer Men.' Photo of nobody chasing a bunch of little green guys through a cornfield. I repeat: 'photo of *no*body.' "

I slammed down the receiver. Broke it, I hope. I stared again at the cover of the *National Revealer*, and then threw it down.

Picked it up again and called back. Hadn't quite broken the phone, it just hissed a little in my ear.

"You calmed down a little now?" Bernie said.

"Jesus Christ!" I said, "Jesus *Christ*, Bernie: 'Liz Takes Monkey Lover'? *That's* the lead story? 'Liz Takes Monkey Lover'?"

"Hey," he said. "We're an honest rag here at the *Rev*. We give people what they really want. Not what the government wants them to hear, like those other rags. 'Vampire saves earth' is great news, it's just too bad both stories broke at the same time. Liz comes first. Pretty much no matter *what* happens, Liz comes first." He paused.

"Besides," he chuckled, "that monkey's a pretty cute little guy."

I just stood there staring at the receiver. Maybe I *had* broken it.

"Don't you find that monkey lover stuff kind of . . . well . . . revolting, Bernie?"

"Frankly, I find it sort of refreshingly piquant," he said in a sincere tone of voice.

This time I put the receiver down gently. I'd probably want to use it again sometime, I realized.

Outside the booth it was a bright shiny day. Beautiful weather. *Wonder what Liz does on days like this*, I thought to myself. I'm kind of getting interested, I realized, with a start. Maybe I'm front page potential after all.

STABLE STRATEGIES FOR MIDDLE MANAGEMENT

Eileen Gunn

"Stable Strategies for Middle Management" was purchased by Gardner Dozois, and appeared in the June 1988 issue of Asimov's, *with an illustration by Marc Davis. It went on to be one of our most popular stories that year, and Gunn has subsequently sold several other popular stories to the magazine. She is not a prolific writer, but, like her friend Howard Waldrop, her stories are well worth waiting for—she has a twisted perspective on life unlike anyone else's, and a strange and pungent sense of humor all her own. She has been a Nebula and Hugo finalist several times, has also sold stories to markets such as* Amazing, Proteus, Tales by Moonlight, *and* Alternate Presidents, *and is currently at work on her first novel. She lives in Seattle, Washington, where she is involved in the administration of the Clarion West workshop.*

In the strange and funny story that follows, she outlines for us one of the most bizarre career-advancement ploys that anyone is ever likely to see....

Our cousin the insect has an external skeleton made of shiny brown chitin, a material that is particularly responsive to the demands of evolution. Just as bioengineering has sculpted our bodies into new forms, so evolution has shaped the early insect's chewing mouthparts into her descendants' chisels, siphons, and stilettos, and has molded from the chitin special tools—pockets to carry pollen, combs to clean her compound eyes, notches on which she can fiddle a song.

> From the popular science
> program *Insect People!*

I awoke this morning to discover that bioengineering had made demands upon me during the night. My tongue had turned into a stiletto, and my left hand now contained a small chitinous comb, as if for cleaning a compound eye. Since I didn't have compound eyes, I thought that perhaps this presaged some change to come.

I dragged myself out of bed, wondering how I was going to drink my coffee through a stiletto. Was I now expected to kill my breakfast, and dispense with coffee entirely? I hoped I was not evolving into a creature whose survival depended on early-morning alertness. My circadian rhythms would no doubt keep pace with any physical changes, but my unevolved soul was repulsed at the thought of my waking cheerfully at dawn, ravenous for some wriggly little creature that had arisen even earlier.

I looked down at Greg, still asleep, the edge of our red and white quilt pulled up under his chin. His mouth had changed during the night too, and seemed to contain some sort of a long probe. Were we growing apart?

I reached down with my unchanged hand and touched his hair. It was still shiny brown, soft and thick, luxurious. But along his cheek, under his beard, I could feel patches of sclerotin, as the flexible chitin in his skin was slowly hardening to an impermeable armor.

He opened his eyes, staring blearily forward without moving his head. I could see him move his mouth cautiously, examining its internal changes. He turned his head and looked up at me, rubbing his hair slightly into my hand.

"Time to get up?" he asked. I nodded. "Oh, God," he said. He said this every morning. It was like a prayer.

"I'll make coffee," I said. "Do you want some?"

He shook his head slowly. "Just a glass of apricot nectar," he said. He unrolled his long, rough tongue and looked at it, slightly cross-eyed. "This is real interesting, but it wasn't in the catalog. I'll be sipping lunch from flowers pretty soon. That ought to draw a second glance at Duke's."

"I thought account execs were expected to sip their lunches," I said.

"Not from the flower arrangements . . ." he said, still exploring the odd shape of his mouth. Then he looked up at me and reached up from under the covers. "Come here."

It had been a while, I thought, and I had to get to work. But he did smell terribly attractive. Perhaps he was developing aphrodisiac scent glands. I climbed back under the covers and stretched my body against his. We were both developing chitinous knobs and odd lumps that made this less than comfortable. "How am I supposed to kiss you with a stiletto in my mouth?" I asked.

"There are other things to do. New equipment presents new possibilities." He pushed the covers back and ran his unchanged hands down my body from shoulder to thigh. "Let me know if my tongue is too rough."

It was not.

Fuzzy-minded, I got out of bed for the second time and drifted into the kitchen.

Measuring the coffee into the grinder, I realized that I was no longer interested in drinking it, although it was diverting for a moment to spear the beans with my stiletto. What was the damn thing for, anyhow? I wasn't sure I wanted to find out.

Putting the grinder aside, I poured a can of apricot nectar into a tulip glass. Shallow glasses were going to be a problem for Greg in the future, I thought. Not to mention solid food.

My particular problem, however, if I could figure out what I was supposed to eat for breakfast, was getting to the office in time for my ten AM meeting. Maybe I'd just skip breakfast. I dressed quickly and dashed out the door before Greg was even out of bed.

• • •

Thirty minutes later, I was more or less awake and sitting in the small conference room with the new marketing manager, listening to him lay out his plan for the Model 2000 launch.

In signing up for his bioengineering program, Harry had chosen specialized primate adaptation, B-E Option No. 4. He had evolved into a text-book example: small and long-limbed, with forward-facing eyes for judging distances and long, grasping fingers to keep him from falling out of his tree.

He was dressed for success in a pin-striped three-piece suit that fit his simian proportions perfectly. I wondered what premium he paid for custom-made. Or did he patronize a ready-to-wear shop that catered especially to primates?

I listened as he leaped agilely from one ridiculous marketing premise to the next. Trying to borrow credibility from mathematics and engineering, he used wildly metaphoric bizspeak, "factoring in the need for pipeline throughout," "fine-tuning the media mix," without even cracking a smile.

Harry had been with the company only a few months, straight from business school. He saw himself as a much-needed infusion of talent. I didn't like him, but I envied his ability to root through his subconscious and toss out one half-formed idea after another. I know he felt it reflected badly on me that I didn't join in and spew forth a random selection of promotional suggestions.

I didn't think much of his marketing plan. The advertising section was a textbook application of theory with no practical basis. I had two options: I could force him to accept a solution that would work, or I could yes him to death, making sure everybody understood it was his idea. I knew which path I'd take.

"Yeah, we can do that for you," I told him. "No problem." We'd see which of us would survive and which was hurtling to an evolutionary dead end.

Although Harry had won his point, he continued to belabor it. My attention wandered—I'd heard it all before. His voice was the hum of an air conditioner, a familiar, easily ignored background noise. I drowsed and new emotions stirred in me, yearnings to float through moist air currents, to land on bright surfaces, to engorge myself with warm, wet food.

Adrift in insect dreams, I became sharply aware of the bare skin of Harry's arm, between his gold-plated watchband and his rolled-up sleeve, as he manipulated papers on the conference room table. He smelled greasily delicious, like a pepperoni pizza or a charcoal-broiled hamburger. I realized he probably wouldn't taste as good as he smelled, but I was hungry. My stiletto-like tongue was there for a purpose, and it wasn't to skewer cubes of tofu. I leaned over his arm and braced myself against the back of his hand, probing with my stylets to find a capillary.

Harry noticed what I was doing and swatted me sharply on the side of the head. I pulled away before he could hit me again.

"We were discussing the Model 2000 launch. Or have you forgotten?" he said, rubbing his arm.

"Sorry. I skipped breakfast this morning." I was embarrassed.

"Well, get your hormones adjusted, for chrissake." He was annoyed, and I couldn't really blame him. "Let's get back to the media allocation issue, if you can keep your mind on it. I've got another meeting at eleven in Building Two."

Inappropriate feeding behavior was not unusual in the company, and corporate etiquette sometimes allowed minor lapses to pass without pursuit. Of course, I could no longer hope that he would support me on moving some money out of the direct-mail budget. . . .

During the remainder of the meeting, my glance kept drifting through the open door of the conference room, toward a large decorative plant in the hall, one of those oases of generic greenery that dot the corporate landscape. It didn't look succulent exactly—it obviously wasn't what I would have preferred to eat if I hadn't been so hungry—but I wondered if I swung both ways?

I grabbed a handful of the broad leaves as I left the room and carried them back to my office. With my tongue, I probed a vein in the thickest part of a leaf. It wasn't so bad. Tasted green. I sucked them dry and tossed the husks in the wastebasket.

I was still omnivorous, at least—female mosquitoes don't eat plants. So the process wasn't complete. . . .

I got a cup of coffee, for company, from the kitchenette and sat in my office with the door closed and wondered what was happening. The incident with Harry disturbed me. Was I turning into a mosquito? If so, what the hell kind of good was that supposed to do me? The company didn't have any use for a whining loner.

There was a knock at the door, and my boss stuck his head in. I nodded and gestured him into my office. He sat down in the visitor's chair on the other side of my desk. From the look on his face, I could tell Harry had talked to him already.

Tom Samson was an older guy, pre-bioengineering. He was well versed in stimulus-response techniques, but had somehow never made it to the top job. I liked him, but then that was what he intended. Without sacrificing authority, he had pitched his appearance, his gestures, the tone of his voice, to the warm end of the spectrum. Even though I knew what he was doing, it worked.

He looked at me with what appeared to be sympathy, but was actually a practiced sign stimulus, intended to defuse any fight-or-flight response. "Is there something bothering you, Margaret?"

"Bothering me? I'm hungry, that's all. I get short-tempered when I'm hungry."

Watch it, I thought. He hasn't referred to the incident; leave it for him to bring up. I made my mind go blank and forced myself to meet his eyes. A shifty gaze is a guilty gaze.

Tom just looked at me, biding his time, waiting for me to put myself on the spot. My coffee smelt burnt, but I stuck my tongue in it and pretended to drink. "I'm just not human until I've had my coffee in the morning." Sounded phony. Shut up, I thought.

This was the opening that Tom was waiting for. "That's what I wanted to speak to you about, Margaret." He sat there, hunched over in a relaxed way, like a mountain gorilla, unthreatened by natural enemies. "I just talked to Harry Winthrop, and he said you were trying to suck his blood during a meeting on marketing strategy." He paused for a moment to check my reaction, but the neutral expression was fixed on my face and I said nothing. His face changed to project disappointment. "You know, when we noticed you were developing three distinct body segments, we had great hopes for you. But your actions just don't reflect the social and organizational development we expected."

He paused, and it was my turn to say something in my defense. "Most insects are solitary, you know. Perhaps the company erred in hoping for a termite or an ant. I'm not responsible for that."

"Now, Margaret," he said, his voice simulating genial reprimand. "This isn't the jungle, you know. When you signed those consent forms, you agreed to let the B-E staff mold you into a more useful corporate organism. But this isn't nature, this is man reshaping nature. It doesn't follow the old rules. You can truly be anything you want to be. But you have to cooperate."

"I'm doing the best I can," I said, cooperatively. "I'm putting in eighty hours a week."

"Margaret, the quality of your work is not an issue. It's your interactions with others that you have to work on. You have to learn to work as part of the group. I just cannot permit such backbiting to continue. I'll have Arthur get you an appointment this afternoon with the B-E counselor." Arthur was his secretary. He knew everything that happened in the department and mostly kept his mouth shut.

"I'd be a social insect if I could manage it," I muttered as Tom left my office. "But I've never known what to say to people in bars."

For lunch I met Greg and our friend David Detlor at a health-food restaurant that advertises fifty different kinds of fruit nectar. We'd never eaten there before, but Greg knew he'd love the place. It was already a favorite of David's, and he still has all his teeth, so I figured it would be okay with me.

David was there when I arrived, but not Greg. David works for the company too, in a different department. He, however, has proved remarkably resistant to corporate blandishment. Not only has he never undertaken B-E, he hasn't even bought a three-piece suit. Today he was wearing chewed-up blue jeans and a flashy Hawaiian shirt, of a type that was cool about ten years ago.

"Your boss lets you dress like that?" I asked.

"We have this agreement. I don't tell her she has to give me a job, and she doesn't tell me what to wear."

David's perspective on life is very different from mine. And I don't think it's just that he's in R&D and I'm in Advertising—it's more basic than that. Where he sees the world as a bunch of really neat but optional puzzles put there for his enjoyment, I see it as . . . well, as a series of SATs.

"So what's new with you guys?" he asked, while we stood around waiting for a table.

"Greg's turning into a goddamn butterfly. He went out last week and bought a dozen Italian silk sweaters. It's not a corporate look."

"He's not a corporate *guy*, Margaret."

"Then why is he having all this B-E done if he's not even going to use it?"

"He's dressing up a little. He just wants to look nice. Like Michael Jackson, you know?"

I couldn't tell whether David was kidding me or not. Then he started telling me about his music, this barbershop quartet that he sings in. They were going to dress in black leather for the next competition and sing Shel Silverstein's "Come to Me, My Masochistic Baby."

"It'll knock them on their tails," he said gleefully. "We've already got a great arrangement."

"Do you think it will win, David?" It seemed too weird to please the judges in that sort of a show.

"Who cares?" said David. He didn't look worried.

Just then Greg showed up. He was wearing a cobalt blue silk sweater with a copper green design on it. Italian. He was also wearing a pair of dangly earrings shaped like bright blue airplanes. We were shown to a table near a display of carved vegetables.

"This is great," said David. "Everybody wants to sit near the vegetables. It's where you sit to be *seen* in this place." He nodded to Greg. "I think it's your sweater."

"It's the butterfly in my personality," said Greg. "Headwaiters never used to do stuff like this for me. I always got the table next to the espresso machine."

If Greg was going to go on about the perks that come with being a butterfly, I was going to change the subject.

"David, how come you still haven't signed up for B-E?" I asked. "The company pays half the cost, and they don't ask questions."

David screwed up his mouth, raised his hands to his face, and made small, twitching, insect gestures, as if grooming his nose and eyes. "I'm doing okay the way I am."

Greg chuckled at this, but I was serious. "You'll get ahead faster with a little adjustment. Plus you're showing a good attitude, you know, if you do it."

"I'm getting ahead faster than I want to right now—it looks like I won't be able to take the three months off that I wanted this summer."

"Three months?" I was astonished. "Aren't you afraid you won't have a job to come back to?"

"I could live with that," said David calmly, opening his menu.

The waiter took our orders. We sat for a moment in a companionable silence, the self-congratulation that follows ordering high-fiber foodstuffs. Then I told them the story of my encounter with Harry Winthrop.

"There's something wrong with me," I said. "Why suck his blood? What good is that supposed to do me?"

"Well," said David, "*you* chose this schedule of treatments. Where did you want it to go?"

"According to the catalog," I said, "the No. 2 Insect Option is supposed to make me into a successful competitor for a middle-management niche, with triggerable responses that can be useful in gaining entry to upper hierarchical levels. Unquote." Of course, that was just ad talk—I didn't really expect it to do all that. "That's what I want. I want to be in charge. I want to be the boss."

"Maybe you should go back to BioEngineering and try again," said Greg. "Sometimes the hormones don't do what you expect. Look at my tongue, for instance." He unfurled it gently and rolled it back into his mouth. "Though I'm sort of getting to like it." He sucked at his drink, making disgusting slurping sounds. He didn't need a straw.

"Don't bother with it, Margaret," said David firmly, taking a cup of rosehip tea from the waiter. "Bioengineering is a waste of time and money and millions of years of evolution. If human beings were intended to be managers, we'd have evolved pin-striped body covering."

"That's cleverly put," I said, "but it's dead wrong."

The waiter brought our lunches, and we stopped talking as he put them in front of us. It seemed like the anticipatory silence of three very hungry people, but was in fact the polite silence of three people who have been brought up not to argue in front of disinterested bystanders. As soon as he left, we resumed the discussion.

"I mean it," David said. "The dubious survival benefits of management aside, bioengineering is a waste of effort. Harry Winthrop, for instance, doesn't need B-E at all. Here he is, fresh out of business school, audibly buzzing with lust for a high-level management position. Basically he's just marking time until a presidency opens up somewhere. And what gives him the edge over you is his youth and inexperience, not some specialized primate adaptation."

"Well," I said with some asperity, "he's not constrained by a knowledge of what's failed in the past, that's for sure. But saying that doesn't solve my problem, David. Harry's signed up. I've signed up. The changes are under way and I don't have any choice."

I squeezed a huge glob of honey into my tea from a plastic bottle shaped like a teddy bear. I took a sip of the tea; it was minty and very sweet. "And now I'm turning into the wrong kind of insect. It's ruined my ability to deal with Product Marketing."

"Oh, give it a rest!" said Greg suddenly. "This is *so* boring. I don't want to hear any more about corporate hugger-mugger. Let's talk about something that's fun."

I had had enough of Greg's lepidopterate lack of concentration. "Something that's *fun?* I've invested all my time and most of my genetic material in this job. This is all the goddamn fun there is."

The honeyed tea made me feel hot. My stomach itched—I wondered if I was having an allergic reaction. I scratched, and not discreetly. My hand came out from under my shirt full of little waxy scales. What the hell was going on under there? I tasted one of the scales; it was wax all right. Worker bee changes? I couldn't help myself—I stuffed the wax into my mouth.

David was busying himself with his alfalfa sprouts, but Greg looked disgusted. "That's gross, Margaret," he said. He made a face, sticking his tongue part way out. Talk about gross. "Can't you wait until after lunch?"

I was doing what came naturally, and did not dignify his statement with a response. There was a side dish of bee pollen on the table. I took a spoonful and mixed it with the wax, chewing noisily. I'd had a rough morning, and bickering with Greg wasn't making the day more pleasant.

Besides, neither he nor David has any real respect for my position in the company. Greg doesn't take my job seriously at all. And David simply does what he wants to do, regardless of whether it makes any money, for himself or anyone else. He was giving me a back-to-nature lecture, and it was far too late for that.

This whole lunch was a waste of time. I was tired of listening to them, and felt an intense urge to get back to work. A couple of quick stings distracted them both: I had the advantage of surprise. I ate some more honey and quickly waxed them over. They were soon hibernating side by side in two large octagonal cells.

I looked around the restaurant. People were rather nervously pretending not to have noticed. I called the waiter over and handed him my credit card. He signaled to several bus boys, who brought a covered cart and took Greg and David away. "They'll eat themselves out of that by Thursday afternoon," I told him. "Store them on their sides in a warm, dry place, away from direct heat." I left a large tip.

I walked back to the office, feeling a bit ashamed of myself. A couple days of hibernation weren't going to make Greg or David more sympathetic to my problems. And they'd be real mad when they got out.

I didn't use to do things like that. I used to be more patient, didn't I? More appreciative of the diverse spectrum of human possibility. More interested in sex and television.

This job was not doing much for me as a warm, personable human being. At the very least, it was turning me into an unpleasant lunch companion. Whatever had made me think I wanted to get into management anyway?

The money, maybe.

But that wasn't all. It was the challenge, the chance to do something new, to control the total effort instead of just doing part of a project. . . .

The money too, though. There were other ways to get money. Maybe I should just kick the supports out from under the damn job and start over again.

I saw myself sauntering into Tom's office, twirling his visitor's chair around and falling into it. The words "I quit" would force their way out, almost against my will. His face would show surprise—feigned, of course. By then I'd have to go through with it. Maybe I'd put my feet up on his desk. And then—

But was it possible to just quit, to go back to being the person I used to be? No, I wouldn't be able to do it. I'd never be a management virgin again.

I walked up to the employee entrance at the rear of the building. A suction device next to the door sniffed at me, recognized my scent, and clicked the door open. Inside, a group of new employees, trainees, were clustered near the door, while a personnel officer introduced them to the lock and let it familiarize itself with their pheromones.

On the way down the hall, I passed Tom's office. The door was open. He was at his desk, bowed over some papers, and looked up as I went by.

"Ah, Margaret," he said. "Just the person I want to talk to. Come in for a minute, would you." He moved a large file folder onto the papers in front of him on his desk, and folded his hands on top of them. "So glad you were passing by." He nodded toward a large, comfortable chair. "Sit down."

"We're going to be doing a bit of restructuring in the department," he began, "and I'll need your input, so I want to fill you in now on what will be happening."

I was immediately suspicious. Whenever Tom said "I'll need your input," he meant everything was decided already.

"We'll be reorganizing the whole division, of course," he continued, drawing little boxes on a blank piece of paper. He'd mentioned this at the department meeting last week.

"Now, your group subdivides functionally into two separate areas, wouldn't you say?"

"Well—"

"Yes," he said thoughtfully, nodding his head as though in agreement. "That would be the way to do it." He added a few lines and a few more boxes. From what I could see, it meant that Harry would do all the interesting stuff and I'd sweep up afterwards.

"Looks to me as if you've cut the balls out of my area and put them over into Harry Winthrop's," I said.

"Ah, but your area is still very important, my dear. That's why I don't have you actually reporting to Harry." He gave me a smile like a lie.

He had put me in a tidy little bind. After all, he was my boss. If he was going to take most of my area away from me, as it seemed he was, there wasn't much I could do to stop him. And I would be better off if we both pretended that I hadn't experienced any loss of status. That way I kept my title and my salary.

"Oh, I see." I said. "Right."

It dawned on me that this whole thing had been decided already, and that Harry Winthrop probably knew all about it.

He'd probably even wangled a raise out of it. Tom had called me in here to make it look casual, to make it look as though I had something to say about it. I'd been set up.

This made me mad. There was no question of quitting now. I'd stick around and fight. My eyes blurred, unfocused, refocused again. Compound eyes! The promise of the small comb in my hand was fulfilled! I felt a deep chemical understanding of the ecological system I was now a part of. I knew where I fit in. And I knew what I was going to do. It was inevitable now, hardwired in at the DNA level.

The strength of this conviction triggered another change in the chitin, and for the first time I could actually feel the rearrangement of my mouth and nose, a numb tickling like inhaling seltzer water. The stiletto receded and mandibles jutted forth, rather like Katharine Hepburn. Form and function achieved an orgasmic synchronicity. As my jaw pushed forward, mantis-like, it also opened, and I pounced on Tom and bit his head off.

He leaped from his desk and danced headless about the office.

I felt in complete control of myself as I watched him and continued the conversation. "About the Model 2000 launch," I said. "If we factor in the demand for pipeline throughout and adjust the media mix just a bit, I think we can present a very tasty little package to Product Marketing by the end of the week."

Tom continued to strut spasmodically, making vulgar copulative motions. Was I responsible for evoking these mantid reactions? I was unaware of a sexual component in our relationship.

I got up from the visitor's chair and sat behind his desk, thinking about what had just happened. It goes without saying that I was surprised at my own actions. I mean, irritable is one thing, but biting people's heads off is quite another. But I have to admit that my second thought was, well, this certainly is a useful strategy, and should make a considerable difference in my ability to advance myself. Hell of a lot more productive than sucking people's blood.

Maybe there was something after all to Tom's talk about having the proper attitude.

And, of course, thinking of Tom, my third reaction was regret. He really had been a likeable guy, for the most part. But what's done is done, you know, and there's no use chewing on it after the fact.

I buzzed his assistant on the intercom. "Arthur," I said, "Mr. Samson and I have come to an evolutionary parting of the ways. Please have him re-engineered. And charge it to Personnel."

Now I feel an odd itching on my forearms and thighs. Notches on which I might fiddle a song?

THE FAITHFUL COMPANION AT FORTY

Karen Joy Fowler

"The Faithful Companion at Forty" was purchased by Gardner Dozois, and appeared in the July 1987 issue of Asimov's, *with an illustration by John Lakey; it went on to be a Hugo and Nebula finalist that year. Fowler made her first professional sale to* Asimov's *in 1985, to Shawna McCarthy, and later became a frequent contributor to the magazine under two different editors. In 1986, she won the John W. Campbell Award as the year's best new writer; 1986 also saw the appearance of her first book, the collection* Artificial Things, *which was released to an enthusiastic response and impressive reviews. Her first novel,* Sarah Canary, *was released in 1991, and greeted with even more enthusiasm. Fowler lives in Davis, California, has two children, did her graduate work in North Asian politics, and occasionally teaches ballet.*

In the surreal and funny story that follows, she gives us an intriguing look beyond those thrilling days of yesteryear. . . .

His first reaction is that I just can't deal with the larger theoretical issues. He's got this new insight he wants to call the Displacement Theory and I can't grasp it. Your basic, quiet, practical minority sidekick. The *limited* edition. Kato. Spock. Me. But this is not true.

I still remember the two general theories we were taught on the reservation which purported to explain the movement of history. The first we named the Great Man Theory. Its thesis was that the critical decisions in human development were made by individuals, special people gifted in personality and circumstance. The second we named the Wave Theory. It argued that only the masses could effectively determine the course of history. Those very visible individuals who appeared as leaders of the great movements were, in fact, only those who happened to articulate the direction which had already been chosen. They were as much the victims of the process as any other single individual. Flotsam. Running Dog and I used to be able to debate this issue for hours.

It is true that this particular question has ceased to interest me much. But a correlative question has come to interest me more. I spent most of my fortieth birthday sitting by myself, listening to Pachelbel's *Canon,* over and over, and I'm asking myself: Are some people special? Are some people more special than others? *Have I spent my whole life backing the wrong horse?*

I mean, it was my birthday and not one damn person called.

Finally, about four o'clock in the afternoon, I gave up and I called him. "Eh, Poncho," I say. "What's happening?"

"Eh, Cisco," he answers. "Happy birthday."

"Thanks," I tell him. I can't decide whether I am more pissed to know he remembered but didn't call than I was when I thought he forgot.

"The big four-o," he says. "Wait a second, buddy. Let me go turn the music down." He's got the *William Tell Overture* blasting on the stereo. He's always got the *William Tell Overture* blasting on the stereo. I'm not saying the man has a problem, but the last time we were in Safeway together he claimed to see a woman being kidnapped by a silver baron over in frozen foods. He pulled the flip top off a Tab and lobbed the can into the ice cream. "Cover me," he shouts, and runs an end pattern with the cart through the soups. I had to tell everyone he was having a Vietnam flashback.

And the mask. There are times and seasons when a mask is useful; I'm the first to admit that. It's Thanksgiving, say, and you're an Indian so it's never been one of your favorite holidays, and you've got no family because you spent your youth playing the supporting role to some macho creep who couldn't commit, so here you are, *standing in line,* to see "Rocky IV" and someone you know walks by. I mean, I've been there. But for everyday, for your ordinary life, a mask is only going to make you *more* obvious. There's an element of exhibitionism in it. A large element. If you ask me.

So now he's back on the phone. He sighs. "God," he says. "I miss those thrilling days of yesteryear."

See? We haven't talked twenty seconds and already the subject is *his* problems. *His* ennui. *His* angst. "I'm having an affair," I tell him. Two years ago I wouldn't have said it. Two years ago he'd just completed his EST training and he would have told me to take responsibility for it. Now he's into biofeedback and astrology. Now we're not responsible for anything.

"Yeah?" he says. He thinks for a minute. "You're not married," he points out.

I can't see that this is relevant. "She is," I tell him.

"Yeah?" he says again, only this "yeah" has a nasty quality to it; this "yeah" tells me someone is hoping for sensationalistic details. This is not the "yeah" of a concerned friend. Still, I can't help playing to it. For years I've been holding this man's horse while he leaps onto its back from the roof. For years I've been providing cover from behind a rock while he breaks for the back door. I'm forty now. It's time to get something back from him. So I hint at the use of controlled substances. We're talking peyote *and* cocaine. I mention pornography. Illegally imported. From Denmark. Of course, it's not really *my* affair. Can you picture me? My affair is quiet and ardent. I borrowed this affair from another friend. It shows you the lengths I have to go to before anyone will listen to me.

I may finally have gone too far. He's really at a loss now.

"Women," he says finally. "You can't live with them and you can't live without them." Which is a joke, coming from him. He had that single-man-raising-his-orphaned-nephew-all-alone schtick working so smoothly the women were passing each other on the way in and out the door. Or maybe it was the mask and the leather. What do women want? Who has a clue?

"Is that it?" I ask him. "The sum total of your advice? She won't leave her husband. Man, my *heart* is broken."

"Oh," he says. There's a long pause. "Don't let it show," he suggests. Then he signs. Again. "I miss that old white horse," he tells me. And you know what I do? I hang up on him. And you know what he *doesn't* do? He doesn't call me back.

It really hurts me.

So his second reaction, now that I don't want to listen to him explaining his new theories to me, is to say that I seem to be sulking about something, he can't imagine what. And this is harder to deny.

The day after my birthday I went for a drive in my car, a little white Saab with personalized license plates. KEMO, they say. Maybe the phone is ringing, maybe it's not. I feel better when I don't know. So, he misses his horse. Hey, *I've* never been the same since that little pinto of mine joined the Big Round-up, but I try not to burden my friends with *anything*. I just nurse them back to health when the Cavendish gang leaves them for dead. I just come in the middle of the night with the medicine man when little Britt has a fever and it's not responding to Tylenol. I just organize the surprise party when a friend turns forty.

You want to bet even *Attila the Hun* had a party on his fortieth? You want to bet he was one hard man to surprise? And who blew up the balloons and had everyone hiding under the rugs and in with the goats? This name is lost forever.

I drove out into the country, where every cactus holds its memory for me, where every outcropping of rock once hid an outlaw. Ten years ago the terrain was still so rough I would have had to take the International Scout. Now it's a paved highway straight to the hanging tree. I pulled over to the shoulder of the road, turned off the motor, and I just sat there. I was remember-

THE FAITHFUL COMPANION AT FORTY 105

ing the time Ms. Emily Cooper stumbled into the Wilcox bank robbery looking for her little girl who'd gone with friends to the swimming hole and hadn't bothered to tell her mama. We were on our way to see Colonel Davis at Fort Comanche about some cattle rustling. We hadn't heard about the bank robbery. Which is why we were taken completely by surprise.

My pony and I were eating the masked man's dust, as usual, when something hit me from behind. Arnold Wilcox, a heavy-set man who sported a five o'clock shadow by eight in the morning, jumped me from the big rock overlooking the Butterfield trail and I went down like a sack of potatoes. I heard horses converging on us from the left and the right and that hypertrophic white stallion of his took off like a big bird. I laid one on Arnold's stubbly jaw, but he cold-cocked me with the butt of his pistol and I couldn't tell you what happened next.

I don't come to until it's after dark and I'm trussed up like a turkey. Ms. Cooper is next to me and her hands are tied behind her back with a red bandanna and there's a rope around her feet. She looks disheveled, but pretty; her eyes are wide and I can tell she's not too pleased to be lying here next to an Indian. Her dress is buttoned up to the chin so I'm thinking at least, thank God, they've respected her. It's cold, even as close together as we are. The Wilcoxes are all huddled around the fire, counting money, and the smoke is a straight white line in the sky you could see for miles. So this is more good news, and I'm thinking the Wilcoxes were always a bunch of dumb-ass honkies when it came to your basic woodlore. I'm wondering how they got it together to pull off a bank job, when I hear horse's hooves and my question is answered. Pierre Cardeaux, Canadian French, hops off the horse's back and goes straight to the fire and stamps it out.

"Imbeciles!" he tells them, only he's got this heavy accent so it comes out "Eembeeceeles."

Which insults the Wilcoxes a little. "Hold on there, hombre," Andrew Wilcox says. "Jess because we followed your plan into the bank and your trail for the getaway doesn't make you the boss here," and Pierre pays him about as much notice as you do an ant your horse is about to step on. He comes over to us and puts his hand under Ms. Cooper's chin, sort of thoughtfully. She spits at him and he laughs.

"Spunk," he says. "I like that." I mean, I suppose that's what he says, because that's what they always say, but the truth is, with his accent, I don't understand a word.

Andrew Wilcox isn't finished yet. He's got this big chicken leg which he's eating and it's dribbling onto his chin, so he wipes his arm over his face. Which just spreads the grease around more, really, and anyway, he's got this hunk of chicken stuck between his front teeth, so Pierre can hardly keep a straight face when he talks to him. "I understand why we're keeping the woman," Andrew says. "Cause she has—uses. But the Injun there. He's just going to be baggage. I want to waste him."

"Mon ami," says Pierre. "Even *pour vous,* thees stupiditee lives me spitchless." He's kissing his fingers to illustrate the point as if he were really French and not just Canadian French and has probably never drunk really good wine in his life. I'm lying in the dust and whatever they've bound my wrists with is cutting off the circulation so my hands feel like someone is jabbing them with porcupine needles. Even now, I can remember smelling the smoke which wasn't there any more and the Wilcoxes who were and the lavender eau de toilette that Ms. Cooper used. And horses and dust and sweat. These were the glory days, but *whose* glory you may well ask, and even if I answered, what difference would it make?

Ms. Cooper gets a good whiff of Andrew Wilcox and it makes her cough.

"He's right, little brother," says Russell Wilcox, the runt of the litter at about three hundred odd pounds and a little quicker on the uptake than the rest of the family. "You ever heared tell of a man who rides a white horse, wears a black mask, and shoots a very pricey kind of bullet? This here Injun is his compadre."

"Oui, oui, oui, oui," says Pierre agreeably. The little piggie. He indicates me and raises his eyebrows one at a time. *"Avec le sauvage* we can, how you say? Meck a deal."

"Votre mere," I tell him. He gives me a good kick in the ribs and he's wearing those pointy-toed kind of cowboy boots, so I

feel it all right. Finally I hear the sound I've been waiting for, a hoot-owl over in the trees behind Ms. Cooper, and then *he* rides up. He hasn't even gotten his gun out yet. "Don't move," he tells Pierre. "Or I'll be forced to draw," but he hasn't finished the sentence when Russell Wilcox has his arm around my neck and the point of his knife jabbing into my back.

"We give you the Injun," he says. "Or we give you the girl. You ain't taking both. You comprendez, pardner?"

Now, if he'd *asked* me, I'd have said, hey, don't worry about *me,* rescue the woman. And if he'd hesitated, I would have insisted. But he didn't ask and he didn't hesitate. He just hoisted Ms. Cooper up onto the saddle in front of him and pulled the bottom of her skirt down so her legs didn't show. "There's a little girl in Springfield who's going to be mighty happy to see you, Ms. Cooper," I hear him saying, and I've got a suspicion from the look on her face that they're not going straight to Springfield anyway. And that's it. Not one word for me.

Of course, he comes back, but by this time the Wilcoxes and Pierre have fallen asleep around the cold campfire and I've had to inch my way through the dust on my side like a snake over to Russell Wilcox's knife, which fell out of his hand when he nodded off, whittling. I've had to cut my own bonds, and my hands are behind me so I carve up my thumb a little, too. The whole time I'm right there beneath Russell and he's snorting and snuffling and shifting around like he's waking up so my heart nearly stops. It's a wonder my hands don't have to be amputated, they've been without blood for so long. And then there's a big shoot-out and I provide a lot of cover. A couple of days pass before I feel like talking to him about it.

"You rescued Ms. Cooper first," I remind him. "And that was the right thing to do; I'm not saying it wasn't; don't misunderstand me. But it seemed to me that you made up your mind kind of quickly. It didn't seem like a hard decision."

He reaches across the saddle and puts a hand on my hand. Behind the black mask, the blue eyes are sensitive and caring. "Of course I wanted to rescue you, old friend," he says. "If I'd made the decision based solely on my own desires, that's what I would have done. But it seemed to me I had a higher responsibility to the more innocent party. It was a hard choice. It may have felt quick to you, but, believe me, I struggled with it." He withdraws his hand and kicks his horse a little ahead of us because the trail is narrowing. I duck under the branch of a Prairie Spruce. "Besides," he says, back over his shoulder. "I couldn't leave a woman with a bunch of animals like Pierre Cardeaux and the Wilcoxes. A pretty woman like that. Alone. Defenseless."

I start to tell him what a bunch of racists like Pierre Cardeaux and the Wilcoxes might do to a lonely and defenseless Indian. Arnold Wilcox wanted my scalp. "*I remember the Alamo*," he kept saying and maybe he meant Little Big Horn; I didn't feel like exploring this. Pierre kept assuring him there would be plenty of time for "trophies" later. And Andrew trotted out that old chestnut about the only good Indian being a dead Indian. None of which was pleasant to lie there listening to. But I never said it. Because by then the gap between us was so great I would have had to shout, and anyway the ethnic issue has always made us both a little touchy. I wish I had a nickel for every time I've heard him say that some of his best friends are Indians. And I know that there are bad Indians; I don't deny it and I don't mind fighting them. I just always thought I should get to decide which ones were the bad ones.

I sat in that car until sunset.

But the next day he calls. "Have you ever noticed how close the holy word 'om' is to our Western word 'home'?" he asks. That's his opening. No hi, how are you? He never asks how I am. If he did, I'd tell him I was fine, just the way you're supposed to. I wouldn't burden him with my problems. I'd just like to be asked, you know?

But he's got a point to make and it has something to do with Dorothy in the *Wizard of Oz*. How she clicks her heels together and says, over and over like a mantra, "There's no place like home, there's no place like home," and she's actually able to travel through space. "Not in the book," I tell him.

"I *know*," he says. "In the movie."

"I thought it was the shoes," I say.

And his voice lowers; he's that excited. "What if it was the *words?*" he asks. "I've got a mantra."

Of course, I'm aware of this. It always used to bug me that he wouldn't tell me what it was. Your mantra; he says, loses its power if it's spoken aloud. So by now I'm beginning to guess what his mantra might be. "A bunch of people I know," I tell him, "all had the same guru. And one day they decided to share the mantras he'd given them. They each wrote their mantra on a piece of paper and passed it around. And you know what? They all had the *same* mantra. So much for personalization."

"They lacked faith," he points out.

"Rightfully so."

"I gotta go," he tells me. We're reaching the crescendo in the background music and it cuts off with a click. Silence. He doesn't say goodbye. I refuse to call him back.

The truth is, I'm tired of always being there for him.

So I don't hear from him again until this morning when he calls with the great Displacement Theory. By now I've been forty almost ten days, if you believe the birth certificate the reservation drew up; I find a lot of inaccuracies surfaced when they translated moons into months. So that I've never been too sure what my rising sign is. Not that it matters to me, but it's important to him all of a sudden; apparently you can't analyze personality effectively without it. He thinks I'm a Pisces rising; he'd love to be proved right.

"We can go *back,* old buddy," he says. "I've found the way back."

"Why would we want to?" I ask. The sun is shining and it's cold out. I was thinking of going for a run.

Does he hear me? About like always. "I figured it out," he says. "It's a combination of biofeedback *and* the mantra 'home.' I've been working and working on it. I could always leave, you know, that was never the problem, but I could never *arrive.* Something outside me stopped me and forced me back." He pauses here and I think I'm supposed to say something, but I'm too pissed. He goes on. "Am I getting too theoretical for you? Because I'm about to get more so. Try to stay with me. The key word is *displacement*." He says this like he's shivering. "I couldn't get back because there was no room for me there. The only way back is through an exchange. Someone else has to come forward."

He pauses again and this pause goes on and on. Finally I grunt. A redskin sound. Noncommittal.

His voice is severe. "This is too important for you to miss just because you're sulking about god knows what, pilgrim," he says. "This is travel through space *and* time."

"This is baloney," I tell him. I'm uncharacteristically blunt, blunter than I ever was during the primal-scream-return-to-the-womb period. If nobody's listening, what does it matter?

"Displacement," he repeats and his voice is all still and important. "Ask yourself, buddy, *what happened to the buffalo?*"

I don't believe I've heard him correctly. "Say *what?*"

"Return with me," he says and then he's gone for good and this time he hasn't hung up the phone; this time I can still hear the *William Tell Overture* repeating the hoofbeat part. There's a noise out front so I go to the door, and damned if I don't have a buffalo, shuffling around on my ornamental strawberries, looking surprised. "You call this grass?" it asks me. It looks up and down the street, more and more alarmed. "Where's the plains, man? Where's the railroad?"

So I'm happy for him. Really I am.

But I'm not going with him. Let him roam it alone this time. He'll be fine. Like Rambo.

Only then another buffalo appears. And another. Pretty soon I've got a whole herd of them out front, trying to eat my yard and gagging. And whining. "The water tastes funny. You got any water with locusts in it?" I don't suppose it's an accident that I've got the same number of buffalo here as there are men in the Cavendish gang. Plus one. I keep waiting to see if any more appear; maybe someone else will go back and help him. But they don't. This is it.

You remember the theories of history I told you about. Back in the beginning? Well, maybe somewhere between the great men and the masses, there's a third kind of person. Someone who listens. Someone who tries to *help*. You don't hear about these people much so there probably aren't many of them. Oh, you hear about the failures, all right, the shams: Brutus, John Alden, Rasputin. And maybe you think there aren't any at all, that nobody could love someone else more than he loves himself. Just because *you* can't. Hey, I don't really care what you think. Because I'm here and the heels of my moccasins are clicking together and I couldn't stop them even if I tried. And it's okay. Really. It's who I am. It's what I do.

I'm going to leave you with a bit of theory to think about. It's a sort of riddle. There are good Indians, there are bad Indians and there are dead Indians. Which am I?

There can be more than one right answer.

SOMETHING RICH AND STRANGE

R. A. Lafferty

"Something Rich and Strange" was purchased by Gardner Dozois, and appeared in the July 1986 issue of Asimov's, *with an illustration by Arthur George. Lafferty is another of those authors who doesn't appear frequently enough in the magazine to really suit us, but he made a number of sales to* Asimov's *under George Scithers, and a handful more under Gardner Dozois, and each has been memorable. Lafferty started writing in 1960, and in the years before his retirement in 1987, he published some of the freshest and funniest short stories ever written in the genre, as well as a string of vivid and unforgettable books such as the novels* Past Master, The Devil Is Dead, The Reefs of Earth, Okla Hannali, The Fall of Rome, Arrive at Easterwine, *and* The Flame Is Green, *and landmark collections such as* Nine Hundred Grandmothers, Strange Doings, Does Anyone Else Have Something Further to Add?, Golden Gate and Other Stories, *and* Ringing the Changes. *Lafferty won the Hugo Award in 1973 for his story "Eurema's Dam," and in 1990 received the World Fantasy Award, the prestigious Life Achievement Award. We still hope to coax him out of retirement to do some more work for us.*

Here he spins a very funny yarn about aliens and . . . teeth. Yes, teeth. And damn big *teeth at that . . .*

SOMETHING RICH AND STRANGE

> I am the biggest and the best,
> I'm full of jive and juices.
> I wear my heart outside my breast.
> My teeth are like a moose's.
>
>   Buck Tooth Boogie, Anonymous.

George Dander had two front buck teeth bigger than those of any other man or beaver or bull moose in the world. George Dander heard voices, a recent circumstance with him. George Dander was conditionally engaged to an enlarging and charming person named Mary Deare. Except for those three items, he was much like everybody else, pleasant, prodigal, talkative, a bit eccentric, opinionated, and mistaken fifty-one percent of the time.

Except for his two buck teeth he was handsome, and he was larger and louder than life. Except for the voices he'd been hearing, he had never had any self-doubts at all: but the new voices did have a doubtful quality to them. Except for Mary Deare (a metamorphic creature who was sometimes called the Unwreckable Mary Deare) his life might have been as empty as are the lives of so many billions of other persons.

Three other young men were also engaged to Mary. The conditions she had imposed on George Dander were that he should get rid of those damned buck teeth, and that he should make a million dollars. He could probably make a million dollars if he put his mind to it. But he sure didn't want to get rid of his buck teeth which were his trademark and his manhood. Ah well, the conditions that Mary Deare had put on her other three fiancés were even more stringent.

When the voices first came to George Dander he had trouble understanding them because of their foreign accent. But he and the voices soon adjusted to each other. The voices seemed to be right in the middle of George's head and nobody except himself could hear them—except, apparently, the sharp-eared Mary Deare a little bit sometimes.

But when George was alone (alone with the voices, for he was never really alone since they came to him) he questioned them.

"Who are you really?" he asked them. "What is your name?"

"Our name is Multitude because there are many of us," they answered him.

"That line has been used before, approximately," George told them. "Where are you really, the rest of you? Wherever in the world are you?"

"We are not in this world at all," they said. "The Name of our world is Synnephon-Ennea or Cloud-Nine Planet. Its direction from here is celestial north."

"Why do you send your voices here?"

"Because we're friendly. We like to talk to all sorts of people. And we like to upgrade the ideas of all sorts of people."

"Do you ever visit any other worlds in person, in the flesh?"

"Oh yes. Perhaps we will visit your world in some very near future: after we have made preparations and shaped the public apperceptions there so we won't appear too shocking to you."

"Why did you pick me to talk in my head?"

"We always seek good paired receptors. Really, we have to have them or we can't make ourselves heard at all. In you we found one of the three best sets of paired receptors on your world. It's a joy to make contact with such an excellent set of receptors as yours."

"You mean my buck teeth? Do I pick you up through my buck teeth?"

"Yes. Does such a thing startle you?"

"Not entirely. There's a bull moose in the Bronx Zoo who picks up radio programs with his buck teeth. He mostly gets New York City boogie music programs, and the nearby animals listen appreciatively to them too. I had guessed that my case was something like that."

"When we come into our kingdom there in your world, one of the first things we will suppress is boogie radio stations. And in the meanwhile we will work through you and through others (especially your girlfriend who has an exceptionally good opportunistic brain) to try to upgrade this world's ideas of beauty. That will have to be done before the time of our coming. Now, to show our friendship, is there anything we can do to make you happier?"

SOMETHING RICH AND STRANGE   115

The seven answers had been in seven different voices.

"Can you see into the future?" George Dander asked them.

"We can't see into our own future, but we can see into yours. Our temporal direction is the opposite of yours. Our past is your future. Our future is your past. What would you like to know?"

"The names of the eight horses who will win the eight races at Blue Ribbon Downs this afternoon."

"Gilded Lily in the first." "Red Beans in the second." "Cactus Joe in the third." "Fly-by-Night in the fourth." "Bangabout in the fifth." "Copperhead in the sixth." "Gandy Dancer in the seventh." "Burglar Dan in the eighth." The eight answers came in eight different voices.

George Dander picked up the phone and placed the eight bets, each horse to win in its race. But he was a little bit doubtful of what he had done.

"Even granting that you've been in the future where the races will be run this afternoon, how could you have all the winners' names so glibly?" he asked.

"We're smart," one of the voices said.

"And if your past is my future and your future is my past, how come we are together so long? Why haven't we passed in less than a moment?"

"We will always be in the same present, but we will always have arrived at that present from opposite directions," a voice said.

"And if Cloud-Nine World (usually regarded as legendary) is four-and-a-half light years from here (even as a legend it is firmly located in the Centauri system) why isn't there a four-and-a-half-year delay in every exchange of ours?"

"There's an explanation, but it's pretty mathematical and we don't believe you could understand it," one of the voices said.

All eight of the horses that George Dander bet on did win their races at Blue Ribbon Downs that afternoon, and George was ahead quite a few bucks. Mary Deare met George as he came back to his house after picking up his winnings. She knew all about it, and she couldn't have known.

"Don't relax, George, don't even think of relaxing," she said. "Have your voices give you the names of the one hundred stocks that will rise most sharply tomorrow. While you're getting them down, I'll phone your broker to have supper with us at the Steak and Ale. And draw a check for twenty thousand dollars, and we'll get our order to buy in to your broker tonight."

"I don't have twenty thousand dollars, Mary."

"Yes you do, honey. You have twenty thousand two hundred and eleven dollars and nineteen cents in your checking account. Why do you try to conceal things from me when we are conditionally engaged and are practically flesh of one flesh?"

Thirty-three days later, after hectic betting and buying and selling and manipulating futures with never a slip, George Dander was a millionaire. Mary Deare knew that he had reached it before George knew it himself. She had a quicker mind and she kept closer track of such things.

"We'll get married at nine o'clock tomorrow morning," she told George. "It's all working out beautifully."

"Good, good," George said. "Then you're waiving the other requirement."

"I'm waiving nothing. You have an appointment with the dentist in twenty-two minutes. We'd better get down there now. We're going to get those unsightly buck teeth jerked out of your mouth."

"But, Mary, don't you realize that I, we, wouldn't be millionaires if it weren't for my buck teeth and my voices? You're killing the golden goose, the golden fleece, the golden buck teeth!"

"Trust me, honey! I always know what I'm doing. I'm not killing that golden goose. I'm going to put it on a business basis."

The dentist pulled George Dander's two priceless buck teeth which were one of the three best sets of paired receptors in the world. And George felt terrible about it.

SOMETHING RICH AND STRANGE

"Don't let them throw them away!" he protested as he came out from under the gas. "Maybe something can be done with them if—"

"They won't be thrown away," Mary Deare reassured him. "My, you do talk funny without them! I have them here in my purse. I told you that I was going to put them on a business basis. Come along now. We'll get married in the morning, and then we'll go on a two-day honeymoon."

"Why only a two-day honeymoon?" George Dander asked. (He sure *did* talk funny without his buck teeth.) "Why for only two days?"

"Because *I* have a dental appointment on the third day," Mary Deare said.

2.
Nothing of her that does fade
But does suffer a sea-change
Into something rich and strange.
Sea-Nymphs hourly ring her knell
Ding-Dong—
Hark, I hear them,
Ding-Dong Bell!
The Tempest, Shakespeare

George Dander had mixed feelings at his wedding. He had a great and worrisome emptiness in the front of his mouth, and he had an awkward and floppy upper lip that was now relieved of its job of at least partly covering his buck teeth. He felt somewhat unmanned.

On the other hand, he was marrying the Unwreckable Mary Deare, an enchanting creature, a metamorphic creature, a pearl beyond price ("That paltry million dollars is only the beginning, honey," she had whispered to him, "we'll be *big* rich"), the Iris goddess at the end of the rainbow. It should be fun. And perhaps he *would be* more handsome without his big buck teeth (which would now, somehow, be put on a business basis).

And it *was* fun, for the two days of their honeymoon. They went to Bald Eagle Cove on Keystone Lake. They ate crawfish tails and Gored Ox Surprise and drank Boilermakers and Sazarac Cocktails. They waterskied and caught catfish and made love. One night they went to a movie at Mannford, and the other night they went to a cow-pasture Rock Concert near New Prue. Yes, all these things were fun when done with the metamorphic Mary Deare.

And they came back on the morning of the third day because Mary Deare had a dental appointment that day.

George Dander was absolutely dumbfounded by the appearance of his cherished wife Mary Deare Dander when she came back from the dentist's.

"No, no, no!" he said (or he made a pitiful attempt at saying). Try to say "No, no, no" with your two front teeth out: try to say *anything* with your two front teeth out. "Never, never!" George declared, and he was shaking like a whole treeful of aspen leaves. "Thomebody thay it ithn't tho!" he begged.

"You'll get used to them, honey," the unwreckable Mary Deare assured him.

"*Really* you will, George," sounded a muffled voice that used to be one of George Dander's own "voices," and it was coming somehow from Mary Deare's mouth. "It is essential that you not only get used to them, but that you learn to love them, that you come to find them things of beauty. You *do* understand that this world's ideas of beauty will have to be upgraded before the time of our coming."

George Dander tried to scream, but it was somehow pathetic. (Try to scream effectively sometime with your two front teeth gone and your upper lip flapping loosely.)

And George Dander began to run, and he disappeared over the horizon still running.

His was surely an odd reaction to his wife's coming home with two large and handsome buck teeth gleaming in the front of her face in place of six smaller upper front teeth that had never done much for her.

But George Dander had always been a little bit eccentric.

SOMETHING RICH AND STRANGE 119

• • •

George Dander came home again after about a month.

"Oh, hi, George!" his wife Mary Deare spoke pleasantly. "It's good to see you."

"It's good to see you too," George said, but he didn't really see her. He couldn't yet stand to look at her. One glimpse out of the corner of his eye was enough. George Dander was tired and dirty and discouraged.

"You'll feel better when you get your bridge with your two new teeth from the dentist," Mary Deare Dander said. "They've been ready for you for a month. He fitted you for them when you were still out from the gas when he pulled your two buck teeth. You will be nice-looking when you have two ordinary-sized front teeth and your upper lip has unextended itself."

"I will be nice-looking then, but I won't be me," George Dander said. "Mary, let me give you a little history of the world, and of my family, and of my teeth.

"When the great Indo-Aryan migration from central Asia to Europe began thirty centuries ago, its languages and words began to diverge. Of their original words, only about a hundred are still to be recognized in most of its branches. There isn't any common word for ocean, for they hadn't lived on the ocean. There isn't any common word for elephant or palm tree for they didn't know these things before their split-up. But there is a common word for teeth, for all of them had teeth. It was *don'di* in Greek, *dens* in Latin, and *dantis* in Lithuanian. It is *dent* in French and *diente* in Spanish. The word isn't recognized in English, but we still have *dental* and *dentist*. It is *tand* in Dutch and Scandinavian. With the greatest tribe of all of them (and there are now less than a hundred members of our 'tribe' left in the world) the word for tooth is *dand* and its plural is *dander*. So my name is George Dander which is George Teeth, and my family name has been 'teeth' for a hundred generations. We've always known that our buck teeth were receptors, part of the 'ivory grapevine.' People with *outstanding* teeth have always been in rapport with each other and have known each others' thoughts. Outsiders who noticed this didn't understand it and they thought that it was telepathy at work. Our buck teeth have been handed down from father to son (but never has any female member of the Dander family shown any signs of buck-teethism) for a hundred generations, growing always larger and more beautiful, and they climaxed in me. This isn't the first time we have picked up voices from the stars with our front teeth. But now I am shorn of them."

"Poor George!" the unwreckable Mary Deare said. "But look at it *this* way. Your wonderful teeth are in good hands now, which is to say in good mouth now, mine. Now *my* name is teeth, and the line won't be broken. Your son, of whom I am gravid now, will have the finest buck teeth ever in the history of the world."

"The fact is, George," said a muffled voice that had been one of George's own "voices" a month before, "we needed good paired receptors *combined* with brains, with *opportunistic* brains, to use for our deployments. You had the good paired receptors. Mary Deare had the fine opportunistic brains. So we made a deal."

"And now, honey, we will be rich beyond your fondest expectations," Mary Deare told George.

"I no longer have any fond expectations," George Dander said sadly, and he went away again.

But Mary Deare Dander thrived. Those first couple of million dollars had been only peanuts. Now, with the aid of the "voices" she became fabulously rich, and in exchange for it she had only to become a sort of famous role model.

"Some of them laughed at me for a while, at the way I looked," she said. "But they laughed at me to their peril. Laughing people, do you ever know who *really* owns the company from which you have your living? It is dangerous to laugh at the richest woman in the world." For, by the time that Mary Deare Dander gave birth to George Dander the one-hundred-and-first (Oh, the buck teeth on that new-born baby!) she really was the richest woman in the world, and in three more days she would be the richest person in the world.

SOMETHING RICH AND STRANGE

• • •

There is nothing so unpredictable as the changes in fads and fashions, especially the fads and fashions of beautiful women. And one of the strangest fashions ever to be taken up was the *Dente Sporgente* Look (pronounce it Dentay Sporgentay). Who would believe that the *Dente Sporgente* Look would be equated with having chic, with having elegance, with having total charm?

Indeed, Marcel Buffon, the greatest beauty expert in the world, writing in the French fashion magazine Lendemain Elegant, wrote "The new *Dente Sporgente* Look is like nothing ever seen before. It is something new in beauty, it is something new in excitement, it is something new in bla." It is true that this was the last thing that Marcel Buffon ever wrote, for immediately after writing that he opened his veins and died. He had always been a puzzling man.

But the *Dente Sporgente* Look (the English translation of that wonderful and untranslatable name would be the "Protruding Teeth Look") was in. No, you wouldn't have guessed in a hundred guesses that the great new world-wide fashion of that year would be the stylish and beautiful women of the world, millions and millions of them, all having their six upper front teeth pulled out and replaced by a pair of huge buck teeth, implanted in the bone and growing there (they wouldn't be good receptors unless they were growing from the bone because good receptors require the complete bone skeleton to serve as an antenna). And you wouldn't have guessed in a hundred-and-one guesses that these women would universally be regarded as ravishingly beautiful after the toothy change had been made in them. Whoever effected such a change anyhow, and by what means? (Ah, the *Dente Sporgente* was almost something new in newness.)

It isn't certain who effected it, but the person who turned the greatest profit from it was that richest woman in the world, that metamorphic creature, Mary Deare Dander. Of the three thousand companies and corporations that she now owned, three hundred of them were part of the Buck Tooth Cartel.

• • •

One day, a gnarled and knobby space-traveler who happened to be on World for a short stopover, saw Mary Deare Dander herself, and he reeled back aghast.

"It is one of the natives of Synnephon-Ennea on Cloud-Nine Planet," he groaned, "the most repulsive creatures in the Universe. If they have already begun to arrive here, then World would be better off to die the death."

"But Cloud-Nine Planet is usually deemed to be a legendary place," said the travel agent who was expediting the space-traveler, "and it's also said that it is impossible to go to it or leave it."

"Cloud-Nine Planet is approximately as real as this planet here under my feet, and it is about as easy to get to or leave. Of course, one must always arrive at Cloud-Nine from the future because it's in a time-reversal eddy. But it's real, and one can go to and from it with a little trickery. Ugh, isn't she ugly!"

"She is accounted the most beautiful woman on World," the travel-agent said.

"I see now that she is *not quite* a Cloud-Nine person yet," the space-traveler mused. "But she is a metamorphic, and she is turning into a Cloud-Nine person. If one isn't already a Cloud-Nine person, one will become such after a bit of trafficking with the Cloud-Niners. The Cloud-Niners are real, but they destroy the reality of every world they infest."

And then the old space-traveler seemed to be literally pulled apart. His four limbs and his head were all separated from his torso by giant and invisible hands, so it seemed. Old space-travelers often talk too much and they suffer the consequences of talking too much. The travel-agent, being a fastidious man, disassociated himself from the scattered remains of the old space-traveler and walked stiffly away.

The "voices" from Cloud-Nine Planet now had about fifty million good paired receptors that they could use on World, and that was about all they needed for right now.

Beaver teeth, wild stallion teeth, moose and elk most of all! How could there have been enough of them to satisfy the demand? If the price is set high enough, there will always be enough, either genuine or counterfeit.

The only still living giant Irish elk in the world had its two front teeth torn out of its mouth in the Dublin zoo one night. "Shame, Shame, Shame," read the headlines of all the Irish papers, but that pair of giant elk buck teeth was known to bring a hundred and fifty thousand dollars on the black market.

Behemoth teeth were the best of all, matched pairs of behemoth front teeth.

But the behemoth is a fabulous creature.

So are the prices for its buck teeth fabulous.

You say that the behemoth front teeth are really plastic and cost only thirty-five cents a pair to produce? Well, with a base price of thirty-five cents, and approximately a hundred thousand dollars a sale going into advertising and hype, a million dollars a throw for them still yields a tidy profit for somebody, somebody named Mary Deare Dander.

> Somewhere in distant Space and Time
> Is wetter water, slimier slime.
> And there (we trust) there swimmeth one
> Who swam ere rivers were begun.
> Immense, of fishy form and mind,
> Squamous, omnipotent, and kind.
>
> Rupert Brooke

Mary Deare Dander now had large and glittering thousand-facet insect-type eyes. They would have appeared very ugly to anybody who was born before yesterday, but there were now no such persons. Now everybody was wearing a button that read "I was born anew this morning." Such persons will soon come to accept and even love thousand-faceted, ugly, insect-type eyes. At least a dozen of the facets of the strange eyes were meaningful, for with them Mary could focus in on scenes on a dozen different worlds including Cloud-Nine Planet. This might be an advantage some time. The enlarged eyes were too big to remain in Mary's head, so now they were two throbbing, living, baseball-sized, bloodshot-in-seven-colors eyes on the front of Mary Deare's face.

These new eyes would be the next fashion for the beautiful women of the world, the Augen-Laugen or Lye-in-the-Eye look. Already such orbs were being installed in leading ladies at a million dollars a throw, and both the numbers of them and the price would pick up. Oh yes, objectively they were very ugly, but who was still objective nowadays? Their introduction was part of the upgrading of the sense of beauty for the people of World, the upgrading that would have to be completed before the Cloud-Nine people themselves could appear.

George Dander, when he left home that second time, believed that he would never laugh again. And he did not laugh again until a year and a day after his wedding. Then one aspect of the happenings struck him as very, very droll.

(Hippopotamus front teeth, they were still going well now. They hadn't much shape or style, but they *were* mouth-fillingly *big*. They were second class, but there was always a strong market for the second class. And the most important dealer in the world in hippopotamus front teeth was the metamorphic Mary Deare Dander.)

"I wonder what the 'voices' really look like!" George Dander chortled in glee when the droll mood hit him one day. (Try to chortle some time without any front teeth.) "If they have to effect 'upgradings' of this world's ideas of beauty, like these present capers of theirs, before they can appear at all, boy-o-boy-o-boy! what must they really look like!"

"Music has charms to soothe a savage breast," the great Congreve wrote three hundred years ago, and the music that charmed the savage breasts of the worldlings in that season was a series of very strange tunes and songs. One of them had the strange name "Five Footfalls; glooch, klownk, geeze, klupple, bonk" and the name was far from the strangest thing about that song. Well, it was a real recording of the footsteps of the people of Cloud-Nine Planet. The five-legged persons of Cloud-Nine Planet had their five feet and legs all different, and those were the sounds of their footfalls when they walked. And wordlings would have to get used to the sound and the fact of the Cloud-Niners walking before the Cloud-Niners arrived. World persons could not help listening to such strange pieces of music as this. Some people found those sounds delightful and enchanting. And some people quivered with fear at the sound of the murderously stalking, fearsome, five-footed Cloud-Niners.

Mary Deare Dander now practiced an hour a day at walking on five different sorts of stilts at the same time. Mary Deare had become a prototype and a role-leader at many things.

The metamorphosis of Mary Deare was coming along nicely, and all the substance of it came to her over the ivory grapevine and through the dozen special facets of her thousand-faceted eyes.

She was the richest and most beautiful person in the world, and the most enchantingly strange.

> Oh noble teeth and noble eyes
> Beyond all reasoned uses!
> None other like her shall arise
> In land of Golden Gooses.
>
> Buck Tooth Boogie.

And how was the visit of the Cloud-Nine people when they finally came?

It was cryptic: that is the only word for it. But it did fulfill the Niners' old crab-tree Latin motto: *"Eveneunt, Eridiunt, Exiviunt"* which is rendered "They arrived, they laughed, they departed again."

The Cloud-Niners had specified only a medium-sized meeting hall and, adjoining it, a spacious withdrawing room with padded floor and walls.

Only one hundred world people saw them at all, and that for only a few moments. The Cloud-Nine people were clad in a neutral sort of space vestiture and were normal of teeth and eyes and feet. Well yes, the only way you could describe them was as "Squamous, omnipotent, and kind."

The one hundred VIP worldlings were splendid with hippopotamus teeth and thousand-faceted giant insect eyes. And they were wobbly on five-stilted asymmetric contraptions.

Mary Deare Dander, of course, was the spokesperson for the worldlings.

"Our meeting is of the highest historical importance—" she began, and each of the Cloud-Niners pointed a finger at one of the Worldlings. The sign probably meant "Prodigious Welcome" or something like that.

"Let history stand still and be humbled," Mary Deare was saying. "This is the first moment of a new era."

The Cloud-Niners were absolutely twinkling and gurgling with some sort of delight or anticipation. They pointed their fingers at the worldlings again, and several of them seemed on the verge of speaking. But then all of them rushed into the padded withdrawing room, and you wouldn't believe what happened there!

They leapt and tumbled and beat their heads on the padded floor and walls. They laughed and laughed and laughed with a whooping rowdiness which is a little bit beyond the capacity of humans. What an orchestration of laughter! It was like ten million of those old milk cans banging down ten million steps of a celestial stairway. It was like a million donkeys laughing at one of the seven outrageous donkey jokes.

Twice the Nine-Clouders controlled themselves a little bit and came back into the hall with the worldlings.

"This is First Encounter," Mary Deare Dander spoke around her hippopotamus teeth. "This is—"

But the Cloud-Niners each pointed a finger at a worldling, and then rushed into the padded withdrawing room again overcome with a high hilarity about something.

And then, after an especially loud hurricane of merriment, the Cloud-Niners all went up through the ceiling in that droll way of theirs, and entered into hover-cars that they had whistled down

SOMETHING RICH AND STRANGE

from the low sky. Then they were gone, and their laughter fell like hunks of happy thunder down onto the earth.

Yes, the visit of the Cloud-Niners would have to be called "cryptic." That's the only word for it.

Of course the laughter of the Cloud-Niners had all been recorded. And of course an attempt at decoding it was made. There would surely be treasures of information to be got from it when it was properly interpreted. And of course Mary Deare Dander was in charge of the great project. Well, who would *you* put in charge of it? Who else had sufficient prestige to head such a world-wide project?

But as yet the "Project Decode Laugh" has not borne significant fruit.

> The "Niners" were pleasant and squamous and stout,
> But what in the hell were they *laughing* about?
> 					Buck Tooth Boogie.

JESSE REVENGED

Don Webb

"Jesse Revenged" was purchased by Gardner Dozois, and appeared in the December 1986 issue of Asimov's, *with an illustration by John Lakey. It was another one of those stories, like Neal Barrett's "Perpetuity Blues," that became an underground cult classic almost as soon as it hit print—in fact, connoisseurs of the gonzo still speak admiringly of it. It may well be one of the weirdest "Wild West" stories ever written, as you'll soon discover. . . .*

In addition to several more sales to Asimov's, *each as exuberantly unclassifiable as the last, Don Webb is also a small-press veteran whose fiction has appeared in over sixty magazines in the United States, Great Britain, France, Norway, and India. His stories have also been included in* Interzone, Amazing, New Pathways, Fantasy Tales, When the Music's Over, *and elsewhere, and he is also the author of the very strange "collection" called* Uncle Ovid's Exercise Book. *He lives with his wife Rosemary in Austin, Texas.*

The community of Oneida has become Amarillo, Tascosa is beginning to fade into the dust, and, a few weeks ago, Admiral Sampon blockaded the navy of Admiral Cervera in Santiago Bay. It is the summer of 1898. Robert Ford, the man who shot Jesse James in the back, has left the Ozarks and moved to Amarillo. He lives in the third floor of the yellow-painted wooden Amarillo Hotel. He's changed his name to Aubrey

JESSE REVENGED

Sorrentino and affected an Italian accent.

He sits on the wide porch of the Amarillo and slowly fans himself. Lesser men would be blinded by the gleam from his refulgent ebon leather boots. But Aubrey sits with his boots up, face lit by the black light, and very slowly sips a Texas Tumbleweed.

Aubrey doesn't know that his doom is already coming by train from California.

He's plotting how to extend his hotel bill. Maybe he'll borrow money from a wealthy rancher using his phony Count title and his phony Old World charm. The reward money from shooting Jesse seventeen years ago has long since been converted to wine, women, and song. He'll have another cigar by and by.

Heavy rain last night, and the ridiculous wooden cobbles the city bought in the spring have begun to swell. Every now and then one pops out of the grid, shooting eight or ten feet into the air. The horses hitched in front of the hotel are getting a mite skittish. Aubrey wishes it were cooler.

In California, having completed his lecture on philosophical conceptions and practical results, William James boards an eastbound train. His brother Henry had arrived a week before, ostensibly to autograph copies of the just-released *In the Cage* at a Navajo bookstore in nearby Arizona. They have a private car.

William doesn't speak to Henry until they pass through Tombstone. He's just corrected proofs of *Human Immortality*. He's still peeved at Henry for siding with Frank and against him on the idea of the specious present. In Tombstone he recites the James brothers' creed to break the silence, "Never rob from a friend, a Southerner, a preacher, or a widow. Amen."

"Amen," says Henry.

Henry opens up a small hand-tooled leather valise. Inside are two pairs of pearl-handled revolvers. One pair had been Jesse's, the other is Frank's, who is too old for this. Henry hands Jesse's guns to William.

William says, "I see you're already interested in the dense

symbolism and complicated characterization that will come to dominate your later work."

Henry nods grimly.

As the warm stars of the Panhandle night begin to shine through the lavender and orange Texas sunset, Aubrey makes his way to his room. He opens his last bottle of Kentucky bourbon and dips his pen in the inkwell the Chinese boy has brought. The two civilizing claims that the six-year-old city of Amarillo has are a five-story hotel and two Chinese gofers, Joe Fong Yang and Joe Fong Yin. Aubrey begins the thirty-seventh chapter of his autobiography, *Robert Ford My Story*. Aubrey writes, "To Carthage I come, where a cauldron of unholy loves sang about my ears. Since I had developed elephantiasis in my testicles six months ago in New Orleans I was tone-deaf. So I went to Amarillo." He is referring to Carthage, Texas, but the words—at least the first string of them—are St. Augustine's. The man who shot Jesse James in the back is not above plagiarism. Aubrey takes a long swig of bourbon and decides to stretch his legs. He locks his bio carefully away in a Confederate Army strongbox.

When Aubrey reaches the door of the Amarillo, no more sunset remains. He walks toward the depot, a thousand schemes hatching in his brain. A swarthy gypsy lights a kerosene lamp in front of a buffalo hide tent.

Madam Rose

Reader and Advisor

Palm Head and Cards
Read

The tent's new. The hides smell and look a little stiff. Aubrey walks up to the swarthy man. "How much?"

JESSE REVENGED

"Palm read ten cents. Head read ten cents. Cards read fifteen cents. Triple reading thirty cents."

Aubrey hands the man a quarter and a nickel. The gypsy sticks his head through the folds and says, "Triple reading." Aubrey enters. The man walks up the street toward the saloon.

Rosa, an ancient and enigmatic gypsy, quietly and efficiently does the three readings. Across the candles, she stares sad and sullen at the elderly stranger. Finally she says, "You've got troubles."

"Like what?"

"Like death. I can see in your palm that someone's coming to kill you. Someone influenced by the novels of Ivan Turgenev. Someone who's an excellent marksman and a damn fine writer."

Aubrey feels his bowels turn into cold aspic. He's naked without a gunbelt. But he still appreciates the value of money, he'll get his thirty cents worth. He asks Rosa, "This someone, does he come alone?"

"No. I feel he's traveling with an older bearded man. An older man who distrusts all monistic absolutisms."

"Anyone else?"

"No. Just the two. Coming from the direction of the setting sun."

Aubrey knows the first man is Henry, the writer. The second could be either Frank or William. Both are good shots—maybe as good as Jesse. He can't remember if the subject of monistic absolutisms came up when they were planning bank jobs.

"Are they going to kill me?"

"They'll try. I think the younger one will succeed."

"But it's not certain?"

"Mister, if I thought the future was fixed, would I charge thirty cents trying to help people avoid it?"

Aubrey is relieved.

Outside the tent another wooden cobble rockets into the air.

The train stops around midnight to take on water and coal near the eastern Arizona border. Henry awakens. He's forgotten the photographer. Dammit. He'd promised John Singer Sargent pictures of the shootout. Henry wonders if they should call the whole thing off. They've done that too often waiting to the end of this novel or that book. Maybe they can hire a photographer in Amarillo. The train begins rolling.

Aubrey Sorrentino buys the swarthy man another watered whiskey. Four drunk cowpokes simulate a poker game near the saloon door. Aubrey shows the Romani a wad of bills. The outer bills are U.S. currency, the inner and more numerous are Confederate boodle. The Romani smiles and pulls a knife from his belt. He plunges the knife into a photo of Henry James, pinning it to their wobbly table. The chai has bad teeth. Aubrey buys the man a bottle and then heads back to his hotel.

Aubrey's sleep is fitful but no more fitful than any night since he shot Jesse. Phantoms of the remaining James brothers appear every night. Sometimes singly. Sometimes the whole gang: Frank James, William James, Henry James, Josiah Royce, Hermann von Helmholtz, William Dean Howells, and Doc Holiday.

They'd had their petty revenges over the years, but now they were going for hot lead. Aubrey's cheeks still burn at the thought of Henry's devastating review of Aubrey's first novel, *Missouri Christmas,* in the *North American Review.* That review had closed publishers' doors on two continents. But he'd show them. He'd kept in shape and could outshoot all of them except maybe Frank or Henry.

The train pulls into Amarillo about an hour after dawn. The gypsy waits in the shadow of the depot. The James brothers step down. They travel light, only a bag apiece. Their eyes are as cold as an Amarillo winter. The gypsy draws his bowie knife, presses himself flat against the wooden frame of the station. The James brothers talk. William's going to rent a room. Henry's going to try getting a photographer. William walks southward and Henry walks northward, gypsyward.

The gypsy shifts slightly preparing to spring. Henry's predator hearing informs him. Henry drops the suitcase and jumps around the depot's corner facing the gypsy. The gypsy lunges, but Henry's gun is quicker. A bright red rose blooms in the gypsy's chest. Henry asks the falling man if he knows of any photographers working in the Amarillo area, but it is too late. Henry pauses to cut another notch in his pistol grip.

The dining room of the Amarillo Hotel opens onto the main lobby. Aubrey sits, back against the wall, watching the lobby and shoveling down biscuits and gravy. Aubrey chokes as William walks in. William turns without breaking his stride and flashes Aubrey a huge smile. Aubrey knows how George Armstrong Custer, old Yellow Hair himself, felt when he looked up the canyon walls at Little Bighorn.

William signs in. The manager says, "Gee, Mr. James, it's an honor to have you and your brother here. I surely enjoyed *The Will to Believe and Other Essays in Popular Philosophy.*"

"Thanks," says William.

William pages back through the hotel's register until he finds Aubrey Sorrentino. He draws a line through the name and writes in Robert Ford. He pushes the register back to the manager. The manager's eyes widen but he says nothing, only (and almost imperceptibly) nods.

Robert Ford runs up to his room for the security of his guns. Later on he will almost shoot a chambermaid.

William makes himself comfortable in his fourth-floor room. He sips on the glass of buttermilk he'd got in the dining room. About eleven, Henry comes in. From Henry's haggard hangdog look, William knows there's not a photographer to be had.

When noon comes, the James brothers go to the wide porch of the hotel. William pulls a revolver and motions everybody off the street. It's quiet and hot. William steps into the street and shouts, "Robert Ford, I am calling you out."

The waiting is intolerable.

Then Ford appears in an all-black outfit. His black Stetson is edged with Mexican silver. He walks calmly out of the hotel, nodding amicably to Henry, who sits on a bench. He steps off the porch. His eyes lock on William with rattlesnake intensity.

He goes for his gun.

As William goes for his gun, one of the rain-soaked wooden cobbles shoots into the air between him and Ford. William shoots the cobble. He has a flash of satori concerning human cognitive processes.

Robert isn't distracted. His bullet tears into William just below the rib cage.

Robert wheels and fires at Henry. Henry's on his feet shooting. Robert misses. Henry doesn't.

Henry runs to his dying brother.

He says, "William, you've got to make it."

"I'm a goner. But we got him. We got Ford."

"I don't want to lose two brothers to Ford."

"Get Frank out of retirement. Get him to take up my career so I can be remembered. In my bag I've got some notes on the variety of religious experience he should find invaluable." William's breathing stops.

Henry stands. The silence is deafening.

THE CRITIC ON THE HEARTH

Isaac Asimov

"The Critic on the Hearth" was purchased by Gardner Dozois, and appeared in the November 1992 issue of Asimov's. *It was one of a long series of stories about the curious misadventures of George and Azazel that have appeared in the magazine under four separate editors, since the first one was published by George Scithers; the majority of them have been assembled in the collection* Azazel. *In this one, George and his multidimensional demonic pal square off against the dreaded Critical Establishment itself—which, of course, proves to be no match for them at all. . . .*

*A good case could be made for the proposition that the late Isaac Asimov was the most famous SF writer of the last half of the twentieth century. He was the author of more than four hundred books, including some of the best-known novels in the genre (*The Caves of Steel, I, Robot, *and the* Foundation *trilogy, for example); his last several novels kept him solidly on the nationwide bestseller lists throughout the '80s; he won two Nebulas and two Hugos, plus the prestigious Grandmaster Nebula; he wrote an enormous number of nonfiction books on a bewilderingly large range of topics, everything from the Bible to Shakespeare, and his many books on scientific matters made him perhaps the best-known scientific popularizer of our time; his nonfiction articles appeared everywhere from* Omni *to* TV Guide; *he was one of the few SF writers* *whose face was recognizable to the general public, due to his frequent appearances on late-night and daytime talk shows (he even did television commercials)—and he is also the only SF writer famous enough to ever have had an SF magazine named after him,* Asimov's Science Fiction *magazine. A mere sampling of Asimov's other books, even restricting ourselves to fiction alone (we should probably say to SF alone, since he was almost as well known in the mystery field), would include* The Naked Sun, The Stars Like Dust, The Currents of Space, The Gods Themselves, Foundation's Edge, The Robots of Dawn, Robots and Empire, *and* Foundation and Earth. *His most recent fiction titles include two expansions of famous Asimov short stories into novel form,* The Ugly Little Boy *and* Nightfall, *written in collaboration with Robert Silverberg. Upcoming is his last novel,* Forward the Foundation.

I had been brooding a bit during the course of the dinner with George, but I finally said, "Would you like to hear what Samuel Taylor Coleridge thought of critics?"

"No," said George.

"Good! Then I'll tell you." He said, 'Reviewers are usually people who would have been poets, historians, biographers, etc. if they could; they have tried their talents at one or at the other, and have failed; therefore they turn critics.' Percy Bysshe Shelley said almost the same thing. Mark Twain said, 'The trade of critic, in literature, music, and the drama, is the most degraded of all trades.'

"Lawrence Sterne said, 'Of all the cants which are canted in this canting world . . . the cant of criticism is the most tormenting.' Twenty-three centuries ago, the Greek artist, Zeuxis, said, 'Criticism comes easier than craftsmanship.' Lord Byron said, 'Critics all are ready made, with just enough learning to misquote.' He also said, 'As soon seek roses in December,

THE CRITIC ON THE HEARTH

ice in June, Hope constancy in wind, or corn in chaff. Believe a woman or an epitaph, Or any other thing that's false, before you trust in critics.'—I could go on and on."

"You are going on and on," said George. "What do you do? Memorize these things?"

"Yes, I have lots more."

"Don't quote them."

"I have two of my own comments. The first is that every critic ought to become a garbage collector. He will be doing more useful work and he will have a higher social position. The second is that every critic ought to be thrown into the fireplace."

"And become the critic in the hearth, eh? And all this, I gather, because one of your miserable productions received a truthful review from some hard-working artisan who had been forced to read through your swill."

At this point, a brilliant idea crossed my mind. "George," I said, "have you ever known a critic and tried to help him?"

"What do you mean?"

"Well, you have bent my ear most grievously with your tales of your little demon, what's his name, and the miseries he has inflicted through you on innocent victims. Surely, there has been an occasion when you have inflicted the miseries on someone well worth it—a critic, in other words."

George said, thoughtfully, "There is indeed the case of Lucius Lamar Hazeltine."

"A critic?"

"Yes, but I doubt that you have ever heard of him. He doesn't work with your kind of trash, as a general rule."

"And you tried to help him?"

"I did."

For the first time in our long acquaintanceship, I made no effort to abort one of his stories. "Give me all the details," I said, gloatingly.

Lucius Lamar Hazeltine [said George], although a critic, is a most remarkably handsome young man. In fact, I have never known anyone more handsome than he except for myself in my somewhat younger days.

It is to his good looks entirely that I attribute his ability to remain a critic for ten long years and yet retain an unscarred face and an unbroken nose. As you, of all people, know very well, critics are constantly faced with the possibility of being struck with generous force by writers who object to being described as "meretricious purveyors of organic dreck."

Hazeltine, however, had so nearly the look of an angel from heaven with his clear, blue eyes, his golden curls, his pink complexion, his beautiful nose and manly chin that one could see writer after writer striding toward him with malevolent intent, only to waver and turn away. They did not want to be responsible for spoiling perfection. Undoubtedly, they cursed their own weakness, and it must have occurred to them that if one among them, but one, were to consent to bang up Hazeltine a bit, his perfection would be gone and the rest could then pounce on him with unrestrained fury.

However, none wished to be the villain of the piece.

For a while, the hopes of the writing fraternity rested on Agatha Dorothy Lissauer. Perhaps you have heard of her. She writes murder mysteries that delve ferociously into the inner workings of psychotics. Her stories are so replete with details of the most repellant sort that even critics find themselves irresistibly drawn to her. One critic said, "For slime, Agatha Dorothy Lissauer cannot be touched." Another said, "Horrifying disgust fills every sentence."

Naturally, a delicately nurtured young woman would feel glee and delight at having her work described in this fashion and, at a meeting of the Crime Writers Association, she was the only writer to stand up and defend the art of criticism, to the slack-jawed astonishment of every decent writer in the place.

It was, however, Lucius Lamar Hazeltine, who taught her better. He had ignored her first dozen books totally, but her new book, *Wash Your Hands in My Blood* seemed to attract his attention. He said, among other things, "*Wash Your Hands in My*

Blood attempts to upset the stomach and at times I became aware of a very mild feeling of nausea, but nothing more than that. I find myself astonished that any young woman cannot do better. The book might as well have been written by a man."

On reading this, Agatha Dorothy Lissauer burst into tears and then, afterward, her lips set firmly, and a cold hard look in her glorious eyes, she went from livery stable to livery stable pricing horse-whips.

Hazeltine, she knew, was a member of the Critics Congregation, a gathering of the profession who met in an obscure tenement in the wilds of South Bronx, where they felt, quite justifiably, no one would dare follow them. Miss Lissauer, however, caught up in the grip of stormy emotion, threw caution to the winds. It was her intention to find the Congregation, wait till Hazeltine emerged and then, showing no mercy whatever, whip and lash him into a bloody pulp.

This she would crtainly have done, cheered on by a happily drooling membership of the Crime Writers Association, until she actually came face to face with him. She had seen photographs of him, but had never seen him in three-dimensional proximity.

The sight of his lovely face changed everything for her. Throwing away her horsewhip, she collapsed in tears. I might have mentioned that Miss Lissauer had the same heavenly beauty that Hazeltine had, except that her hair was russet, and her eyes a heavenly brown. Her nose was tip-tilted, her lips bee-stung, her complexion a delicate peach and, to be as brief as possible, the two fell instantly in love.

I met Hazeltine not long afterward. We were good friends, partly because, as a critic, hardly anyone would speak to him, and he was always grateful to me that I consented to do so.—But then, you know me, old man. Hazeltine was generous with his luncheon hospitalities and I am the kind of person who is a true democrat. I will accept refreshments from any hands, however lowly.

"Lucius," I said, "congratulations. I hear that you have won the heart of the loveliest writer in all the world."

"Yes, I have," he said, with an oddly strained expression, "and she has won the heart of the loveliest critic in all the world—myself. It is, however, an ill-fated love. It can never be, George."

"Why not?" I said, puzzled.

"She is a writer. I am a critic. How, then, may we love?"

"Why, the usual way. Having obtained a motel room with a comfortable bed, you—"

"I am not speaking of the physical manifestations of love, George, but of the inner and spiritual beauty. You might as well expect oil and water to mix, fire and sand to coexist, dolphins to cohabit with deer, as to expect writers and critics to love. Could I refrain from reviewing her books?"

"Of course, you can, Lucius. Just ignore them."

"No. Having reviewed *Wash Your Hands in My Blood* I have established reviewing rights, and I must review all her future books including the one she is now writing, a tender tale to be entitled *Hang Me Up by My Intestines.*"

"Well, then, if you do review, say something nice. Emphasize the nausea and disgust."

Hazeltine looked at me with loathing. "How can I do that, George? You forget the Critic's Oath as established in ancient Greek times. Translated into English it reads: 'Though the subject is divine, and the outlook wide and vasty, Put starch into your spine, and utter something nasty.' I cannot break that oath, George, though it destroys my love and tears me apart."

I went to see Ms. Lissauer. I did not know her, but I introduced myself as a close friend of Lucius Lamar Hazeltine. That, combined with my air of stately dignity, worked wonders, and in no time she was bedewing my shirt with her tears.

"I love him; I love him," she said, finding a dry spot on my sleeve with which to wipe her eyes.

I said, "Then why not try to write something he would like?"

"How can I?" she said, eyeing me with loathing. "I could not break the writers' oath."

"There's a writer's oath?"

"It goes back to the ancient Sumerian. Translated into English it states: 'Be always keen and analytic, with the back of your hand to every critic.' "

My heart bled for these two sundered people and I felt that I had to turn to Azazel, whom I proceeded to call from the high-technology continuum in which he lives.

For a wonder, he was in a good mood. His little red face, with its nubbins of horns, smiled at me, and his inch-long tail wobbled to and fro.

"Oh, Wonder of the Cosmos," I said, "You seem happy."

"Indeed, I am," he said, "I have written a zyltchik which has been greeted with universal approbation."

"What is a zyltchik?"

"A witticism. All have laughed. It is a great triumph for me."

"Would that I could report triumphs for two young hearts that are steadily breaking. But, obviously, since your zyltchik met with universal approbation, there are no such things as critics on your world."

"Are there not?" said Azazel, in sudden indignation. "There you reveal your puny ignorance. We have these fossil remnants of Hades among us. It was only last week, in discussing another zyltchik I had perpetrated—I mean, composed—that a critic said, 'Horsabelum desoderatim andeviduali stinko.' Can you credit the ignorance and vile personality of anyone who would say that?"

"What does it mean in English?"

"I wouldn't sully my lips to explain."

He was becoming furious and I could see his willingness to cooperate beginning to disappear, so I hastened to put the situation before him.

He listened closely, and said, "You have this critic and you want me to ameliorate his behavior."

"Yes."

"Impossible. Even I could not do that. A critic is beyond

all help, at any level of technology."

"Could you in some way, then, manage to make him something other than a critic."

"Again impossible. Surely you understand that a critic is totally unable to succeed at any other line of endeavor. If he had a trace of talent at anything, would he choose to be a critic?"

"There is something to that," I said, rubbing my chin.

"However," said Azazel, "let me think. There is a second person involved. A writer."

"Yes," I said, with sudden enthusiasm. "Could you manage to make her write something bland enough to avoid criticism."

"You know that's impossible. Nothing is so bland, or, for that matter, so good, that a critic will refrain from tearing it to shreds. Where else lies the point of criticism? However—"

"However," I said, tensely.

"If I can't change the two together. That is—I can turn the critic into a writer and the writer into a critic, by making use of the Law of Professional Conservation, and perhaps each one, having experienced the other side of the fence, so to speak, may then approach each other with newer eyes."

"Wonderful," I said. "I think you have the solution, O Master of the Infinite."

About a week later, I went to see Lucius Hazeltine and, sure enough, the virus was working.

He heaved a sigh in my direction and said, "I have grown tired of being a critic, George. The social obloquy that meets me on all sides; the hatred; the scorn and contumely; wearies me. Even the keen ecstasy of finding new ways of being unfairly nasty and vile in my estimates of literature no longer makes up for it."

"But what will you do instead?" I asked, anxiously.

"I will be a writer."

"But, Lucius, you can't write. You can stumble through critical invective, but that's about all."

"I will write poetry. That's easy."

THE CRITIC ON THE HEARTH

"Are you sure?"

"Of course. You bung in a rhyme or two and count the feet and if it's modern poetry, it doesn't even have to make sense. For instance, here is a morceau I have just tossed off. I call it 'The Vulture.' It goes:

> "*He clasps the crag with crooked claws;*
> *Close to the Sun without a pause,*
> *Ringed with the azure world because*
> *He watches for prey from mountain sides,*
> *Then down like a thunderbolt he glides.*"

I said, thoughtfully, "Lucius, that sounds derivative."

"Derivative? What do you mean?"

"There's a poem entitled 'The Eagle' that starts with 'He clasps the crag with crooked hands.' "

Hazeltine glared. "An eagle? With hands? Anyone knows an eagle doesn't have hands. To be ignorant of so elementary a fact of natural history must make the poet a fool of no common size. Who wrote that poem you mention?"

"It was Alfred, Lord Tennyson, actually."

"Never heard of him," said Hazeltine. (He undoubtedly never had, for, after all, he had been a literary critic.)

"Let me read you some additional pieces," he said. He intoned:

> "*Listen, my children, and you will find*
> *That I'll tell you a story, if you don't mind,*
> *About the Land of the Rising Sun*
> *On the Seventh of December, forty-one,*
> *Almost all who remember are over and done—*"

I interrupted. "What do you call this one, Lucius? The Daylight Snooze of Kimmel and Short?"

He stared at me narrowly. "How did you know?"

"A wild guess," I said.

He then went on to recite, "That's my last mother-in-law painted on the wall—" and "You know, we Yanks stormed Anzio, and on the trysting day—"

I had to stop him when he began what would clearly be a long, long ballad. It started:

> *"It was an ancient sailing man*
> *And he stoppeth one of five.*
> *'If you don't unhand me, graybeard loon,*
> *You won't be long alive.'"*

I staggered away. It wasn't as bad as being a critic, but it wasn't much better.

I went to see Ms. Lissauer. I found her in her study, drooping sadly over a manuscript.

"I don't seem to be able to write any longer, George," she murmured softly. "The whole process no longer seems to grab me. My book *Hang Me Up by My Intestines* is doing well despite the cruel and vicious review of it by my beloved Lucius, but this new one palls. It is called *Skin Me to the Bone*, but I can't seem to put my heart into the skinning."

"But what are you going to do instead, Agatha?" I asked.

"I have decided to be a critic. I have sent in my curriculum vitae to the Critics Congregation, including documentary proof that I beat my aged grandmother and that I have stolen milk from babies on numerous occasions. I believe that will qualify me for the profession."

"I'm sure it will. And is it your intention to be a literary critic?"

"Not quite. I am, after all, a writer, and what does any writer know about literature? No, indeed, I am going to be a poetry critic."

"Poetry?"

"Of course. That's easy. The pieces are usually short so you don't get a headache reading them. And if they're modern you don't have to strain to understand them, because they're not supposed to have meaning of any kind. Naturally, I shall find a post with *Booksellers Weekly*, which publishes anonymous reviews. I am certain I can really fulfill myself if no one ever finds out who said the nasty things I plan to say."

"But, Agatha, you probably have not heard of this, but your beloved Lucius is no longer a critic. He is writing poetry."

"Wonderful," said Lissauer. "I will review his books."

"Gently, I hope," I said.

She eyed me with loathing. "Are you mad? And be fired from my post by *Booksellers Weekly*? Never."

I suppose you see the end.

Hazeltine's book of poetry was published under the title of *Fragrant Reminiscences* and was reviewed anonymously by Ms. Lissauer. This time it was Hazeltine who went about the livery stables, testing out horsewhips for the necessary springiness. He stormed the offices of *Booksellers Weekly* and before they could get in a squadron of police to remove him, he had found Ms. Lissauer cowering in a corner.

"Yes, yes," she said. "It was I who wrote the review."

Hazeltine threw away his horsewhip and burst into tears. As they dragged him off, he said, "She well deserves a lashing but I could not bring myself to raise welts on that glorious skin."

But it is still the same. Despite the changeover, they are still critic and writer and their love, which is as deep and as passionate as ever, must remain forever unfulfilled.

I had listened closely to the story and, when it was done, I said, "Let me get this straight, George. Lucius Lamar Hazeltine, who had been a literary critic, is still suffering, is he?"

"He is suffering the agonies of the damned."

"Wonderful. And Agatha Dorothy Lissauer, who became a critic, is also still suffering, is she not?"

"If anything, more than Hazeltine is."

"And they will continue to suffer forever?"

"I am sure of it."

"Well," I said, "no one can ever say that I am a vicious person or that I hold grudges. All who know me speak favorably of my sunny disposition and my ability to forgive and forget. But I do make some exceptions. George, for once you don't have to ask me for anything. Here is twenty dollars. If Azazel has any use for Earthly money, give him half."

THE DAY THE INVADERS CAME

O. Niemand

"The Day the Invaders Came" was purchased by Shawna McCarthy, and appeared in the Mid-December 1984 issue of Asimov's, *with a clever illustration by O. Niemand himself. O. Niemand is the pseudonym of a well-known SF writer, who, for a number of years now, has been producing a string of SF stories written as homages in the voices of various prominent dead American authors. In the past, Niemand has given us brilliant homages to authors such as Steinbeck, Hemingway, Damon Runyon, and Flannery O'Connor—several of these have appeared in* Asimov's, *under two different editors now. In fact, to my knowledge, O. Niemand is the only pseudonymous author ever to have had a cover story in* Asimov's (*the late James Tiptree, Jr. had a cover story here, but that was after the secret of her identity was generally known). I hope to coax Niemand to contribute more of these little gems in the future.*

Here, Niemand turns his attention to one of the funniest American writers ever published, James Thurber, and manages to catch him exactly—if Thurber ever *had written science fiction, then, by golly, this is just what it would have been like!*

Some readers have written to me about the way I portray my grandfather in these stories. They complain that he's shown as a cranky, cantankerous old galoot, and that he was shut up in the attic just because he sometimes forgot what year it was. "You're awful cruel, son," wrote one correspondent, "so let that nice old codger out from the attic for a change!" Well, I suppose there is some truth in the accusation, although it was never I who put him up there—mostly grandfather retreated to the attic when the rest of our excitable family started to give him the nervous jimjams. He came downstairs often enough when he felt better, and whenever he did he caused some kind of ruckus. That's what happened the day he defended Springfield when the invaders came.

We were living in a big white house at 154 State Street, about a half mile from the wall of the dome. We were so close to the dome that from the attic window, which we could look out of only when grandfather was out of the house on one of his mysterious errands, we thought we could see beyond to the lifeless black face of the asteroid itself. My father tried to explain that we simply couldn't see craters from our house, because the dome was tinted a deep green and the artificial sunlight made it impossible to see out. That didn't stop me from believing that I could see craters. My younger brother, Parren, told a story for years about the dinosaur he had glimpsed creeping among the rills and ridges beyond the dome. We all told him that was impossible, too, but he just got stubborn and maintained that he'd seen what he had seen. My mother had the experience once of imagining that she'd observed a large three-masted sailing vessel scudding across the barren landscape, sails billowing full in the wind. My father almost went berserk. "There isn't any wind out there," he argued. My mother just shook her head defiantly. She said that she had awakened Parren, who slept in the same room with her, and pointed it out to him; but Parren reported that nothing of the sort had happened. My mother tried to make a deal with him, offering to believe in his dinosaur if he'd believe in her ship, but Parren didn't care about such a thing. He knew he had seen his dinosaur, and he didn't need mother's insincere testimony to support his claim.

Grandfather was also fascinated by the forbidding territory beyond the dome. He disappeared sometimes, and when he returned he brought back wild tales of his adventures out on the nightside of the asteroid. He generally had one of two kinds of stories: either he prospected among the low hills, certain that gold and jewels and other riches were just waiting to be discovered; or else he fancied that the treacherous Cycladians were planning a sneak attack on Springfield, and that he had to hurry to his observation post. Grandfather had been in the army during the war with the Cycladians, but that had been more than sixty years ago, and peace had been made with them a long time ago. Even during the war, they had never come nearer to Springfield than four or five light-years. Grandfather had never seen any Cycladians in his entire life. He didn't even know what they looked like.

Still, every few months he borrowed father's groundcar and raced across the asteroid to an abandoned shack near the dayside. That is what happened on the morning of the day the invaders came. Our maid, Mella, came into the kitchen with a tray. "The old gennamun he ain't there," she said. She put grandfather's breakfast on the table, and my older brother, Rys, who had finished his own, began to eat grandfather's.

Mother's expression grew worried. She looked at me. "Go tell your father," she said. "Wake him up and tell him that grandfather's gone again." I didn't like the job of waking my father, but you didn't argue with mother about things like that. You didn't argue with her about anything.

My father's reaction was less concerned. He had been through all of this many times before; it just meant renting another groundcar and fetching grandfather home again. Whether grandfather was poking around for gold or keeping a weather eye out for the Cycladians, our task would be long and tiresome.

My brothers and I always looked forward to these expeditions, but my mother continued to fret and my father was just plain annoyed. We climbed into the rented groundcar, my parents in the front and the three of us behind them. Mother, as was her habit, gave my father directions in an appalled tone of voice,

THE DAY THE INVADERS CAME

convinced of the imminent destruction of her entire family and her with it. My father, in retaliation, kept growling that we should lay off the arguing and wrestling in the back seat. And so the time passed as we emerged from the nightside portal and hurried toward grandfather's fortress.

We did not get outside the dome very often, so these drives were something of a treat, although the truth was that one part of the asteroid looked exactly like any other part. The darkness and the silence frightened my mother, I know, and my father was never enthusiastic about leaving the dome, either; but my brothers and I always stared with wide-open eyes at the grim terrain. "Here's where the dinosaur was," said Parren at one point. I heard my father sigh.

"How can you tell?" demanded Rys.

"I can see its tracks," replied my younger brother. We were all tired of hearing about his dinosaur, so no further inquiry was made. We weren't far, in any event, from our destination.

We checked each other's pressure suits and climbed out of the groundcar. Father led us through the shack's airlock, and when we were safely inside we shucked out of the heavy suits. Grandfather was astonished to see us, but it put him in good spirits. "Boy howdy," he cried, "reinforcements!"

"The Cycladians are coming again," said my mother sadly.

"I smell them varmints," said grandfather. "They'll attack at dawn."

One of grandfather's other little crotchets was his distrust of certain modern conveniences. He had no truck with any sort of power that came out of atoms. The shack was equipped with nuclear-generated electrical lights and heat, but grandfather had long ago supplied the place with lanterns and a pot-bellied stove. We looked at each other in the flickering dimness and knew there was nothing we could do until grandfather's mood changed. He grasped his ancient rifle, ready to prevent any of us from leaving the outpost. He always was a strict one for discipline, even among green recruit reinforcements like us.

My father, knowing that it was very likely a hopeless task, attempted to reason with grandfather. "This asteroid has a nightside and a dayside," he said. "There isn't going to be a dawn. Ever."

"Ye be as skeered as a duck in thunder," cried grandfather. "Don't worry, boy. They can't creep up on me."

"But if you stand there looking out that port and waiting for the sun to come up, you're going to have a long wait!" shouted father in exasperation.

Grandfather gave a short, courageous smile. "They reckon they're goin' t' ketch me unawares, but I know they're comin'. That's my secret, boy."

"I'm hungry," said Parren.

"You new men air purt near allus hungry," said grandfather sternly. "We're on short rations here. It's your skin ye ought t' be worried about, not your stummick."

"And I'm cold, too," complained my younger brother. There was a small box filled with coal, and Parren scooped some of the black lumps into the stove. The fire flared and the temperature in the shack fluttered up a degree or two.

Father had made no progress with his calm approach, and he had no more success with any other. Mother joined him in begging grandfather to come home with us, but the old coot only became angry. "Ye're askin' me to desert my post!" he shouted. "What air ye, spies for them varmints? Is that it? Just think o' your mothers and sisters, dependin' on ye at home!"

"We don't have any sisters," said Rys. "And mother's here with us."

"All the more reason," snarled grandfather. He turned back to his duty. The hours passed, the shack got colder, and dawn was as far away as ever. Eventually Parren got tired and fell asleep in mother's lap. Rys threw the rest of the coal into the stove and huddled up against me for warmth. Father glowered by himself in one corner, and grandfather stood wakeful and watchful at the shack's single port.

When we awoke we had no idea what time it was. It was still night, of course, but several hours at least had passed. It was very cold in the shack, because the fire in the pot-bellied stove had gone out. Grandfather sat on the floor beneath the port, his rifle

THE DAY THE INVADERS CAME

beside him. He was studying us closely. "It's time ye woke up," he said.

"Didn't you sleep, Pa?" asked mother.

"How could I sleep?" demanded grandfather. "It's colder'n a freezer full o' shorn sheep."

"Put some more coal in the stove," said Rys, yawning and shivering.

"Coal?" asked grandfather. "Air ye crazy? What coal?"

Father explained that the previous night Parren had dumped a boxful of coal into the stove; and, he asked, was there any more? Grandfather grimaced and made some remarks about how weak-minded the younger people were these days. He usually didn't spend very much time in the cold shack, he said, because he'd rather be out in the hills, looking for gold and jewels. It was very obvious to all of us that grandfather had forgotten all about the Cycladian menace, and this was good news all around. It meant that we might be able to go home soon.

Grandfather had similar suspicions. "Ye come out here t'honeyfogle me back t' the goddam dome with ye," he snapped.

Father wore a strained smile and he patted the air in what he must have thought was a reassuring gesture. "It's cold here," he said, "and it's nice and warm at home." Grandfather snorted. "But d'ye have gold and jewels layin' about at home?" I was going to point out that grandfather didn't have gold and jewels laying about here either, but I kept my thought to myself. I learned at an early age that in a situation of this delicacy, sense and logic have little place.

It developed in the end that grandfather, in his less militant frame of mind, was easily persuaded. We let him think that he might slip away from us another day, and that the gold and jewels weren't going anywhere. At last, mummified once again in our pressure suits, we made our way from the old shack to the groundcars. Grandfather wanted to drive, but my mother wouldn't allow it. Father drove his own car, and Rys drove the rented one.

The trip home was made in relative peace; grandfather lapsed into a sulky silence, and Parren and I dozed. Just before we arrived at the nightside portal, however, grandfather said something that roused us. "What was all that flummery about coal?" he wanted to know. Mother repeated the story of the night before, but grandfather shook his head vigorously. "Don't ye know where coal comes from, girl?" he cried. "There ain't ever been anything alive on this goddam asteroid. Ye'd be as like to find coal here as tits on a boar hog. It'd be worth more'n its weight in gold and jewels." We just looked at each other. Back in the dome, the coal would have made everyone change their ideas about where Springfield had come from. Maybe our chunk of space debris had once been part of some larger world. It was too late for idle guesses now, though. We'd burned every bit of evidence.

Later we tried to find out where grandfather had found the coal, but he refused to admit that it ever existed. He got so tired of the argument that he never went prospecting again. From that day on, whenever he disappeared, it was to go fight the Cycladian invaders. That made it even more difficult to fetch him home, and soon my father didn't want to have anything more to do with the matter. My older brother, Rys, took over the job of going after grandfather.

My mother, however, only let out a wistful sigh now and then. "It sure would have been nice to've saved a piece of that coal," she would say. "It sure would have been nice to be rich." She was probably right about that.

NINE TENTHS OF THE LAW

Susan Casper

"Nine Tenths of the Law" was purchased by Sheila Williams (to whom buying authority had been delegated in this case by Casper's husband, Gardner Dozois), and appeared in the July 1991 issue of Asimov's, *with an illustration by Bob Walters. It was one of several sales Casper has made to the magazine, going all the way back to the second issue we ever published, in 1977, for which she contributed a word-search puzzle. Susan Casper has also sold fiction to* Playboy, Amazing, The Magazine of Fantasy and Science Fiction, The Twilight Zone Magazine, *and to many original horror anthologies. She is co-editor, with Gardner Dozois, of the horror anthology* Ripper! *and has just completed her first novel,* The Red Carnival.

Here she gives us a wry look at a woman who discovers that she's not quite herself after surgery. . . .

Mrs. Birnbaum found herself looking down at her own body. She had read about things like that in *The National Enquirer*, and *The Star*, but she was never really sure that she believed everything she read in those newspapers. She felt the sudden urge to reach out toward herself and found that the arm stretched out in front of her was thick and muscular, covered in dark black hair. The nails on the hand were neatly clipped rather than sculpted. It was then that she glanced at herself. She was wearing surgical greens and her chest was actually flat enough to allow her to see her shoes—

ugly affairs with gum soles and velcro closures. "Minor surgery. What could go wrong?" she wailed. To her horror, the words came out in a deep, masculine voice.

"Mike, pull yourself together," someone shouted. It took a moment for her to realize that he was talking to her. "There wasn't anything we could do." He reached out a hand in comfort.

"Mike-Schmike," she answered, pushing the offending hand away. "I don't know what you're talking about." She turned and marched out of the operating room.

Across the hall was a small, glassed-in area. She spotted her doctor, Dr. Sanderson, talking to her daughter, Sharon. The sound of his voice didn't reach her, but Sharon was in tears. How dare he upset the poor girl like that. Mrs. Birnbaum walked into the room.

"I'm sorry," Dr. Sanderson was saying. "We didn't expect it. We don't know exactly what happened yet. There's always some risk involved in surgery. We did everything that we could."

"What are you telling her?" Mrs. Birnbaum asked. Before he could answer, Sharon leapt off the chair and threw her arms around Mrs. Birnbaum and began weeping piteously on her shoulder. "There, there," Mrs. Birnbaum said, patting her daughter's back. At least someone knew who she was.

"Oh, Mike," Sharon sobbed.

"Dr. Cohen, I'll leave her with you," Dr. Sanderson said.

"So what's this Dr. Cohen stuff?" she asked, looking around to see who else was there. The three of them were alone.

"Dr. Cohen, your humor seems very inappropriate," Dr. Sanderson said. At the same time, Sharon pulled back and said, "Mike?"

"Why does everyone keep calling me Mike Cohen? You know perfectly well that I," she said, puffing out her chest and putting her chin up, "am Reba Birnbaum. And you . . ." she added, turning to Sharon, "you ungrateful little girl. Denying your own mother. After all I went through for you. All the sacrifices. I carried you for nine months. Almost ten. You weren't an easy delivery, you know. I almost died."

Dr. Sanderson turned and stormed out of the room.

"Mother?" Sharon said, staring up at her quizzically. Her face was ashen.

"It's okay. Grab your coat. I'll explain everything in the car," Mrs. Birnbaum said, only what was there to explain? She had no idea herself what had happened. She took Sharon's hand and led her down the hall. "So where's your father?" she asked as they walked.

"He's home. He doesn't know yet," Sharon answered.

"Great! I'm dying and Nate's in bed watching football."

"That's not fair," Sharon snapped. "Mother told him not to come. I mean you told . . . I mean . . . oh, I'm so confused." She began to cry again.

"Stop that," her mother ordered. "Where did they put my coat?" She led Sharon to the elevator and pressed for the fifth floor. Her hospital room was 515. The door was closed and the little curtain drawn, but Mrs. Birnbaum paid no attention. She pushed the door open and dragged Sharon inside. A nurse was bending over the patient in bed A.

"You can't come in. . . . Oh, hello, Dr. Cohen," she said, the tone of her voice sweetening.

"You see what this boyfriend of yours is like at work," she called over her shoulder to Sharon. The girl needed a lot of looking after. Well, that was okay. She was here to look after her. "You have to keep an eye on these men or there's no telling what they might do." She had always kept a very good eye on Nathan . . . not that he'd ever done much, except lie on the couch and watch football. There was a cabinet on the window side, labeled "B bed" with sticky tape. She removed the bag with her clothing. Her good cloth coat was hanging on the hook. She took it and started to put it on. The sleeves were very tight, and, as she forced her arms into them, a distinct ripping sound was heard. Mrs. Birnbaum pulled off the coat and laid it over her shoulders. The nurse was staring at her, her mouth agape. "It's okay," Mrs. Birnbaum said. "I'll sew it when I get home."

Nathan Birnbaum, as expected, was lying in bed watching TV when his wife and daughter entered. "Is your mother out of surgery?" he asked Sharon.

"Oh, she's out all right," Sharon said, a little hesitantly.

"A lot you care," Mrs. Birnbaum said.

"Say, what are you doing in my bedroom?" Nathan shouted.

"*Your* bedroom? Well, I like that," Mrs. Birnbaum said, seating herself abruptly on the bed. She folded her arms across her chest and stared out the window, refusing to notice him.

"Dad," Sharon said, sitting beside him and taking his hand, "there's been a little problem."

"Problem?" he said. Mrs. Birnbaum turned to look at him. "Problem. Is she all right?"

"No, Dad. She isn't," Sharon said.

"Oh no. Oh, my Reba. My poor Reba. Is she . . ." Sharon nodded, then glanced at Mrs. Birnbaum and shrugged. Mr. Birnbaum began to cry. His wife softened. She got up and walked around the bed, pushed Sharon aside and took the place where she had been sitting. Nathan's head was in his hands. She put her arms around him and pulled his head to her chest.

"Shhh, shhh, it's okay," she said.

Nathan squirmed out of her arms, pushing her roughly away. "What do you think you're doing?" he asked.

"What do you mean, 'what am I doing?' I'm comforting you," she said.

"Well, stop it," he said.

"Nathan, I'm your wife," Mrs. Birnbaum said.

"You're not *my* wife, you little pervert," Nathan said. "Get the hell out of here."

"Well, I like that! After thirty years of marriage." Mrs. Birnbaum turned on her heel and stalked right out of the room.

The bathroom was a mess. Towels were strewn everywhere and the toothpaste had been left capless to drip on the sink. So this was how Nathan lived when he wasn't expecting her home. How like a man. She cleaned up the room, even before she looked herself over in the bathroom mirror. She did look a bit like Mike Cohen. What an ape. She wondered what it was that

Sharon saw in him. Although, now that she got a real close look, he was much better looking than she had thought. Still, there would have to be changes made. She looked inside her mouth and examined the teeth. Not too many fillings. She seemed to be in good health. Well, that was a bonus. She ran her fingers through the short, dark, curly hair and wondered how long it would take it to grow. Nathan hated short hair, she knew.

Her bladder had behaved quite nicely. It had been several hours since she'd last had to pee. Still, she had learned, in those last days of her illness, to take advantage of such opportunities as they came to her. Old habits die hard. She examined the pants for a button and found instead a tie. How unusual. Sort of like Nathan's pajamas. She pulled the string and let them fall. The jockey shorts were tight, unlike Nathan's boxer shorts, but otherwise similar to her own baggy panties. She'd never seen a pair before, other than in advertisements. She pulled them down to her knees.

"Oh my," she said. And she had thought Nathan was well built. She wondered if Sharon knew. No, she decided. Not *her* daughter. Still, this was going to be a problem. In all her life she had never touched any organ but Nathan's. She certainly wasn't going to start now. Not even with her own. But how did one use it? She tried cautiously and found she could sit on the toilet and let it dangle into the bowl.

Sharon was sitting in the kitchen. The girl had her head on the table and was sobbing softly. Mrs. Birnbaum's heart went out to her. Poor thing. Always thinking of her mother. But how could Mrs. Birnbaum make the girl see that this wasn't such an awful thing? After all, look at the alternative. She could be lying dead on the operating table. She put a hand on the child's shoulder and stroked her hair. "It's okay, baby," she said. She helped Sharon up and gave her a hug. "Really. It's okay." Sharon pulled her head back and stared deeply into Mrs. Birnbaum's eyes. *She sees me,* Mrs. Birnbaum thought. *She alone, of all the people in the world really sees me.* The girl raised herself up on her tiptoes and kissed her. But wait. This was all wrong. Sharon was trying to stick her tongue in Mrs. Birnbaum's mouth. She pushed the child away.

"Ugh. That's disgusting," Mrs. Birnbaum said.

"I'm sorry," Sharon said. Her cheeks burned red.

"You should be. A nice girl like you. I didn't know you did things like that. You should be ashamed," Mrs. Birnbaum said.

"Mom," Sharon said, using the word as if she'd just learned it, "Where *is* Mike? Don't you think he might want to come back?"

"So who's stopping him?" Mrs. Birnbaum asked.

"You are, Mother," Sharon said. "You're using *his* body. You aren't supposed to be there. You're dead."

"Dead?" Mrs. Birnbaum said. "Of course I'm not dead. How can I be dead? I'm standing here, right in front of you."

"Yes, Mom, but you're standing there in Mike's body. Suppose he wants to use it?"

Nathan Birnbaum picked that moment to sweep into the room. "Are you still here?" he asked. "I thought you'd left. Sharon, are you aware that this boyfriend of yours is a little *faygeleh?*"

"Is he?" Mrs. Birnbaum asked. "How do you know? Maybe I won't let him come back after all."

"Daddy, what *are* you talking about?" Sharon asked.

"Just now, upstairs, when you left the bedroom . . . he tried to kiss me," Nathan said.

"Oh Nate, that was just me," Mrs. Birnbaum said.

"You see? He admits it!"

"Dad, go away for a while. I need to talk to Mike alone, please," Sharon said.

"Good. Give him what for," Mr. Birnbaum said. In a moment they could hear his footsteps on the carpeted stairs. It was only then that Sharon started talking.

"Mom, I love you. You've been a good mother, always. But this is Mike's body. Dad will never recognize you in it. Neither will the girls from Hadassah. None of your clothes will fit. Your jewelry would all look silly. Why, your ears aren't even pierced. You can't be Mrs. Reba Birnbaum in this body. It's the body of a young man. A doctor. You always wanted me to marry a doctor, didn't you?"

"Honey, I don't care who you marry, as long as he's a man who can make you happy. It's just that I thought a doctor, a lawyer, someone who makes good money, could, maybe, make you a little happier than anybody else."

"Mom . . . Mike makes me happy."

Mrs. Birnbaum looked thoughtful. There was something in what Sharon was saying. She'd look awfully silly in her furs like this. Nathan would be embarrassed to walk with her on his arm. True, her daughter still needed looking after, but Nathan was there. Maybe it was time to go. She took one last look at her house and her daughter, her prides and her joy. If this was the price of her daughter's happiness, who was she to deny her? "Okay," she said at last. "If that's what's best for you." She seated herself at the table and a moment later her eyes closed.

It wasn't a moment before they opened again. "Where the hell am I?" Mike said.

"You're at my house," Sharon answered. Her eyes were brimmed with tears, but she was smiling. "It's a long story, but I'll explain later."

"Oh, Sharon, your mother. I'm so sorry." He jumped up and took her in his arms and kissed her, and for quite a few moments they were much too busy to talk.

"Now that wasn't the least bit motherly," Sharon said at last.

By the day of the wedding, Sharon had almost convinced herself that the whole thing had never happened. Mrs. Birnbaum's funeral had been a lovely affair with all of her friends and family in attendance. Nathan took it well. Within months he was safely ensconced in a Florida condo, where he could watch ball games to his heart's content. The honeymooners landed in Hawaii without a hitch and attended a luau held in their honor. It had been a perfect day, and an even better night. The two lovers fell easily into an exhausted sleep.

That night, Mrs. Birnbaum sat up in bed. She looked over at Sharon sleeping next to her. There were some sacrifices a mother had to make for her children, and one of them was learning to share. Mike wouldn't mind. After all, half was better than none. Sharon might think she was all grown up, but you're never too old to need a mother's guidance. Mrs. Birnbaum smiled with satisfaction and softly patted her daughter on the back. "Now I can *really* keep an eye on you."

THE HEMSTITCH NOTEBOOKS

John M. Ford

"The Hemstitch Notebooks" was purchased by Gardner Dozois, and appeared in the August 1989 issue of Asimov's, *with an illustration by Robert Shore. It was one of a long series of* Asimov's *sales for Ford, starting with his first sale to George Scithers and continuing under two other editors; the bulk of Ford's short fiction has appeared in* Asimov's, *in fact, although he has also made sales to* Omni, Liavek, Ripper! Under the Wheel, *and elsewhere. Ford won the prestigious World Fantasy Award in 1984 for his alternate-world fantasy novel* The Dragon Waiting. *His other books include* Web of Angels *and* The Princes of the Air, *and two* Star Trek *novels,* The Final Reflection, *and the comic extravaganza* How Much for Just the Planet? *which may well be the weirdest* Star Trek *novel ever written. His latest book is the novel* Casting Fortunes.

In the strange little piece that follows, he gives us a biting satire of the work of a certain Very Well Known Writer, one we think you'll recognize. . . .

Elliot Hemstitch (1896?–1954?!?) occupies a place in the literary firmament somewhere between the discount gun shop and the all-night liquor store. An unshakeable believer in the principle that there are certain things a man is required to do, and after doing them throw up, he distilled the products of his experience, particularly his experience of the products of distilleries, into a series of writings that will endure forever, not least because they are not very long, use no big words, and contain a great deal of sex and shooting things.

Until recently, it was believed that all of Hemstitch's work was in print and earning someone money. (The exception, of course, is Hemstitch's unpublished first novel, the manuscript having disappeared when, during a long sea voyage, Hemstitch ate it.) This changed when the present author moved into an apartment formerly rented by screenwriter Patrick Hobby. While attempting to place cartons of rat poison, cartons containing a number of Hemstitch's unpublished notes were discovered. The find led to considerable excitement in the present author's circle, especially among his creditors. These are definitely genuine material, written with the authentic blue crayon in original Little Engine That Could and Cuddly Bear notebooks. The present author emphasizes again that the work is by Hemstitch himself, and anyone who says differently should be very careful starting his car.

The present author has plans to return to the closet corner in search of further literary material, perhaps Hitler's photo album or something negotiable with Howard Hughes's name on it. But that is a subject for another time and another book contract. Now, we are pleased to present the following excerpts from the work of a man who shot straight at life and rarely missed, especially at very close range.

For Whom the Bird Beeps

The furry one came into the cantina. He did not walk as a coyote should, he flowed like brown fuzzy water along the floor to the bar and held up a finger, and though he did not speak the owner poured him a drink and he drank it. It poured over his teeth and around his tongue and down his gullet and past his duodenum and into his flat coyote belly, and then he filled out and stood up straight like a man coyote does, and his eyes had the light of those who have had the very big rock fall on them, or been blown up by the Acme dynamite, or have fallen off the high cliff and hit the telegraph wires and bounced up again. When a man coyote knows these things they do not go away from him. The coyote walked out of the cantina, straight with the tire marks down his back like sergeant's stripes.

The cantina owner came over to me and put the bottle of Acme mezcal with the Acme worm in the bottom between us. "Always he comes here," said the owner, "and always he goes out again to chase the fast bird of the road. But never does he catch the bird. It is sad."

"It would be sad for the bird if he were caught," I said, and the owner smiled at me as those who understand these things smile at those who do not understand these things and he said, "You do not understand these things. Always does the furry one chase the small fast one across the desert and the balancing rocks and the very deep canyons and the atomic test sites. Many things does he send away for from the Acme company, so that if not for him the Acme company would fail, and the Acme company people would have to take jobs in television, and would this be a good thing?"

"No," I said.

"No," said the owner. "It is what we call *queserasera*, the Doris Day thing."

"Fate," I said.

"No, that is a magazine," said the cantina owner. "You are a stupid *gringo,* but I like you. You can drink the Acme mezcal so that it goes between your teeth and past your uvula and down your esophageal tract and not get the worm stuck in your mustache. It is good that a man should do these things."

I wanted to ask him some more about the furry one, but then the cantina doors swung wide, and an old one came in, and a young one, and a not so old one in a vest, and an extremely furry one, and they began to talk of the ships that go faster than light, and I turned away, for I do not like fast ships, especially after a lot of mezcal with the worm in the bottle.

Outside, the big Acme truck was delivering packages. There was an Acme rocket sled and an Acme cruise missile and an

Acme compact-disc player with wireless remote, and that was all I needed to know.

The Banana Also Rises

One of the young people who tells me they will overthrow the Republic or die stands in a small clearing, looking through binoculars. He wears a polyester jacket of a blue not found in nature, bell-bottomed trousers, white shoes and a matching belt. He is smiling, perhaps not knowing he does, showing teeth that are neither white nor even.

We are deep in the Republic's wilderness, a long way from its cantinas and its big malls. It is almost dawn. The young ones ask me not to describe the place too well. It is hard to hide when one wears Hawaiian shirts and Mondrian dresses with crude imitations of the Yves Saint Laurent label sewn in crookedly. But it is how they will dress. It is what they are.

"There," says the young man in the blue jacket, and hands me the binoculars. They are not good glasses. They are of plastic, and say "Souvenir of Rock City" on the side. I squint through them, and see a line of the Republic's loyalists. All wear khaki bush jackets and baggy cotton trousers. All have epaulets with leather straps hooked through them, supporting small leather cases in odd shapes. One I know is a musette bag from the Army of Schleswig-Holstein.

The binoculars start to hurt my eyes. As I hand them back, a lens falls out.

"Our foreign aid," the young man says bitterly.

"That is not how they see it," I say. "They say you have the backing of the big stores. That you are the puppets of the warehouse discounters, and want only to plant their flags in the Republic's outlets."

The young one spits on a gila monster. "That is how all you people see the world. It is always your stores and the other stores. But I tell you we will have stores of our own one day. They may not be big stores, but the prices will be fair."

"And will they take the credit cards?" I say.

The young one frowns. "When the people are ready for the credit cards," he says, and turns away, so I can see the label on his jeans. It says CALVIN KOOLIDGE. I say nothing.

At the back of the line there is an American. He tells me to call him Brad, though the pink bowling shirt he wears says "Louie" on the pocket. He has the look of a man who has eaten radicchio and sashimi but now eats macaroni and cheese and canned tamales, which is a look that stays with a man, from somewhere a little north of his stomach.

I ask him why he is here.

"I couldn't look in the mirror any longer," he says. "Not without seeing the wrinkles. In my sleeves, my back, my knees—oh, God, the wrinkles."

I ask him the same thing again. I have been here long enough to know that it is never the wrinkles. The ones like Brad have other ones to do their ironing.

"All right," he says. "It was Meryl Streep. But I don't blame her."

I have heard this many times too, but I believe it. For so many of them it was Meryl Streep, playing Isak Dinesen in the big film that sold many tickets. But they never blame her.

When the sun comes up there is a battle. There is no way to tell about a battle. You either know of it or you do not, and if you do not there are no words for the noise and confusion and horror that will make you know, no words that are worth the rates this magazine pays to go and get them. Maybe in the book to come later, the big book with the hard covers, it will be different.

But I do have a minimum contract length, so I will tell you this: when it was over, there was much cotton on the field, getting rotten so that you could not pick very much of it. There was much polyester as well, still pressed neatly. I thought of the gingham dog and the calico cat.

The young man in the blue jacket was lying still, with one of the women in a silver Lurex jumpsuit kneeling beside him. "Is it all right?" the young man said, and the woman said, "Yes, it is fine," though when one hundred percent polyester begins to smell like that, all the fabric softener in the world is no use.

In the camp of the rebels, they are drinking generic beer and eating sandwiches on white bread filled with the pasteurized food product of the cheese. The American has connected a guitar to the portable generator and is singing "Cielito Lindo" and the theme from *The Patty Duke Show*.

One of the rebels pulls my sleeve, a very young one in pajamas with a picture of a Japanese robot that sometimes becomes a Buick Electra. "Are you going back to America soon?" he says.

"Yes," I say, "soon."

"Tell them we know they love us, no matter what the media says," the very young one says. He is so small to know words like "media," I have no heart to point out that it is a plural noun. "I know they love us in America. I have a picture of the President's wife." He shows me the picture, which is autographed, and I nod and agree with him that it is very fine. There is no way that I can tell him that the woman in the picture is Fawn Hall.

Glitz in the Afternoon

The mall is a cold place in the middle of the day. Those who have gone into the mall are all in the restaurants eating the burgers and the drinks that fizz, and the wide corridors are empty and the air conditioning makes them very cold then. The people in the stores are cold too, because they all wish they were doing the lunch-break thing. It is then that a man knows whether he has come to the mall to do the hanging-out, or the shopping.

Even at the cold hour there are many people in the mall. There are the women, and the children, and the skateboard ones, and the old ones with their cheap wine in the bags of paper. The elevator music is very loud and the restrooms are for those with steel in their hearts. It is much like the bazaars of the east except that the children are not for sale.

There are other men there, but there are never many. Most look straight ahead, thinking only of the thing they have come to buy, and plan a route that leads them on a true line from the trackless seas where their cars are parked to the store where they must buy the thing. Their eyes may be drawn aside by the stores that sell the good lingerie, or by the young ones who wear the high-heeled shoes, as in the videos of the heavy metal, but they do not stop. They order the good lingerie by mail, which a man may have many reasons to do, and they know well about the charge of the messing around with the a little bit too young ones in the spike heels. They go only to the store where the thing they want is, and they buy it and go away.

That is good and clean and honest. But it is not shopping.

To shop is to go into the mall alone, carrying only the card and a little cash for food from the places that will not accept the card. A man does not know what he will shop for before he sees it, but when he sees it he will know. It may be in a window or on a table or behind a glass case, but it will call to him. Maybe he has seen it before, in the possession of another at a restaurant where the tablecloth tastes better than the food does, or in the magazine with the pages that fold out of the middle, the pages that fold out suddenly when you are trying to buy it and stick it inside a copy of the *National Review*. The thing he shops for will smell good and it will please the eye and it will probably be matte black. It will cost like a bastard. Men know this. It is why so few men shop well.

I went through the mall, watching the young ones play the games of video and shoplifting and the sales ones chasing them and the display ones setting up the Christmas decorations, for it would be October soon. There was a strong smell of bayberry, and the sharp cry that the Styrofoam makes when it is wounded. I went back and forth, past the cards and the cheese and the Benetton of many colors and the good lingerie. I went many times past the good lingerie.

I knew the thing before I saw it. I turned, already reaching for my card, and there it was, just between the two pillars that make the terrible noise when the sales one forgets to remove the tag. I have seen pillars like that in Egypt. I do not know if their sales ones ever forgot to remove the tag, but the Pharaohs were hard men and it must have been very bad when they forgot.

I went in. The sales one, who was a young one, said "May I help you?" but she had the look that said she knew she could not help me and the clothes that asked to be helped with and the body that said if I offered to help her with the clothes she would hit me hard in the places that when they are broken do not get strong again soon.

I moved around the store. You must stalk the thing even though you know it is there. There is a chance that another man, one of those who already knows what he wants, will come in and make the buy before you, and when this happens you must let him do it. This is the difference between those who shop and those who only buy. If you then go back into the parking lot before him and do the small wrench thing to the brakes of his BMW, this is all right, too.

No one came in. I took the thing, took it to the counter and laid it down. It looked helpless there, as the animal that shows its throat, but men who shop know this is a lie. The truth about the thing only comes when you have thrown away the store receipt and cannot return it anymore.

"Will that be cash or charge?" the sales one said. I did not speak, but took out my card of platinum and put it on the counter. The sales one shoved it into the machine, and then began what the true shoppers call the moment of truth. Either the machine will make the good beep that means your purchase is approved, or the bad beep that means you have shopped more than a man may shop. Some cannot stand the pressure, and take back the card and throw down the money that folds. In the great stores of the Champs Elysees they call it *le card cafard*, and it is a worse thing than to wear *les souliers bruns* with *le smoking*.

The machine made the good beep. The sales one put the bought thing in a shopping bag, a big one with the name of the store on the outside, so that all the other men in the mall would know that I had made my buy.

It was nearly sunset before I found my car in the big lot. It was not always so, when a man would drive all day in a car with the big fins and the name of a jungle animal. Now the cars have no fins and names like the old ones give to poodles.

When it was all over and I was home again, I sat before the box. The box was dark and quiet but I could see the numbers on

THE HEMSTITCH NOTEBOOKS

the dial, and it was tuned to the channel of those who sell shoddy things to those who do not go into the mall.

There must be many reasons why a man will not go into the mall, alone as a man should, with only his card of platinum and the sizes of his women. Yet I have seen the very old ones go in, though they could no longer see or hear because of the neon and the elevator music. And the young one who wrote funny, Jack Kerouac, would have gone into the mall, and when the blue light flashed for a special on motor oil, he would have bought motor oil.

I sat before the silent box, and cleaned the remote control. It was cool in my hand. I rested my finger on the button.

PICKMAN'S MODEM

Lawrence Watt-Evans

"Pickman's Modem" was purchased by Gardner Dozois, and appeared in the February 1992 issue of Asimov's. *Although Watt-Evans was already a well-known novelist, and had sold some short fiction to gaming magazines, he made his first short fiction sale to a mainline science fiction magazine in 1988, with his widely popular* Asimov's *story "Why I Left Harry's All-Night Hamburgers," a story that won our annual Readers' Award, and later went on to win a Hugo Award as well. A frequent contributor since then, Watt-Evans has won the* Asimov's *Readers' Award on two other occasions as well, including a win for the year's Best Poem. He has also published widely in markets such as* Amazing, Pulphouse, Aboriginal SF, *and* The Magazine of Fantasy and Science Fiction. *His many books include the novels* The Wizard and the War Machine, Denner's Wreck, The Cyborg and the Sorcerers, With a Single Spell, Shining Steel, *and* Nightside City, *the anthology* Newer York, *and a collection of his short fiction,* Crosstime Traffic. *He lives in the Maryland suburbs of Washington, D.C., with his wife and two children.*

In the wry but Eldritch story that follows, he warns us of an Indescribable Horror that could even now be traveling over your *telephone line. . . .*

I hadn't seen Pickman on-line for some time; I thought he'd given up on the computer nets. You can waste hours every day reading and posting messages, if you aren't careful, and the damn things are addictive; they can take up your entire life if you aren't careful. The nets will eat you alive if you let them.

Some people just go cold turkey when they realize what's happening, and I thought that was what had happened to Henry Pickman, so I was pleased and surprised when I saw the heading scroll across my monitor screen, stating that the next post had originated from his machine. Henry Pickman was no Einstein or Shakespeare, but his comments were usually entertaining, in an oafish sort of way. I had rather missed them during his absence.

"From the depths I return and greet you all," I read. "My sincerest apologies for any inconvenience that my withdrawal might have occasioned."

That didn't sound at *all* like the Henry Pickman I knew; surprised, I read on, through three screens describing, with flawless spelling and mordant wit, the trials and tribulations of the breakdown of his old modem, and the acquisition of a new one. Lack of funds had driven him to desperate measures, but at last, by judicious haggling and trading, he had made himself the proud owner of a rather battered, but functional, second-hand 2400-baud external modem.

I posted a brief congratulatory reply, and read on.

When I browsed the message base the next day I found three messages from Pickman, each a small gem of sardonic commentary. I marveled at the improvement in Pickman's writing—in fact, I wondered whether it was really Henry Pickman at all, and not someone else using his account.

It was the day after that, the third day, that the flamewar began.

For those unfamiliar with computer networks, let me explain that in on-line conversation, the normal social restraints on conversation don't always work; as a result, minor disagreements can flare up into towering great arguments, with thousands of words of invective hurled back and forth along the phone lines.

Emotions can run very high indeed. The delay in the system means that often, a retraction or an apology arrives too late to stop the war of words from raging out of control.

These little debates are known as "flamewars."

And Pickman's introductory message had triggered one. Some reader in Kansas City had taken offense at a supposed slur on the Midwest, and launched a flaming missive in Pickman's direction.

By the time I logged on and saw it, Pickman had already replied, some fifty messages or so down the bitstream, and had replied with blistering sarcasm and a vituperative tone quite unlike the rather laid-back Pickman I remembered. His English had improved, but his temper clearly had not.

I decided to stay out of this particular feud. I merely watched as, day after day, the messages flew back and forth, growing ever more bitter and vile. Pickman's entries, in particular, were remarkable in their viciousness, and in the incredible imagination displayed in his descriptions of his opponents. I wondered, more than ever, how this person could be little Henry Pickman, he of the sloppy grin and sloppier typing.

Within four or five days, both sides were accusing the other of deliberate misquotation, and I began to wonder if perhaps something even stranger than a borrowed account might not be happening.

I decided that drastic action was called for; I would drop in on Henry Pickman in person, uninvited, and talk matters over with him—*talk,* with our mouths, rather than type. Not at a net party, or a convention, but simply at his home. Accordingly, that Saturday afternoon found me on his doorstep, my finger on the bell.

"Yeah?" he said, opening the door. "Who is it?" He blinked up at me through thick glasses.

"Hi, Henry," I said, "It's me, George Polushkin—we met at the net party at Schoonercon."

"Oh, yeah!" he said, enlightenment dawning visibly on his face.

"May I come in?" I asked.

Fifteen minutes later, after a few uncomfortable silences and various mumbled pleasantries, we were both sitting in his living room, open cans of beer at hand, and he asked, "So, why'd you come, George? I mean, I wasn't, y'know, *expecting* you."

"Well," I said, "It was good to see you back on the net, Henry . . ." I hesitated, unsure how to continue.

"You're pissed about the flamewar, huh?" He grinned apologetically.

"Well, yes," I admitted.

"Me, too," he said, to my surprise. "I don't understand what those guys are doing. I mean, they're *lying* about me, George, saying I said stuff that I didn't."

"You said that on-line," I said. "But I hadn't noticed any misquotations."

His mouth fell open and he stared at me, goggle-eyed. "But, George," he said, "*Look* at it!"

"I *have* looked, Henry," I said. "I didn't see any. They were using quoting software; they'd have to retype it to change what you wrote. Why would anyone bother to do that? Why should they change what you said?"

"I *don't know,* George, but they *did!*" He read the disbelief in my face, and said, "Come on, I'll show you! I logged everything!"

I followed him to his computer room—a spare bedroom upstairs held a battered IBM PC/AT and an assortment of other equipment, occupying a second-hand desk and several shelves. Print-outs and software manuals were stacked knee-deep on all sides. A black box, red lights glowering ominously from its front panel, was perched atop his monitor screen.

I stood nearby, peering over his shoulder, as he booted up his computer and loaded a log file into his text editor. Familiar messages appeared on the screen.

"Look at this," Henry said, "I got this one yesterday."

I had read this note previously; it consisted of a long quoted passage that suggested, in elaborate and revolting detail, unnatural acts that the recipient should perform, with explanations of why, given the recipient's ancestry and demonstrated proclivities, each was appropriate. The anatomical descriptions were thoroughly stomach-turning, but probably, so far as I could tell, accurate—no obvious impossibilities were involved.

The amount of fluid seemed a bit excessive, perhaps.

To this quoted passage, the sender had appended only the comment, "I can't believe you said that, Pickman."

"So?" I said.

"So, I *didn't* say that," Pickman said. "Of course I didn't!"

"But I read it . . ." I began.

"Not from *me,* you didn't!"

I frowned, and pointed out, "That quote has a date on it—I mean, when you supposedly sent it. And it was addressed to Pete Gifford. You didn't send him that message?"

"I posted a message to him that day, yeah, but it wasn't anything like *that!*"

"Do you have it logged?"

"Sure."

He called up a window showing another file, scrolled through it, and showed me.

"PETE," the message read, "WHY DO'NT YUO GO F*CK YUORSELF THREE WAYS ANYWAY."

I read that, then looked at the other message, still on the main screen.

Three ways. One, two, three. In graphic detail.

I pointed this out.

"Yeah," Pickman said, "I guess that's where they got the idea, but I think it's pretty disgusting, writing something that gross and then blaming me for it."

"You really didn't write it?" I stared at the screen.

The message in the window was much more the old Henry Pickman style, but the other, longer one was what I remembered reading on my own machine.

"Let's look at some others," I suggested.

So we looked.

We found that very first message, which I had read as beginning, "From the depths I return and greet you all. My sincerest apologies for any inconvenience that my withdrawal might have occasioned."

Pickman's log showed that he had posted, "BAck from the pits—hi, Guys! Sorry I wuz gone, didja miss Me?"

"Someone," I said, "has been rewriting every word you've sent out since you got your new modem."

"That's silly," he said. I nodded.

"Silly," I said, "But true."

"How *could* anyone do that?" he asked, baffled.

I shrugged. "Someone is."

"Or something." He eyed the black box atop the monitor speculatively. "Maybe it's the modem," he said. "Maybe it's doing something weird."

I looked at the device; it was an oblong of black plastic, featureless save for the two red lights that shone balefully from the front and the small metal plate bolted to one side where incised letters spelled out, "Miskatonic Data Systems, Arkham MA, Serial #R1LYEH."

"I never heard of Miskatonic Data Systems," I said. "Is there a customer support number?"

He shrugged. "I got it second-hand," he said. "No documentation."

I considered the modem for several seconds, and had the uneasy feeling it was staring back at me. It was those two red lights, I suppose. There was something seriously strange about that gadget, certainly. It buzzed; modems aren't supposed to buzz. Theories about miniature AIs rambled through the back corridors of my brain; lower down were other theories I tried to ignore, theories about forces far more sinister. The brand name nagged at something, deep in my memory.

"It probably is the modem that's causing the trouble," I said. "Maybe you should get rid of it."

"But I can't *afford* another one!" he wailed.

I looked at him, then at the screen, where the two messages still glowed side by side in orange phosphor. I shrugged. "Well, it's up to you," I said.

"It isn't really *dangerous,* anyway," he said, trying to convince himself. "It just rewrites my stuff, makes it better. More powerful, y'know."

"I suppose," I said dubiously.

"I just need to be more careful about what I say," he said, wheedling.

"You don't need to convince *me,*" I said, "It's *your* decision."

We were both staring thoughtfully at the screen now.

"I've always wanted to write like that," he said, "But I just couldn't, you know, get the *hang* of it. All those rules and stuff, the spelling, and getting the words to sound good."

I nodded.

"You know," he said slowly, "I've heard that some magazines and stuff will take submissions by e-mail now."

"I've heard that," I agreed.

"You ready for another beer?"

And with that, the subject was closed; when I refused the offer of more beer, the visit, too, was at an end.

I never saw Pickman in the flesh again, but his messages were all over the nets in the subsequent weeks—messages that grew steadily stranger and more lurid. He spoke of submitting articles and stories, at first to the major markets, and then to others, ever more esoteric and bizarre. He posted long diatribes of stupendous fury and venom whenever a piece was rejected— the usual reason given was apparently that his new style was too florid and archaic.

Sometimes I worried about what he might be letting out into the net, but it wasn't really any of my business.

And then, after the last of April, though old messages continued to circulate for weeks, new ones no longer appeared. Henry Pickman was never heard from on the nets again, except once.

That once was netmail, a private message to me, sent at midnight on April 30.

"Goerge," it began—Henry never could spell—"I boroed another modem to log on, I could'nt trust it anymore, but I think its angry with me now. Its watching me, I sware it is. I unplugged it, but its watching me anyway. And I think its calling someone, I can hear it dialing. #$"

And then a burst of line noise; the rest of the message was garbage.

Line noise? Oh, that's when there's interference on the phone line, and the modem tries to interpret it as if it were a real signal. Except instead of words, you get nonsense. The rest of Henry's message was all stuff like "Iä! FThAGN!Iä!CTHulHu!"

I didn't hear anything from Henry after that. I didn't try to call him or anything; I figured it might all be a gag, and if it wasn't—well, if it wasn't, I didn't want to get involved.

So when I went past his place a couple of weeks later, I was just in the neighborhood by coincidence, you understand, I wasn't checking up on him. Anyway, his house was all boarded up, and it looked like there'd been a bad fire there.

I figured maybe the wiring in that cheap modem had been bad. I hoped no one had been hurt.

Yeah—bad wiring. That was probably it. Very bad.

After that, I sort of tapered off. Telecommunicating made me a bit uneasy; sometimes I almost thought my modem was watching me. So I don't use the nets any more. Ever.

After all, as I've always said, the nets will eat you alive if you let them.

BODY MAN

Avram Davidson

"Body Man" was purchased by Gardner Dozois, and appeared in the June 1986 issue of Asimov's *with an illustration by Arthur George. It was one of a long string of sales to the magazine by Davidson, of both fiction and non-fiction (many of his "Adventures in Unhistory" essays appeared in* Asimov's*), that started under George Scithers and later continued under Gardner Dozois. One of the most eloquent and individual voices in modern SF and fantasy, Davidson is also one of the finest short story writers of our times. He won the Hugo Award for his famous story "Or All the Seas with Oysters," and his short work has been assembled in landmark collections such as* Strange Seas and Shores, The Best of Avram Davidson, Or All the Seas with Oysters, The Redward Edward Papers, Collected Fantasies, *and* The Adventures of Doctor Eszterhazy. *His novels include* The Phoenix and the Mirror, Masters of the Maze, Rork!, Rogue Dragon, *and* Vergil in Averno. *He has also won the Edgar and the World Fantasy Award.*

Here he takes a sardonic look at just how far the modern obsession with looking good may eventually go. . . .

The customer pushed his lower lip into his upper lip, shook his head.

"What," said Birnbaum.

" 'No warts,' I told you, Birnbaum."

" 'No warts,' of course you told me 'no warts.' Who says 'warts'?"

"So why are there warts?"

"What warts, where warts?"

The customer averted his head, pointed. Said: "Look."

Birnbaum looked. He looked the look of one who saw no warts and merely wondered greatly. Then a look of disbelief, then a look of astonishment, then a look of outrage. "I'll kill 'im, I'll kill 'im, that dumb kid assistant! 'No warts,' I told 'im. 'Customer doesn't *care* the present body has warts, customer doesn't want warts on the new body,' I tell 'im; talk to the dumb kid assistant, talk to the wall. Warts." He shook his head from side to side with little stiff jerks. A moment later he said, hopefully, "A, a dermatologist, one—two—three, *zzzzzzzz?*"

"I wanted a dermatologist, Birnbaum, I'd go to a dermatologist. Eight million, eight hundred thousand—"

"*You*'re right, *you*'re right. *O*kay. *O*kay." He flipped through his order book, smeared back the pages, mumbled. " 'Consolidated Factors, two Account Execs,' 'Regular Republican and Democratic District Club, one Politician (attention: Smile), Church of the Former and the Latter Rains, one Spirit-filled Evangelist, customer will supply own Spirit, eighteen and a half percent discount plus regular ten percent clerical discount . . . ' " His mumbling stopped, he gave a quick look up, said, "Two weeks."

"Two, *weeks?*"

"All right. All right. Next Thursday. Ready by five o'clock, quicker than that it couldn't be done, figure it out, 800,000 a day overhead, one customer gets two discounts, one isn't enough, you could live but they won't let you, you think I lick honey in this rotten business, go train a good body man like he was your own son you live in fear and trembling eventually he'll go open his own place with your own customers some of them loyalty doesn't mean a thing, present company exempted, and if you should dast mention to an assistant untactfully a reprimand: right away: the Union."

"Birnbaum."

"Thank God the Summer is a long way off, comes July, August, the pippick people, 'specialists,' you hear? 'specialists,' they start walking out off of even the little bit of a day's work you ever get from them, 'Not only are the pippicks melting but we are also melting too in this terrible weather where you could pass out in any minute,' the specialists—"

"Biographies I don't want, Birnbaum. Warts I don't want, Birnbaum. Next Friday at what time is none of your business Birnbaum I have a very important appointment, God forbid I should have warts, Birnbaum. You hear." The air was tepid and smelled of elastiform.

"You wouldn't, you wouldn't. Thursday at six o'clock."

"Five."

Birnbaum gave a despairing look around the cluttered workshop, slumped into a weary sigh. "So let be five, I'll go with*out* lunch, who has the heart to eat? Five. Not before."

The young assistant had his own problems, but, "Listen, Bobby," said Birnbaum, "I regard you as my own son almost, what, the nose mixture I didn't confide in you, the formula that Kaplan and Kelley I let them eat their hearts out I didn't give, so when it says on the *blue* slip 'No warts,' so why do you put warts?"

Bobby looked up slowly from his sandwich, mayo drip on his lower lip. "You know what she says to me, Morris? 'All you want is my body, Bobby, maybe you been in that business long enough and maybe we been together too long,' how do you like *that*, how do you *like* that?"

Birnbaum, whose wife had long since ceased to make similar accusations, was, despite business pressures, interested. "*Who* said? Sheila?"

"Who else but Sheila, you think I'm some kind of a philander, I have the soul of a great artist, Morris, I'm no philander; what does she mean, '*all* I want,' as though it was a mere nothing of no consequence: *Maron!* You seen the body on her, Morris?"

"I didn't seen."

"Oh my *God* what a body. '*All*,'" he said, bitterly, biting into his sandwich with savage teeth.

Birnbaum breathed a breath or two, nodded. "Yes, but Bobby,

I also was once young, similar stories I could tell you, passion I appreciate completely, at the end of the week when she or any other young lady she demands 'Take me here and take me there or I wouldn't even let you look at it,' and you're reaching into the pockets with both hands and the left foot: so how, so tell me, so explain to me, Bobby, how do you expect you're going to find anything in the pocket, Bobby, if we lose our paying customers because you paying no attention to the *blue* slip where it says, clearly and distinctly, Bobby, 'No warts'?"

Bobby took the last swallow of sandwich, followed it with a long tug at his soft-drink bottle, turned his large and glistening eyes upon his employer, put the bottle down on the spray-tray, asked, "Medium-brown hair slightly receding hairline, 'Reduce obesity by ten pounds' it also says on the *blue* slip?"

Birnbaum, encouraged, nodded and nodded. "The one, that's the one—"

Bobby burped; said, "Morris, to you I may be just a young kid whose erotic impulses, like, overshadow his importance of economic considerations, but let me tell you, Morris, I love artistic integrity above all things, and believe me, Morris: I don't put warts where they don't belong; okay, okay, I see I still got ten minutes left on my lunch hour, but I'll bring it in on the dolly and I'll take a look at it; don't tell the Union."

The next week passed in the usual grind of occupation; Bobby came to work placidly, disconsolately, frenziedly, haggardly. At five on Thursday afternoon a customer perhaps twenty pounds overweight and with a slightly receding line of medium-brown hair came in with his eyebrows raised, followed Birnbaum's finger, examined the work, examined it carefully, gave several nods of more than merely grudging acceptance, verbally expressed his total satisfaction, and microzapped for the 8,800,000; Bobby came to work on Friday morning sullenly and contentedly; he and his employer toiled together without many words, Consolidated Factors' Account Execs (two) were picked up by a mere menial; the Representative of the Regular Republican and Democratic District Club praised the quality of the crafted smile, and, smiling, sold Birnbaum two tickets for a dance and ball, Birnbaum offered them to Bobby: Bobby, with a quick jerk of his head, declined.

He declined lunch, too, was offered and accepted his check plus a small bonus, and helped get the order finished and ready for the Church of the Former and the Latter Rains' Evangelist a bit ahead of time, thus avoiding an opportunity for the Church's representative to engage in prolonged witnessing; "*Two* discounts," said Birnbaum, shaking his head. "Some have the name, whereas others play the game."

At five Birnbaum began to put things together in order to put things away for the weekend, and to sweep and sort; when he looked up to say a parting word for Bobby, Bobby wasn't there. Shortly before six the front door crashed open and a *gor*geous young woman entered, screaming. "You bastard, you son of a bitch, my brothers will *kill* you, wait till I tell them," she shouted, some degree of hoarseness hinting that she had been screaming for some while; "Where *are* you, you bastard, you son of a bitch, they'll tear you apart, what you did to *me*," she cried, ignoring Birnbaum's presence, though Birnbaum did not ignore hers; "Where *is* he, where *is* he," demanded the splendid creature.

She beat upon the doors of the finishing room; "Where is *who?*" queried Birnbaum.

"That son of a bitch who *works* here, that rotten bastard, Bobby—"

She raised her foot to kick the door which Birnbaum at once flung open; "He's not *here,* go look, go look, then calm down; my God what did he *do?*"

All the while Birnbaum was inviting her to look, she was looking: no dice; when he asked the question she swung her unflawed face and gorgeous body around and, looking at him, she screamed her answer: "*Warts! Warts! Warts! Warts!*"

SPACE ALIENS SAVED MY MARRIAGE

Sharon N. Farber

"Space Aliens Saved My Marriage" was purchased by Gardner Dozois, and appeared in the December 1990 issue of Asimov's, *with an illustration by Laura Lakey. It is one of more than eighteen sales that Farber has made to the magazine since her first sale here to George Scithers in 1978, making her one of the magazine's most frequent contributors. She has also made sales to* Omni, Amazing, *and other markets. Born in San Francisco, she now lives in Chattanooga, Tennessee.*

Here she treats us to a holiday Close Encounter of a very different sort—after this *one, if you hear the patting and pawing of tiny hooves on your roof on Christmas Eve, you might not be so sure that it's Santa Claus. . . .*

When I got home from work, Tim was still in the kitchen, drinking coffee and reading the sports page. Construction's slow in December. The kitten began rubbing up against my leg and purring the minute I came in.

"What do you think, honey?" I asked, petting the kitten. "Shouldn't we give Mittens two names? I mean, she does have two heads, and all."

Tim said, "Whatever you want," but Stacy stopped splashing her spoon in her Count Chockula and pointed at each head. "Muffin. Tiffany."

"Good names," I told her, pouring Muffin and Tiffany a saucer of milk. As usual, the two heads began squabbling over their treat.

"Any newspapers, Bobby June?" asked Tim.

When the new tabloids come out, I get to take home the old ones, along with the day old bread and mushy bananas. I'd already read them all, of course. The Quik-Stop-Shop gets real slow after around 2 A.M. "Look here: HOUSEWIFE SEES ELVIS IN LAUNDROMAT. It happened in our town!"

"Forget it," said Tim. "People are always seeing Elvis. Didn't that spaceship, Voyager or whatever it was, see his face on Mars?" This was the longest conversation we'd had since we were visiting my Aunt Martha in Austin, and saw the ghost of Uncle Edgar in the closet. So I figured, maybe this is the time to bring it up.

"Tim honey, it's Christmas Eve tomorrow. Don't you have any relatives you'd like to invite for dinner, to meet me and Stacy and all?"

"No," he said, and went off to read the papers somewhere else.

I have trouble sleeping when I work third-shift, so I took Stacy shopping for shoes. It's incredible how quick she seems to outgrow them—she's only four, and already in a grownup size 6. She has her dad's feet, I guess, but luckily she has my nose.

Anyway, the mall was pretty crowded, what with it being the day before the day before Christmas. We did a little last-minute shopping for presents, and we were buying this cute little dog and cat salt and pepper set for Jesse, my friend-at-work, when a woman shrieked.

"Oh, my god!" she yelled, pointing up at a black velvet painting of Elvis. Tears seemed to be pouring from his eyes.

"Why's he crying, Mommy?" asked Stacy.

The clerk got up on a ladder and pulled down the painting, to check for leaks or something in the wall, but nothing else was wet.

SPACE ALIENS SAVED MY MARRIAGE

The woman who'd seen it first reached over and touched the tears, then raised her finger to her mouth. "It's salty," she said. "Those are real tears!"

I looked at the painting, and it seemed that the wet eyes were staring deep into my own. And suddenly this thought was there, in my mind. *You'd better go to County Mercy General. There's been an emergency.*

When we got to the hospital, it seemed they'd been looking for me. Grannie had had this bad stomach ache, and they'd been worried she'd bled into a big old fibroid tumor she'd had for a long time, only they hadn't wanted to operate before, what with her being so old and all, but now they'd had to operate after all, and her doctor wanted to talk with me, right outside the operating room.

He was still wearing green clothes and a paper hat and booties, just like on TV. He didn't mince words, just started right out. "Your grandmother's had a baby."

"But that's impossible," I said. "Gran's seventy-eight!"

He got that narrow-eyed little look that doctors get when they think you don't believe them, and said, "Of course it's possible—it happened. It seems your grandmother had been pregnant with twins over fifty years ago, but only one of them actually got born."

Then he talked about ovulation, and hibernation, and a lot of other complicated stuff I didn't get, cause I mean, I dropped out in eleventh grade to work and all. But the long and the short of it seemed to be that this baby had been in her womb for fifty-five years, and in fact was my late daddy's twin. They'd compared footprints, and it was true.

"But that's not the end of it," the doctor continued. "I've seen a lot of weird stuff—I've delivered babies wearing ancient Egyptian amulets, or tattooed with holy symbols, and once I saw a woman give birth to a Cabbage Patch Doll. But never in all my years of practicing has one of my newborns ever spoken in the delivery room before!"

"What'd he say?"

"When I slapped his little behind, he didn't even cry, he just looked me in the eye and said 'The Twin returns. Love him tender and don't be cruel.' He wouldn't say anything more, and now he's acting just like a regular baby." The doctor took off his paper hat and scratched his head. "*The Twin.* Must be himself he means, right?"

"No. No, it isn't." I didn't know yet what he meant, back then, but I knew that something big was going on, or about to happen.

What with staying with Gran all afternoon, and then making dinner for Stacy and Tim, I only had a few hours sleep before going to work. I was a couple minutes late, but Ralph always covers for me—he's a real good guy. He was this World War II veteran who they found after drifting alone in a liferaft in the Bermuda Triangle for forty years, but he didn't let that ruin his attitude.

"Congratulate me, I'm gonna get hitched," Ralph told me while he was putting on his muffler and overcoat.

"Who to?" I didn't even know he was dating. As far as I knew, his only real friend was this guy Eddy he'd known in basic training, who'd looked him up after seeing his picture in the paper.

"I'm marrying Eddy," Ralph said, sort of blushing. "No really, it's not like that. See, he was struck by lightning last year, and it turned him into a woman!"

"Wow!" I remembered reading about it, but never realized who it had been. "Well, good luck and everything." We'd have to put on a shower for them.

Jesse had been in back, and now he came in to restock the chips. "Heard about Ralph and Eddy?" he asked. He's got this real velvety deep voice, but I never could figure out his accent.

"I hope they'll be happy," I said, started thinking about me and Tim, and choked a little. Jesse came over to hug me—we're only friends, really—and I told him how me and Tim just didn't seem to communicate anymore. Then I wiped away my tears, and looked at Jesse. "Hey! You've been losing weight."

"It's that *eat all you want and lose a pound a day diet*. Works!" A customer came in to pay for some gas, so Jesse went back to restock the Oreos and Pecan Sandies.

The customer—he was paying with a credit card—said "Your stockclerk looks a lot like Elvis, don't you think?"

"No, not really . . ." I mean, I just thought of him as my friend Jesse, and never really thought much about his face, you know?

"Yeah," continued the customer, pointing to some cigarettes, so I had to ring him up all over again. "Yeah, they've been seeing Elvis all over—the post office in Decatur, a McDonald's in Fresno, the Baseball Hall of Fame. . . . Now I've seen him here in a convenience store. Think I'll make the papers?"

We laughed a little about that. Another customer, buying milk and bread, put her stuff down on the counter. "Don't laugh," she said. "Yesterday, totally unexpected, my cat dragged in an old monophonic record album, looking brand new. It was *Blue Hawaii*!"

We were pretty impressed by how strange that was, including Jesse, who'd come over to listen. "I tell you," the lady continued, "something's brewing. It feels kind of like a storm, about to break." She noticed Jesse. "Hey, anyone ever said you look like Elvis?"

"No ma'am. Maybe Roy Orbison," he answered.

She looked him over again. "Yeah, guess you're right. Well, Merry Christmas everyone."

Things stayed quiet for a while, and around midnight Brian the night supervisor came by to check on us. I didn't like Brian much, he was always acting like he thought you were stealing money from the store, but I was real pleasant, and didn't suspect much when he sent Jesse in back to inventory all the cookies and sodas, to see what we'd need extra to last over the holidays.

"Come here!" Brian called, from over the back aisle, where the candy and toys are.

"Uh oh," I thought. Some kids must've snuck in while I wasn't paying attention, and taken some toys and left the plastic containers behind. They do that if you don't watch careful.

But everything looked okay on the novelty rack. "What's wrong?" I asked.

"Nothing's wrong," said Brian. "I just wanted to wish you a Merry Christmas," and he started to kiss me.

"Hey!" I said, trying to make like it was a joke. I mean, I needed the job, you know? "Hey, there's no mistletoe here." I pushed him away—and then he opened his mouth and showed me these fangs like the plastic Dracula teeth we sell at Halloween, only his looked real.

"Brian, what the . . ."

And suddenly he was biting me on the throat, and I couldn't call for help. . . .

I seemed to be sliding down this long dark tunnel, and there was a light at the end, and my parents, and my grandparents (except for Gran of course), and everyone I knew who ever died including my ninth grade boyfriend who fell in the drainage ditch, and all the dogs and cats I ever owned, were there to welcome me. Only when I got to the end of the tunnel, there was this view like in an old movie house with just one big screen, and it was showing Earth, and this big old rocky asteroid heading right for it. At first I thought it was something out of a Star Trek movie, but then I realized it was for real. And then the space scene was gone, and Elvis was there—Elvis himself—smiling at me. Just smiling. And he raised up one hand and said to me, "Go back and warn them."

Next thing I knew, I was on the floor back in the Quik-Stop-Shop, and Jesse was putting cold rags on my forehead.

"I thought you'd died," he said.

"I did!" I tried to sit up, making it the second time, and noticed the floor was all wet with milk, and this slimy yellow and red gunk I didn't recognize, but smelled awful. "What happened—is that stuff Brian?"

Jesse nodded. "I threw milk on him—it dissolves vampires. Too wholesome or something, I dunno, but it works every time. Mind, you have to use whole milk. Skim or 2 percent just won't work."

"Jesse, you got to listen to this dream I just had." I told him about the tunnel, and the asteroid, and Elvis. Jesse just rocked back and forth on his heels. Finally he said, "It ain't no dream, Bobby June. It's for real, and we must act quick if we're to save the planet."

I was still kind of dazed, what with dying and coming back and all, so I didn't hardly protest when he closed up the store, and we started driving. I didn't even really care where we were going. I just sat wrapped in a blanket—his pickup didn't have heat—and looked out the window at the big old full moon.

"You see, this is the culmination of my stay upon the Earth," Jesse said.

"Huh?"

"I'm the Twin who returned," he said. "The one your little baby uncle was talking about."

"Huh?" The night was weird enough without old Jesse getting bizarre on me. I looked at him like for the first time. He did look like Elvis. "Who are you?"

"Like I said, I'm the Twin. Elvis's twin brother Jesse, who supposedly died at birth, but who was really taken off planet and raised in a UFO."

"You mean the UFO people who steal missing children and eat them?"

"Nope—those guys're from Andromeda."

"Then, the UFO people who take your pets or lawn ornaments for company, and return them a year later?"

"Nope—Betelgeuse."

"Then how about the ones who hover outside your window and won't let you eat junk food?"

"Those busybodies? I should hope not. No, my UFO was from the Southern Cross, and they're real benevolent folk there."

I suddenly began to snuffle. "Poor Jesse. Taken away from your family and raised with weird aliens."

He took his hand off the wheel long enough to pat me on the shoulder. "It wasn't that bad. The scenery was nice, and we got Lucy reruns on the radio telescope. Besides, I'm half-space alien myself, so I had kinfolk."

His face got real sad. "Poor brother Elvis, he never even knew the truth about his heritage. That's why he ate too much, and drank, and did drugs. Earth food didn't have all the essential vitamins and minerals he needed."

"Oh!" Suddenly it made sense, Jesse's always sucking on a Tictac. "Your breath mints are from space too!"

"Right. They're to compensate for dietary deficiencies, and to protect me from the pollution."

Lots more was making sense. Like those Elvis sightings, all over the country. They'd been Jesse, just wandering about waiting for whatever it was he'd been sent to our planet to stop to happen so he could stop it. As he drove, he told me a little about how he traveled around, always one step ahead of reporters, and the KGB, and bad aliens who didn't want him to save the Earth.

Then we got to where we were going, which was the observatory up near the university. I hadn't been there since a field trip in second grade. Jesse got us inside—he could be real impressive—but the egghead types there were snooty, and wouldn't believe us.

"Asteroid coming in to destroy us? Give me a break," said the professor in charge, but then Jesse took him aside and whispered in his ear for a while, and when they came back, the man was pale. "Turn the scope around," he ordered, and began searching the sky.

"What'd you say?" I asked Jesse.

He shrugged. "I just told him things only he knew about himself—like, he really doesn't like sushi, and he always wanted to be a fireman, and he's got this secret crush on Vanna White."

It took a while, but then the professor came back, even paler, said, "You were right!" and began making lots of important phone calls.

Pretty soon—well, really it was hours later, but I slept through the flight to Washington and was still half asleep when we met the President and the Joint Chiefs of Staff—pretty soon we were at the United Nations. They'd let me call Tim from the

White House, and the President's wife, who was pretty nice, told them to send a plane to pick up Tim and Stacy so they could be with me.

So we were all up there at the UN. First the professor talked, and a bunch of other professors from all sorts of countries agreed with him. Then everyone got in a panic, because this asteroid was going to hit the Earth in a month or so, and smash us to bits, and we didn't have any missiles big enough to stop it.

I was kind of mad about that, thinking about Stacy not even getting old enough for kindergarten, and I said to the President, "Here I voted for you, and you spend all this money on bombs and stuff, and you can't even stop one lousy asteroid." He looked sort of upset, which got me feeling bad, so I apologized.

"It's okay," he told me. "We're all a bit on edge."

Then Jesse got up, and talked about how he had a plan and would need lots of cooperation. Our professor did some calculations and said it'd work. But lots of them still didn't believe Jesse.

"I guess I'll just have to convince you, then," he said, and asked someone to fetch him a guitar, and right there in the UN assembly hall, he started to sing. And maybe his voice wasn't much better than his brother's, who you have to admit was the greatest singer ever lived, but Jesse'd been trained by aliens, and he knew how to use that extra nine-tenths of the brain that none of the rest of us uses, so it was the best singing anyone ever thought they'd ever hear. Pretty soon everyone didn't know if they wanted to cry or applaud, and when they'd all calmed down and the medics had taken away the delegates who'd passed out or had heart attacks, everyone voted to go with Jesse's plan.

So there it was, Christmas Eve day, and Jesse had a radio hookup to everywhere on Earth. They asked if he wanted translators, but he said no—and sure enough, when he started talking, slow and kind of loud, everyone understood him, no matter what language they usually talked.

"I want everyone in the Western Hemisphere and Europe and Africa to just stand real still," he said into the radio. I was kind of awed, thinking how everyone all over the world was hearing my friend Jesse's words. And trusting and believing him too, because he sounded like his brother, and everyone on Earth knows about Elvis. "And I want everyone in the East, in China and Japan and . . ." Well, I'll just skip the list of countries, cause I don't exactly know where most of them were, or how to spell them either.

" . . . I want every one of you to go get a kitchen chair exactly eighteen inches tall—that's forty-six centimeters—"

It was real impressive how smart Jesse was.

"You can put some books or plywood on the seat if it isn't exactly eighteen inches. Now I want you to get up on those chairs, every one of you. Come on now." He waited a bit, so folks who were old or young or maybe had arthritis could get onto their chairs. "Now when I say go—hold on, not yet, when I say Go, I want everyone to jump. Okay, all ready?"

He looked over at me, and I smiled and crossed my fingers.

He leaned close to his microphone. "Okay. Ready, set—jump!"

And all over China and Japan and all those other countries, people jumped off their kitchen chairs.

The ground shook a little, and Stacy began to cry. I comforted her, and Tim put his arm around my shoulder.

The professor was talking on the phone to some other scientists, who were somewhere or other doing stuff, and he put his hand over the receiver and shouted. "It worked! It worked! When the Asians all jumped, they pushed the Earth slightly out of its orbit, so now that asteroid is going to miss us. We're saved!"

Everyone began to cheer and hug each other. Then we got quiet, because we'd all noticed a dayglow orange UFO hovering outside the windows.

Jesse came over and took my hands. "You've been a right good friend, Bobby June, and I'm gonna miss you."

Stacy said, "You goin' somewhere, Uncle Jesse?"

He put a hand on her head—and her hair's been blond and naturally curly ever since—and said, "My job, and my brother's, is over, Stacy. I'm going home. But first . . ."

SPACE ALIENS SAVED MY MARRIAGE

He took Tim aside a bit. "Now Tim," he said, "I know you love your wife, but you have to talk with her."

"But if I do, if she learns the truth about me," Tim answered, "she wouldn't love me no more."

"Now, you know that isn't true. Don't be afraid," Jesse told him.

Tim said to me, "Bobby June, I wouldn't blame you if you leave me when I tell you this. The reason we never visit my relatives, and the reason I have so much trouble finding shoes that fit—sweetheart, I'm Bigfoot.

"Well, I'm not really Bigfoot," he continued. "I'm just his little brother. But you get the idea."

I said, "Honey, I wouldn't care if you were the Loch Ness Monster, you're still my man," and I hugged Tim, and Stacy jumped up and down cause she could tell things were going to be okay from now on.

Jesse went to the window, stepping onto a gangplank from the UFO. "Wouldn't you and your family like to spend the holiday with your relatives, Tim?"

"Sure would," said Tim. "But we couldn't get no flight to Oregon on Christmas Eve, and anyway, we don't have no presents either."

"Forget airplanes," grinned Jesse. "We can drop you off on our way. And I'm sure we can find something around the saucer for you to give your folks." He waved us to the gangplank.

"Oh boy!" cried Stacy. "This is going to be the best Christmas ever! And I also predict major conflict in the Mideast, a startling new career development for Linda Evans, and all the dogs in Denver will lose their hair but learn to speak . . ."

DO YA, DO YA, WANNA DANCE?

Howard Waldrop

"Do Ya, Do Ya, Wanna Dance" was purchased by Gardner Dozois, and was published in the August 1988 issue, with an amusing illustration by Bob Walters. Waldrop has only published a few stories in the magazine, far fewer than we'd like, but they have all been worth waiting for. He is widely considered to be one of the best short-story writers in the business, and his famous story "The Ugly Chickens" won both the Nebula and the World Fantasy awards in 1981. His work has been gathered in three collections: Howard Who? All About Strange Monsters of the Recent Past: Neat Stories by Howard Waldrop, *and* Night of the Cooters: More Neat Stories by Howard Waldrop. *Waldrop is also the author of the novel* The Texas-Israeli War: 1999, *in collaboration with Jake Saunders, and of two solo novels,* Them Bones *and* A Dozen Tough Jobs. *He is at work on another solo novel. Waldrop lives in Austin, Texas.*

Here he gives us a hilarious, high-energy look back at the '60s, a look as funny, poignant, and quirky as one would expect from Waldrop, who has been called "the Resident Weird Mind of his generation."

The light was so bad in the bar that everyone there looked like they had been painted by Thomas Hart Benton, or carved from dirty bars of soap with rusty spoons.

"Frank! Frank!" the patrons yelled, like for Norm on *Cheers* before they canceled it.

"No need to stand," I said. I went to the table where Barb, Bob, and Penny sat. Carole the waitress brought over a Ballantine Ale in a can, no glass.

"How y'all?" I asked my three friends. I seemed *not* to have interrupted a conversation.

"I feel like six pounds of monkey shit," said Bob, who had once been tall and thin and was now tall and fat.

"My mother's at it again," said Penny. Her nails looked like they had been done by Mungo of Hollywood, her eyes were like pissholes in a snowbank.

"Jim went back to Angela," said Barb.

I stared down at the table with them for five or six minutes. The music over the speakers was "Wonderful World, Beautiful People" by Johnny Nash. We usually came to this bar because it had a good jukebox that livelied us up.

"So," said Barb, looking up at me, "I hear you're going to be a tour guide for the reunion."

There are terrible disasters in history, and there are always great catastrophes just waiting to happen.

But the greatest one of all, the thing time's been holding its breath for, the *capo de tutti capi* of impending disasters, was going to happen this coming weekend.

Like the *Titanic* steaming for its chunk of polar ice, like the *Hindenberg* looking for its Lakehurst, like the guy at Chernobyl wondering what *that* switch would do, it was inevitable, inexorable, a psychic juggernaut.

The Class of '69 was having its twentieth high school reunion.

And what they were coming back to was no longer even a high school—it had been phased out in a magnet school program in '74. The building had been taken over by the community college.

The most radical graduating class in the history of American secondary education, had, like all the ideals it once held, no real place to go.

Things were to start Saturday morning with a tour of the old building, then a picnic in the afternoon in the city park where everyone used to get stoned and lie around all weekend, then a dance that night in what used to be the fanciest downtown hotel a few blocks from the state capitol.

That was the reunion Barb was talking about.

"I found the concept of the high school no longer being there so existential that I offered to help out," I said. "Olin Sweetwater called me a couple of months ago—"

"Olin Sweetwater? Olin *Sweetwater!*" said Penny. "Geez! I haven't heard that name in the whole damn twenty years." She held onto the table with both hands. "I think I'm having a drug flashback!"

"Yeah, Olin. Lives in Dallas now. Runs an insurance agency. He got my name from somebody I built some bookcases for a couple of years ago. Anyway, asked if I'd be one of the guides on the tour Saturday morning—you know, point out stuff to husbands and wives and kids, people who weren't there."

I didn't know if I should go on.

Bob was looking at me, waiting.

"Well, Olin got me in touch with Jamie Lee Johnson—Jamie Lee Something hyphen Something now, none of them Johnson. She's the entertainment chairman, in charge of the dance. I made a couple of tapes for her."

I don't have much, but I do have a huge bunch of Original Oldies, Greatest Hits albums and other garage sale wonders. Lots of people know it and call me once or twice a year to make dance tapes for their parties.

"Oh, you'll like this," I said, waving to Carole to bring me another Ballantine Ale. "She said 'Spring for some Maxell tapes, not the usual four for eighty-nine cents kind I hear you buy at Revco.' Where you think she could have heard about that?"

"From me," said Barb. "She called me a month ago, too." She smiled a little.

"Come on, Barb." I said. "Spill it."

"Well, I wanted to—"

"I'm not going," said Penny.

We all looked at her.

"Okay. Your protest has been noted and filed. Now start looking for your granny dress and your walnut shell beads," I said.

"Why should I go back?" said Penny. "High school was shit. None of *us* had any fun there, we were all toads. Sure, things got a little exciting, but you could have been on top of Mount Baldy in Colorado in the late '60s and it would have been exciting. Why should I go see a bunch of jerks making fools of themselves trying to recapture some, some *image* of themselves another whole time and place?"

"Oh," said Bob, readjusting his gimme hat, "You really should hang around jerks more often."

"And why's that, Bob?" asked Penny, peeling the label from her Lone Star.

" 'Cause if you watch them long enough," said Bob, "you'll realize that jerks are capable of *anything*."

Bob's the kind of guy who holds people's destinies in his hands and they never realize it. When someone does something especially stupid and life-threatening in traffic, Bob doesn't honk his horn or scream or shake his fist.

He follows them. Either to where they're going, or the city limits, whichever comes first. If they go to work, or shopping, he makes his move then. If they go to a residence, he jots down the make, model and license plate of the car on a notepad he keeps on his dashboard, and comes back later that night.

Bob has two stacks of bumper stickers in the glove compartment of his truck. He takes one from each.

He goes to the vehicle of the person who has put his life personally in jeopardy, and he slaps one of the stickers on the left front bumper and one on the right rear.

The one on the back says SPICS AND NIGGERS OUT OF THE U.S.!

The one he puts on the front reads KILL A COP TODAY!

He goes through about fifty pairs of stickers a year. He's self-employed, so he writes the printing costs off on his Schedule A as "Depreciation."

Penny looked at Bob a little longer. "Okay. You've convinced me," she said. "Are you happy?"

"No," said Bob, turning in his chair. "Tell us whatever it is that'll make us happy, Barb."

"The guys are going to play."

Just *the guys*. No names. No *what guys?* We all knew. I had never before in my life seen Bob's jaw drop. Now I have.

The guys.

Craig Beausoliel. Morey Morkheim. Abram Cassuth. Andru Esposito. Or, taking them in order of their various band names from junior high on: Four Guys in a Dodge. Two Jews, A Wop, and A Frog. The Hurtz Bros. (Pervo, Devo, Sado, and Twisto). The Bug-Eyed Weasels. Those were when they were local, when they played Yud's, the Vulcan Gas Company, Tod's Hi-Spot. Then they got a record label and went national just after high school.

You knew them as *Distressed Flag Sale*.

That was the title of their first album (subtitled *For Sale Cheap One Country Inquire 1600 Pennsylvania Avenue*). You probably knew it as the "blue-cake-with-the-white-stars-on-the-table-with-the-red-stripes-formed-on-the-white-floor-by-the-blood-running- in-seven-rivulets-from-the-dead-G.I." album.

Their second and last was *NEXT!* with the famous photo of the Saigon police chief blowing the brains out of the suspected VC in the checked shirt during the Tet Offensive of 1968, only over the general's face they'd substituted Nixon's, and over the VC's, Howdy Doody's.

Then of course came the seclusion for six months, then the famous concert/riot/bust in Miami in 1970 that put an end to the band pretty much as a functioning human organization.

Morey Morkheim tried a comeback after his time in the *jusgado,* in the mid-70s, as Moe in Moe and the Meanies' *Suck*

My Buttons, but it wasn't a very good album and the times were *already* wrong.

"I can't believe it," said Penny. "None of them have played in what, fifteen years? They probably'll sound like shit."

"Well, I'll tell you what I know," said Barb. "Jamie Lee—Younts-Fulton is the name, Frank—said after his jail term and the try at the comeback, Morey threw it all over and moved down to Corpus where his aunt was in the hotel business or something, and he opened a souvenir shop, a whole bunch of 'em eventually, called Morey's Mementoes. Got pretty rich at it supposedly, though you can never tell, especially from Jamie Lee—I mean, anyone, *anyone* who'd take as part of her second married name a hyphenated name from her *first* husband that was later convicted of mail fraud just because Younts is more sophisticated than Johnson—Johnson Fulton sounds like an 1830 politician from Tennessee, know what I mean?—you just can't trust about things like who's rich and who's not. Anyway, Morey was at some convention for seashell brokers or something—Jamie says about half the shells and junk sold in Corpus come from Japan and Taiwan—he ran into Andru, of all people, who was in the freight business! Like, Morey had been getting shells from this shipping company for ten years and it turns out to belong to Andru's uncle or brother-in-law or something! So they start writing to each other, then somehow (maybe it was from Bridget, you remember Bridget? from UT? Yeah.) she knew where Abram was, and about that time the people putting all this reunion together got a hold of Andru. So the only thing left to do was find Craig."

She looked around. It was the longest I'd ever heard Barb talk in my life.

"You know where he was?"

"No. Where?" we all three said.

"Ever eat any Dr. Healthy's Nut-Crunch Bread?"

"A loaf a day," said Bob, patting his stomach.

"Craig is Dr. Healthy."

"Shit!" said Bob. "Isn't that stuff baked in Georgetown?"

"Yeah. He's been like thirty miles away for fifteen years, baking bread and sweet rolls. Jamie said, like some modern-day Cactus Jack Garner, he vowed never to go south of the San Gabriel River again."

"But now he is?"

"Yep. Supposedly, Andru's gonna fly down to Morey's in Corpus this week and they're going to practice before they come up here. Abram always was the quickest study and the only real musical genius, so he'll be okay."

"That only leaves one question," said Penny, speaking for us all. "Can Craig still sing? Can Craig still *play?* I mean, look what happened after the Miami thing."

"Good question," said Bob. "I suppose we'll all find out in a big hurry Saturday night. Besides," he said, looking over at me, "we always got your tapes."

The name's Frank Bledsoe. I'm pushing forty, which is exercise enough.

I do lots of odd stuff for a living—a little woodwork and carpentry, mostly speakers and bookcases. I help people move a lot. In Austin, if you have a pickup, you have friends for life.

What I mostly do is build flyrods. I make two kinds—a 7' one for a #5 line and an 8'2" one for a #6 line. I get the fiberglass blanks from a place in Ohio, and the components like cork grips, reel seats, guides, tips and ferrules, from whoever's having a sale around the country.

I sell a few to a fishing tackle store downtown. The seven-footer retails for $22, the other for $27.50. Each rod takes about three hours of work, a day for the drying time on the varnish on the wraps. So you can see my hourly rate isn't too swell.

I live in a place about the size of your average bathroom in a real person's house. But it's quiet, it's on a cul-de-sac, and there's a converted horse stable out back I use for my workshop.

What keeps me in business is that people around the country order a few custom-made rods each year, for which I charge a little more.

Here's a dichotomy: as flyfishing becomes more popular, my business falls off.

That's because, like everything else in these post-modernist times, the Yups ruined it. As with every other recreation, they confuse the sport with the equipment.

Flyfishing is growing with them because it's a very status thing. When the Yups found it, all they wanted to do was be seen on the rivers and lakes with a six-hundred-dollar split-bamboo rod, a pair of two-hundred-dollar waders, a hundred-dollar vest, shirts with a million zippers on them, a seventy-five-dollar tweed hat, and a patch from a flyfishing school that showed they'd paid one thousand dollars to learn how to put out enough fly line to reach across the average K-Mart parking lot.

What I make is cheap fiberglass rods, not even boron or graphite. No glamor. And the real fact is that in flyfishing, most fish are caught within twenty feet of your boots. No glory there, either.

So the sport grows, and money comes in more and more slowly.

All this talk about the reunion has made me positively reflective. So let me put 1969 in perspective for you.

Richard Milhous Nixon was in his first year in office. He'd inherited all the good things from Lyndon Johnson—the social programs—and was dismantling them, and going ahead with all the bad ones, like the War in Nam. The Viet Cong and NVA were killing one hundred Americans a week, and according to the Pentagon, we were killing two thousand of them, regular as clockwork, as announced at the five P.M. press briefing in Saigon every Friday. The draft call was fifty thousand a month.

The Beatles released *Abbey Road* late in the year. At the end of the summer we graduated there was something called the Woodstock Festival of Peace and Music; in December there would be the disaster at the Altamont racetrack (in which, if you saw the movie that came out the next year, you could see a Hell's Angel with a knife kill a black man with a gun on camera while all around people were freaking out on bad acid and Mick

Jagger, up there trying to sing, was saying "Brothers and sisters, why are we fighting each other?"). On the nights of August 8 and 9 were the Tate-LaBianca murders in L.A. (Charles Manson had said to his people "Kill everybody at Terry Melcher's house," not knowing Terry had moved. Terry Melcher was Doris Day's son. Chuck thought Terry owed him some money or had reneged on a recording deal or something. When he realized what he'd done, he had them go out and kill some total strangers to make the murders at the Tate household look like the work of a kill-the-rich cult.) On December 17, Tiny Tim married Miss Vickie on the *Tonight Show,* with Johnny Carson as best man.

The Weathermen, the Black Panthers and, according to agents' reports, "frizzy-haired women of a radical organization called NOW," were disturbing the increasingly senile sleep of J. Edgar Hoover of the FBI. He longed for the days when you could shoot criminals down in the streets like dogs and have them buried in handcuffs, when all the issues were clear-cut. Spirotis T. Agnew, the vice-president, was gearing up to make his "nattering nabobs of negativism" speech, and to coin the term Silent Majority. This was four years before he made the most moving and eloquent speech in his, life, which went: *"Nolo contendere."*

We were reading Vonnegut's *Slaughterhouse-Five,* or rereading *The Hobbit* for the zillionth time, or Brautigan's *In Watermelon Sugar.* And on everybody's lips were the words of Nietzsche's Zarathustra: That which does not kill us makes us stronger. (Nixon was working on that, too.)

There were weeks when you thought nothing was ever going to change, there was no wonderment anymore, just new horrors about the War, government repression, drugs. (They were handing out life sentences for the possession of a single joint in some places that year.)

Then, in three days, from three total strangers, you'd hear the Alaska vacation—flannel shirt—last man killed by an active volcano story, all the people *swearing* they'd heard the story from the kid in the flannel shirt himself, and you'd say, yeah, the world is *still* magic . . .

DO YA, DO YA, WANNA DANCE?

I'll really put 1969 in a nutshell for you. There are six of you sharing a three-bedroom house that fall, and you're splitting rent you think is exorbitant, $89.75 a month. Minimum wage was $1.35 an hour, and none of you even has any of *that*.

Somebody gets some money from somewhere, God knows, and you're all going to pile into the VW Microbus which is painted green, orange, and fuchsia, and going to the H.E.B. to score some food. But first, since there are usually hassles, you all decide to smoke all the grass in the house, about three lids' worth.

When you get to the store you split up to get food, and are to meet at checkout lane Number Three in twenty minutes. An hour later you pool the five shopping carts and here's what you have:

Seven two-pound bags of lemon drops. Three bags of orange marshmallow goobers. A Hostess Ding-Dong assortment pack. A twelve-pound bag of Kokuho Rose New Variety Rice. A two-pound can of Beer-Nuts. A fifty-foot length of black shoestring licorice. Three six-packs of Barq's Root Beer. Two quarts of fresh strawberries and a pint of Half and Half. A Kellog's Snak-Pak (heavy on the Frosted Flakes). A five-pound bag of turbinado sugar. Two one-pound bags of Bazooka Joe bubble gum (with double comics). A blue 75-watt light bulb.

It fills up three dubl/bags and the bill comes to $8.39, the last seventy-four cents of which you pay the clerk in pennies.

Later, when somebody finally cooks, everybody yells, "Shit! Rice again? Didn't we just go to the grocery store?"

PS: On July 20 that year we landed on the Moon.

Now I'll tell you about this year, 1989.

The Republicans are in the tenth month of their new Presidency, naturally. After Cuomo and Iacocca refused to run, the Democrats, like always, ran two old warhorses who quit thinking along about 1962. ("If nominated, I refuse to run," said Iacocca, "if elected, I refuse to serve. And that's a promise.")

We have six thousand military advisors in Honduras and Costa Rica. All those guys who went down to the post office and signed their Selective Service postcards are beginning to look a little grey around the gills.

There are 1,800,000 cases of AIDS in America, and 120,000 have died of it.

On Wall Street the Dow Jones just passed the 3000 mark after its near-suicide in '87. "Things are looking just great!" says the new president.

Congress is voting on the new two-trillion-dollar debt ceiling limit.

Things are much like they have been forever. The rich are richer, the poor poorer, the middle class has no choices. The cities are taxing them to death, the suburbs can't hold them. Every state but those in the Bible-belt South has horse *and* dog racing, a lottery, legalized pari-mutuel Bingo *and* a state income tax, and they're still going broke.

Everything is wrong everywhere. The only good thing I've noticed is that MTV is off the air.

You go to the grocery store and get a pound of bananas, a six-foot electric extension cord, a can of powder scent air freshener, a tube of store-brand toothpaste and a loaf of bread. It fits in the smallest plastic sack they have and costs $7.82.

Let me put 1989 in another nutshell for you:

A friend of mine keeps his record albums (his CDs are elsewhere) in what looks like a haphazard stack of orange crates in one corner of his living room.

They're not orange crates. What he did was get a sculptor friend of his to make them. He got some lengths of stainless steel, welded and shaped them to look like a haphazard stack of crates. Then with punches and chisels and embossing tools the sculptor made the metal look like grained unseasoned wood, and then painted them, labels and all, to look like crates.

You can't tell them from the real things, and my friend only paid three thousand dollars for them.

Or to put it another way: And Zarathustra came down from the hills unto the cities of men. And Zarathustra spake unto them, and what he said to them was: "Yo!"

PS: Nobody's been to the Moon in sixteen years.

* * *

MY TRIP TO THE POST OFFICE by FRANK BLEDSOE
AGE 38

I'd finished three rods for a guy in Colorado the day before. I put the clothes back on I'd worn working on them, all dotted with varnish. I was building a bookcase, too, so I hit it a few licks with a block plane to get my blood going in the early morning.

It was a nice crisp fall day, so I decided to ride my bike to the post office substation to mail the rods. I was probably so covered with wood shavings I looked like a Cabbage Patch Kid that had been hit with a slug from a .45.

I brushed myself off, put the rods in their cloth bags, put the bags in the tubes with the packing paper, and put the tubes in the carrier I have on the bike. Then I rode off to the branch post office.

I'm coming out of the substation with the postage and insurance receipts in my hand when I hear a lot of brakes squealing and horns honking.

A lady in a white Volvo has managed to get past two One Way Do Not Enter signs at the exit to the parking lot and is coming in against the traffic, and all the angles of the diagonal parking places. She has a look of calm imperturbability on her face.

Nobody's looking for a car from her direction. As they back out, suddenly there she is in the rear-view mirror. They slam on their brakes and honk and yell.

"Asshole!" yells a guy who's killed his engine in a panic stop. She gets to the entrance of the lot, does a 290-degree turn, and pulls into the Reserved Handicapped spot at the front door, acing out the one-armed guy with Disabled American Vets license plates who was waiting for the guy who was illegally parked against the yellow curbing in the entrance to move so he could get in.

She gets out of the car. She's wearing a silk blouse, a set of June Cleaver double-strand pearls and matching earrings, and a pair of those shorts that make the wearer look like they have a refrigerator stuffed down the back of them.

"Are you handicapped?" I ask.

She looks right through me. She's taking a yellow Attempt to Deliver slip out of her sharkskin purse. She has on shades.

"I said, are you handicapped? I don't see a sticker on your car."

"What business is it of yours?" she asks. "Besides, I'm only going to be in there a minute."

That's what you think. She goes inside. I shrug at the one-armed guy. With some people it was their own fault they went to Korea or Viet Nam and got their legs and stuff blown off, with others it wasn't.

He drives off down the packed lot. He probably won't find a space for a block.

I take my bike tools out of my pocket. I go to the Volvo. In deference to Bob, I undo the valve cores on the left front and right rear tires.

Then I get on my bike and ride down to the pay phone at the bakery three blocks away, call the non-emergency police number, and tell them there's a lady without a handicap sticker blocking the reserved spot at the post office substation.

After mailing the rods and using the quarter for the phone, I have eighty-two cents left—just enough for coffee at the bakery. It's a chi-chi place I usually never go to, but I haven't had any coffee this morning and I know they make a cup of Brazilian stuff that would bring Dwight D. Eisenhower back to life.

I go in. They've got one of those European doorchimes that sets poor people's nerves on edge and lets those with a heavy wallet know they're in a place where they can really drop a chunk of money.

The clerk is Indian or Paki; he's on the phone talking to someone. I start tapping my change on the counter looking around. Maybe ten people in the place. He hangs up and starts toward me.

"Large cuppa—" I start to say.

The chime jingles and the smell hits me at the same time as their voices; a mixture of Jovan Musk for Men and Sassoon styling mousse.

"—game." says a voice. "How many croissants you still got?" says the voice over my shoulder to the clerk.

DO YA, DO YA, WANNA DANCE?

The counterman has one hand on the coffee spigot and a sixteen-ounce styrofoam cup in the other.

"Oh, very many, I think," he says to the voice behind me.

"Give us about—oh, what, John?—say, twenty-five assorted fruit-filled, no lemon, okay?"

The clerk starts to put down the styrofoam cup. In ambiguous situations, people always move toward the voice that sounds most like money.

"My coffee?" I say.

The clerk looks back and forth like he's just been dropped on the planet.

"Could you sort of hurry?" says the voice behind me. "We're double-parked."

I turn around then. There are three of them in warmup outfits—gold and green, blue and orange, blue and silver. They look maybe twenty-five. Sure enough, there's a blue Renault blocking three cars parked at the laundromat next door. The handles of squash racquets stick up out of the blue and orange, blue and silver, gold and green duffles in the back seat.

"No lemon," says the blond-haired guy on the left. "Make sure there's no lemon, huh?"

"You gonna fill our order?" asks the first guy, who looks like he was raised in a meatloaf mold.

"No," I say. "First he's going to get my coffee, then he'll get your order."

They notice me for the first time then, suspicion dawning on them this wasn't covered in their Executive Assertiveness Training program.

The clerk is turning his head back and forth like a radar antenna.

"I thought they gave *free* coffee at the Salvation Army," says the blond guy, looking me up and down.

"*Tres, tres amusant*," I said.

"Are you going to fill our $35 order, or are you going to give him his big fifty-cent cup of coffee?" asked the first guy.

The ten other people in the place were all frozen in whatever attitude they had been in when all this started. One woman actually had a donut halfway to her mouth and was watching, her eyes growing wider.

"My big seventy-five cent order," I said, letting the change clink on the glass countertop. "Any time you come in *any* place," I went on, "you should look around the room and you should ask yourself, who's the only, *only* possible one here who could have taken Taiwanese mercenaries into Laos in 1968? And you should act accordingly."

"Who the fuck do you think *you* are?" asked the middle one, who hadn't spoken before and looked like he'd taken tai-kwon-do since he was four.

"Practically nobody," I said. "But if any of you say *one more word* before I get my coffee, I'm going out to the saddlebag on my bike, and I'm going to take out a product backed by 132 years of Connecticut Yankee know-how and fine American craftsmanship and I'm coming back in here and showing you *exactly* how the rat chews the cheese."

Then I gave them the Thousand Yard Stare, focusing on something about a half mile past the left shoulder of the guy in the middle.

They backed up, jangling the doorbell, out onto the sidewalk, bumping into a lady coming out with a load of wash.

"Crazy fuck," I heard one of them say as he climbed into the car. The tai-kwon-do guy kept looking at me as the driver cranked the car up. He said something to him, jumped around the car and started kicking the shit out of the back tire of the twelve-speed white Concord leaning against the telephone pole out front.

I heard people sucking in their breaths in the bakery.

The guy kicked the bike three times, watching me, breaking out the spokes in a half moon, laughing.

"My bike!" yelled a woman on one of the stools. "That's my bike! You assholes! Get their license number!" She ran outside.

I turned to the clerk, who had my cup of coffee ready. I plunked down eighty cents in nickels, dimes and pennies, and put two cents in the TIPS cup. Then I put saccharine and cream in the coffee.

Out on the sidewalk, the woman was screaming at the tai-kwon-do-looking guy, and she was crying. His two friends were talking to him in low voices and reaching for their billfolds. He looked like a little kid who'd broken a window in a sandlot ball game. People had come out of the grocery store across the street and were watching.

I got on my bike and rode to the corner unnoticed.

A cop car, lights flashing but with the siren off, turned toward the bakery as I turned out onto the street.

It was only 9:15 A.M. It was looking to be a nice day.

I got two-and-three-fourths stars in the 1977 *Career Woman's Guide to Austin Men*. Here's the entry: Working-class bozo, well-read. Great for a rainy Tuesday night when your regular feller is out of town. PS: You'll have to pick up all the tabs.

I'm still friends with about two-thirds of the women I've ever gone with, which I'm as proud of as anything else in my life, I guess. I care a lot, I'm fairly intelligent, and I have a sense of humor. You know, the doormat personality.

At one time, in those days before herpes and AIDS, when everybody was trying to figure out just who and what they were, I was sort of a Last Station of the Way for women who, in Bob's words, "were trying to decide whether to go nelly or not." They usually did anyway, more often than not with another old girlfriend of mine.

(It all started when I was dating the ex-wife of the guy who was then living with my ex-girlfriend. The lady who was then the ex-wife now lives with a nice lady who used to be married to another friend of mine. They each have tattoos on their left shoulders. One of them has a portrait of Karl Marx and under it the words *Hot to Trotsky*.

The other has the Harley-Davidson symbol but instead of the usual legend it says *Born to Read Hegel*.)

No one set out an agenda or anything for me to be their Last Guy on Earth. It just happened, and expanded outward like ripples in a pond.

About two months ago at a party some young kid was listening to a bunch of us old farts talk, and he asked me, "If the Sixties were so great, and the Eighties suck so bad, then what happened in the Seventies?"

"Well," I said. "Richard Nixon resigned, and then, and then . . . gee, I don't know."

Another woman I dated for a while had only one goal in life: to plant the red flag on the rubble of several prominent landmarks between Virginia and Maryland.

We used to be coming home from the dollar midnight flicks on campus (*Our Daily Bread, Sweet Movie, China Is Near*) and we would pass this neat old four-story hundred-year-old house, and every time, she would look up at it and say "That's where I'm going to live after the Revolution."

I'm talking 1976 here, folks.

We'd gone out together five or six times, and we went back to her place and were going to bed together for the first time. We were necking, and she got up to go to the bathroom. "Get undressed," she said.

When she came back in, taking her sweater off over her head, I was naked in the bed with the sheets pulled up to my neck. I was wearing a Mao Tse Tung mask.

It was *wonderful*.

Friday. Reunion Eve.

It was one of those days when everything is wrong. All the work I started I messed up in some particularly stupid way. I started everything over twice. I gave up at three P.M.

Things didn't get any better. I tried TV. A blur of talking heads. Nothing interested me for more than thirty seconds.

Outside the sun was setting past Mt. Bonnell and Lake Austin. Over on Cat Mountain the red winks of the lights on the TV towers came on. A Continental 737 went over, heading towards California's golden climes.

I put on a music tape I'd made and tried to read a book. I got up and turned the noise off. It was too Sixties. I'd hear enough of that tomorrow night. No use setting myself up for a wallow in the good times and peaking too early. I drank a beer that tasted like kerosene. It was going to be a cool clear October night. I closed the windows and watched the moon come up over Manor, Texas.

The book was Leslie Fiedler's *Love and Death in the American Novel*. I tried to read it some more and it began to go *yammer yammer yibble yibble* Twain, *yammer yibble* Hemingway. Enough.

I turned the music back on, put on the headphones and lay down on the only rug in the house, looking up at the cracks in the plaster and listening to the Moody Blues. What a loss of a day, but I was tired anyway. I went to bed at nine P.M.

It was one of those nights when every change in the wind brings an erection, when every time you close your eyes you see penises and vulvas, a lot of them ones you haven't seen before. After staring up at the ceiling for an hour, I got up, got another beer, went into the living room and sat naked in the dark.

I had one of those feelings like I hadn't had in years. The kind your aunt told you she'd had the day your grandfather died, before anybody knew it yet. She told you at the funeral that three days before she'd felt wrong and irritable all day and didn't know why, until the phone rang with the news. The kind of feeling Phil Collins gets on "In the Air Tonight," a mood that builds and builds with no discernible cause.

It was a feeling like in a Raymond Chandler novel, the kind he blames on the Santa Ana winds, when all the dogs bark, when people get pissed off for no reason, when yelling at someone you love is easier than going on silently with the mood you have inside.

Only there were no howling dogs, no sound of fights from next door. Maybe it was just me. Maybe this reunion thing was getting to me more than I wanted it to.

Maybe it was just horniness. I went to the VCR, an old Beta II, second one they ever made, no scan, no timer, all metal, weighs 150 pounds, bought at Big State Pawn for fifty bucks, sometimes works and sometimes doesn't. I put in *Cum Shot Revue #1* and settled back in my favorite easy chair.

The TV going *kskksssssssss* woke me up at 4:32 A.M. I turned everything off. So this is what me and my whole generation come down to, people sleeping naked in front of their TVs with empty beer cans in their laps. It was too depressing to think about.

I made my way to bed, lay down, and had dreams. I don't remember anything about them, except that I didn't like them.

I've known three women the latter part of the twentieth century has driven slapdab crazy.

For one, it was through no fault of her own. Certain chemicals were missing in her body. She broke up with me quietly after six months and checked herself into the MHMR. That was the last time I saw her.

She evidently came back through town about three years ago, *after* she quit taking her lithium. I got strange phone calls from old friends who had seen her. Her vision, and that of the one we call reality, no longer intersected. Having destroyed her present, she had begun to work on the past and the future also.

Last I heard she had run off with a cook she met at a Halfway House; they were rumored to be working Exxon barges together on the Mississippi River.

The second, after affairs with five real jerks in a row in six months, began to lose weight. She'd only been 111 pounds to begin with. People whispered about leukemia, cancer, some wasting disease. Of course it wasn't—in the rest of the world, dying by not getting enough to eat is a right, in America, it's a privilege. She began to look like sticks held together with a pair of kid's blue-jeans and a shirt, with only two brightly-glowing eyes watching you from the head to show she was still alive. She was fainting a lot by then.

One day Bob, who had been her lover six years before, went over to her house. (By then she was forgetting to do things like close and lock the doors, or turn on the lights at night.)

Bob picked her up by her shirt collar (it was easy, she only weighed eighty-three pounds by then) and slapped her, like in the movies, five times as hard as he could.

It was only on the fifth slap that her eyes came to life and filled with fear.

"Stop it, Gabriella," said Bob. "You're killing yourself." Then he kissed her on her bloody, swelling lips, set her down blinking, and walked out her door and her life, and hasn't seen her since.

He saved her. She met another nice woman at the eating disorder clinic. They now live in Westlake Hills, raising the other woman's two boys by her first marriage.

The third one's cat ran away one morning. She went back upstairs, wrote a long apologetic note to her mother, dialed 911 and told them where she was, hung up and drank most of an eleven-ounce can of Crystal Drano.

She lived on for six days in the hospital in a coma with no insides and a raging 107° fever.

Her friends kept checking, but the cat never came back.

"Yo!" said Olin Sweetwater. He and two or three others were standing outside the community college on the cool Saturday morning. He had on a sweatshirt, done up in the old school colors, that said Bull Goose Tour Guide. We shook hands (thumbs locked, sawing our arms back and forth). He was balding; what hair he had left had a white plume across the left side.

The two women, Angela Pardo and Rita Jones when I'd known them, were nervous. Olin handed us sweatshirts that said Tour Guide. We thanked him.

I looked at the brick facade. The school had been an ugly dump in 1969; it was still a dump, but with a charm all its own.

(One of the reasons Olin asked me to help with the tour is that I'd lived with a lady artist for a year who had worked part-time as a clerk in the admissions office of the community college. I guess he thought that qualified me as an Expert.)

The tours were supposed to start at ten A.M. Sleepy college students who had Saturday labs were wandering in and out of the two-and-a-half-story building or some of the other outbuildings the college leased. Olin had pulled lots of strings to let us guide people without any interference, or so he kept telling us.

Around 9:45 people started wandering up, trailing kids, shy husbands, wives, lovers. God, I thought recognizing a few here and there. We're so fucking normal looking. We look like our mothers and fathers did in 1969.

(Remember in 1973 when you saw *American Graffiti* for the first time and everybody laughed at the short haircuts and long skirts, then when you went back to see it in 1981 those parts didn't seem so strange anymore?)

I was talking to one of the few women who'd been nice to me in high school, a quiet girl named Sharon, whose front teeth then had reminded me, sweetly and not at all unpleasantly, of Rocket J. Squirrel's. She was now, I learned, on her second divorce. She introduced me to her kids—Seth and Jason—who looked like they'd rather be on Mars than here.

Sharon stopped talking and stared behind me. I saw other people turning and followed their gaze toward the street. "Jesus," I said. A pink-flowered VW Beetle pulled up to the curb as a student drove away. Out of it came something from Mr. Natural—the guy had hair down to his butthole (a wig, it turned out), headband, walnut shell beads, elephant bell pants with neon green flash panels, a khaki shirt and wool vest, Ben Franklin specs tinted Vicks Salve blue. There was a B-52 peace symbol button big as a dinner plate on his left abdomen, and the vest had a leather stash pocket at the bottom snaps.

Something in the way he moves . . .

Seth and Jason were pointing and laughing, other people were looking embarrassed.

"Peace, Love, and Brotherhood," he said, flashing us the peace sign.

The voice. I knew it after twenty years. Hoyt Lawton.

DO YA, DO YA, WANNA DANCE? 215

Hoyt Lawton had been president of the fucking Key Club in 1969! He'd worn three-piece suits to school even on the days when he didn't *have* to go eat with the Rotarians! His hair was never more than three-eighths of an inch off his skull—we said he never got it cut, it just never grew. He won a bunch of money from something like the DAR for a speech he made at a Young Republicans convention on how all hippies needed was a good stiff tour of duty in Vietnam that would show them what America was all about. Hoyt Lawton, what an asshole!

And yet, there he was, the only one with enough *chutzpah* to show up like we were all supposed to feel. Okay, I'm older and more tolerant now. Hoyt, you're still an asshole, but with a little style.

By about 10:10 there were a hundred people there. Excluding husbands, wives, Significant Others and kids, maybe sixty of the Class of '69 had taken the trouble to show up.

Olin divided us up so we wouldn't run into each other. I started my group of twenty or so (Hoyt was in Olin's group thank god) on the second floor. We climbed the stairs.

"You'll notice they have air conditioning now?" I said. There were laughs. Austin hits ninety-five by April 20 most years. We'd sweltered through Septembers and died in Mays here, to the hum of ineffectual floor fans. The ceilings were twenty feet high and the ceiling fans might as well have been heat pumps.

"How many of you spent most of the last semester here?" I said, pointing. Two or three held up their hands. "This used to be the principal's office; now it's the copy center. Over there was Mr. Dix's office itself." Lots of people laughed then, probably hadn't thought of the carrot-headed principal since graduation day. He'd had it bad enough before someone heard him referred to as "Red" by the Superintendent of Schools one day.

"That used to be the only office that was air-conditioned, remember? At least you could get cool while waiting to be yelled at." I pointed to the air-conditioning vents.

That there air duct I didn't say *is the one that Morey Morkheim got into and took a big dump in one night after they'd expelled him one of those times.* Only in America is the penalty for skipping school expulsion for three days.

Mr. Dix had yelled at him after the absence, "What are you going to do with your life? You'll never amount to anything without an education!"

In seven months Morey was pulling in more money in a weekend than Dix would make in ten years—legally, too.

We moved through the halls, getting curious stares from students in classrooms with closed glass doors.

"Down here was where the student newspaper office was. Over there was the library, which the community college is using as a library." We went down to the first floor.

"Ah, the cafeteria!" It was now the study room, full of chairs and tables and vending machines. "Remember tomato surprise! Remember macaroni and cheese!" "Fish lumps on Friday!" said someone.

Half the student body in those days had come from the parochial junior highs around town. In 1969, parochial was the way you spelled Catholic. Nobody in the school administration ever read a paper, evidently, so they hadn't learned that the Pope had done away with "going to hell on a meat rap" back in 1964. So you still had fish lumps on Friday when we were there. The only good thing about having all those Catholic kids there was that we got to hear their jokes for the first time, like what's God's phone number? ETcumspiri 220!

"Down there, way off to the left," I said "was the band hall. You remember Mr. Stoat?" There were groans. "I thought so. Only musician I ever met who had *absolutely* no sense of rhythm."

Ah, the band hall. Where one morning a bunch of guys locked themselves in just before graduation, wired the intercom up to broadcast all over school, and played "Louie, Louie" on tubas, instead of the National Anthem, during home room period. It was too close to the end of school to expel them, so they didn't let them come to the commencement exercise. In protest of which, when they played "Pomp and Circumstance," about three hundred of us Did the Freddy down the aisles of the municipal auditorium in our graduation gowns.

We passed a door leading to the boiler room, where all the teachers popped in for a smoke between classes, it being forbidden for them to take a puff anywhere on school grounds but in the Teachers' Lounge during their off-hour.

I stopped and opened it—sure enough, it was there, dimmed by twenty years and several attempts to paint over it, but in the remains of smudged-over day-glo orange paint on the top inside of the door it still said: *Ginny and Ray's Motel.*

Ginny Balducci and Ray Petro had come to school one morning ripped on acid and had wandered down to the boiler room and had taken their clothes off. My theory is that it was warm and nice and they wanted to feel the totality of the sensuous space. The school's theory, after they were interrupted by Coach Smetters, was that they had been Fornicating During Home Room Period, and without hall passes, too!

After Ginny came down, and while her father was screaming at Ray's parents across Dix's desk, she said to her father, "Leave them alone. They didn't have *their* clothes off!"

"Young lady," said Dix. "You don't seem to realize what serious trouble you're in."

"What are you going to do?" asked Ginny, looking the principal square in the eye, "Castrate me?"

I answered some questions about the fire escapes that used to be on the south side of the building. "They fell on a community college student one day four years ago," I said. "Good thing we never *had* to use them." We were outside again.

"Over there was the gym. World's worst dance floor, second worst basketball court. Enough sweat was spilled there over the years to float the *Big Mo.* We can't go in, though, they now use it to store visual aids for the Parks and Rec department."

There was the morning when Dix had us all go to the gym for Assembly. His purpose, it went on to appear after he had talked for ten minutes, was to try to explain why the Armed Forces recruiters would be there on Career Day, along with the realtors and college reps and Rotarians who would come to tell you about the wonders of their profession in the Great Big World Out There. (Some nasty posters had appeared on every bare inch of wall in the building that morning questioning not only their presence on Career Day but also their continuing existence on the third rock from the sun.)

He was going on about how they had been there, draft or no draft, war or no war, every Career Day when a small sound started at the back of the ranked bleachers. The sound of two stiffened index fingers drumming slowly but very deliberately dum-dum-thump dum-dum-thump. Then a few other sets of fingers joined in *dum-dum-thump dum-dum-thump*, at first background, then rising, louder and more insistent, then feet took it up, and it spread from section to section, while the teachers looked around wildly Dum-Dum-Thump Dum-Dum-Thump.

Dix stopped in mid-sentence, mouth open, while the sound grew. He saw half the student body—the other half was silent, or like the jocks led by Hoyt Lawton, beginning to boo and hiss— rise to its feet clapping its hands and stamping its feet in time—

DUM DUM THUMP DUM DUM THUMP

He yelled at people and pointed, then he quit and his shoulders sagged. And on a hidden passed signal, everybody quit on the same beat and it was deathly silent in the gym. Then everybody sat back down.

I think Dix had seen the future that morning—Kent State, the Cambodian incursion, the cease fire, the end of Nixon, the fall of Saigon.

He dismissed us. The recruiters were there on Career Day anyway.

I'd almost finished my tour. "One more place, not on the official stops," I said. I took them across the side street and down half a block.

"Ow wow!" said someone halfway there. "The Grindstone!"

We got there. It was a one-story place with real glass bricks across the whole front that would cost $80 a pop these days. The place was full of tools and cars.

"Oh, gee," said the people.

DO YA, DO YA, WANNA DANCE?

"It's now the Skill Shop," I said. "Went out of business in 1974, bought up by the city, leased by the community college."

Ah, the Grindstone! A real old-fashioned cafe/soda fountain. You were forbidden on pain of death to leave the school grounds except at lunch, so three thousand people tried to get in every day between 11:30 and 12:30.

One noon the place was packed. There was the usual riot going on over at UT ten blocks away. All morning you could hear sirens and dull *whoomps* as the increasingly senile police commissioner, who had been in office for thirty-four years, tried dealing with the increasingly complex late twentieth century. *Why, the children have gone mad* he once said in a TV interview.

Anyway, we were all stuffing our faces in the Grindstone when this guy comes running in the front door and out the back at two hundred miles an hour. Somebody made the obvious stoned joke—"Man, I thought he'd *never* leave!"—and then a patrol car slammed up to the curb, and a cop jumped out. You could see his mind work.

A. Rioter runs into the Grindstone. B. Grindstone is full of people. Therefore: C. Grindstone is full of rioters.

He opened the door, fired a tear-gas grenade right at the lunch counter, turned, got in his car and drove away.

People were barfing and gagging all over the place. There were screams, tears, rage. The Grindstone was closed for a week so they could rent some industrial fans and air it out. The city refused to pick up the tab. "The officer was in hot pursuit," said the police commissioner, "and acted within the confines of departmental guidelines." Case closed.

"Ah, the Grindstone," I said to the tour group. "What a *nice* place." A wave of nostalgia swept over me. "Today, shakes and fries. Tomorrow, a lube job and tune-up."

I was so filled with *mono no aware* that I skipped the picnic that afternoon.

The Wolfskill Hotel! Scene of a thousand-and-one nights' entertainments and more senior proms than there are fire ants in all the fields in Texas.

A friend of mine named Karen once said people were divided into two classes: those who went to their senior proms and went on to live fairly normal lives, and those who didn't, who became perverts, mass murderers or romance novelists.

If you were a guy you got maybe your first blow job after the prom, or if a girl a quick boff in the back seat of some immemorial Dodge convertible out at Lake Travis. The hotel meant excitement, adventure, magic.

I hadn't gone to my senior prom. A lot of us hadn't, looking on it as one more corrupt way to suck money from the working classes so that orchids could die all over the vast American night.

There were some street singers outside the hotel, playing jug band music without a jug—two guitars, a flute, tambourine and harmonica. They were fairly quiet. The cops wouldn't hassle them until after eleven P.M. They were pretty good. I dropped a quarter into their cigar box.

You could hear the strains of the Byrds' "Turn! Turn! Turn!" before you got through the lobby. The entertainment committee must have dropped a ton o' bucks on this—they had a bulletin board out front just past the registration table with everybody's pictures from the yearbook blown up, six to a sheet.

It was weird seeing all those people's names and faces—the beginnings of mustaches and beards on the guys, we'd fought tooth and nail for facial hair—long straight hair on the women—names that hadn't been used, or gone back to three or four times, in the last twenty years.

I paid my $10.00 fee (like in the old days. Dance Tonight! Guys fifty cents Girls Free!).

Inside the ballroom people were already dancing, maybe a hundred, with that many more standing around talking and laughing in knots and clumps, being polite to each other, sizing up what Time's Heedless Claws had done to each other's bodies and outlooks.

Bob and Penny were already there. He was in a bluejean jacket and pants and wore a clear plastic tie. Penny was stunning, in a green velour thing, beautiful as she always is early in the evenings, before alcohol turns her into a person I don't know.

I was real spiffed out, for me: a nice sport coat, black slacks, a red silk tie with painted roses wide as the racing stripe on a Corvette.

There were people there in $500 gowns, $300 suits, tuxes, jeans, coveralls. Several were in period costumes; Hoyt had on another, much better than this morning's nightmare, but still what I describe as Early Neil Young. He was, of course, with a slim blonde who had once been a Houston cheerleader, I'm sure.

I saw some faculty members there. They had all been invited, of course. Ten or so, with their husbands or wives, had come. Even Mr. Stoat was there. It hit me as I looked at them that most of them had been in their twenties and thirties when they were trying to deal with us on a daily basis, much younger than we were now. God, what a thankless job they must have had—going off every day like going back up to the Front in WWI, trying to teach kids who viewed you as The Enemy, following along behind everything you did with the efficient erasers in their minds! Maybe I'm getting too mellow—they had it easier with us than teachers do now—at least most of us *could* read, and music was more important than TV to us. Later, I told myself, I'll go over and talk to Ms. Nugent who was always my favorite and who had been a good teacher in spite of the chaos around her.

There were two guys working the tapes and CDs up on the raised stage. I didn't recognize the order of the songs so knew they weren't playing one of my tapes. On the front part of the stage were a guitar and bass, a drum set and keyboards.

So it was true, and seemed the main topic of conversation, although as I passed one bunch of people I heard someone say "Those assholes? Them?"

Barb showed up, without a date, of course. She took my hand and led me toward the dance floor. "Let's dance until our shoulders bleed," she said.

"Yes, ma'am!" I said.

I don't know about you, but I've been hypnotized on dance floors before. Sometimes it seems as if the tune stretches out to accommodate how long and hard you want to dance, or think you can. The guys working the decks were switching back and forth between two cassette players and the music never stopped—occasionally songs *only* I could have recorded showed up. I didn't care. I was dancing.

(I've seen some strange things on dance floors in my life—the strangest was people forming a conga line to a song by the band Reptilikus called "After Today, You Got One Less Day To Live.")

"Ginny's here," I said to Barb. Barb looked over toward the door where Ginny Balducci's wheelchair had rolled in. One weekend in 1973 Ginny had gone off for a ski weekend with an intern, and had come back out of the hospital six months later with a whole different life. "I'll say hi in a minute," said Barb.

We danced to the only Dylan song you can dance to, "I Want You," "Back in the U.S.S.R.," Buffalo Springfield, Blue Cheer, Sam and Dave, slow tunes by Jackie Wilson and Sam Cooke, then Barb went over to talk to Ginny. I was a sweating wreck by then, and the ugly feeling from the night before was all gone.

I started for the *whizzoir*.

"You won't like it," said a guy coming out of the men's room.

The smell hit me like a hammer. Someone had yelled New York into one of the five washbasins. It was half full. It appeared the person had lived exclusively for the last week on Dinty Moore Beef Stew and Fighting Cock Bourbon.

A janitor came in cursing as I was washing my hands.

I went back out to the ballroom. Mouse and the Trapps "Public Execution" was playing—someone who doesn't *dance* recorded that. Then came Jackie Wilson's "Higher and Higher."

"Dance with me?" asked someone behind me. I turned. It was Sharon. She must have Gone Borneo that afternoon. She'd been somewhere where they do things to you, wonderful things. She had on a blue dress and seamed silk stockings, and now she had an Aunt Peg haircut.

"You bet your ass!" I said.

DO YA, DO YA, WANNA DANCE?

About halfway through the next dance, I suffered a real sense of loss. I missed my butthole-length hair for the first time in ten years. The song, of course, was "Hair" off the original Broadway cast recording, Diane Keaton and all, and Joe Morton's wife Patricia, who had never cut hers, it grew within inches of the floor, suddenly grabbed it near her skull with one hand and whipped it around and around her head, the ends fanning out like a giant hand across the colored lights above the stage. Joe continued his Avalon-ballroom-no-sweat dancing, oblivious to the applause his wife was getting.

Then they played the Fish Cheer and we all sang and danced along with "I-Feel-Like-I'm-Fixin'-to-Die-Rag."

Then the lights came up and the entertainment director, Jamie Younts-Fulton, came to the mike and treated us to twenty minutes of nostalgic boredom and forced yoks. The tension was building.

"Now," she said, "for those of you who don't know, we've got them together again for the first time in nineteen years, here they are, Craig Beausoliel, Morey Morkheim, Abram Cassuth, and Andru Esposito, or, as you know them, *Distressed Flag Sale!*"

It was about what you'd expect—four guys in their late thirties in various pieces of clothing stretching across twenty years of fashion changes.

Morey'd put on weight and lost teeth, Andru had taken weight off. Abram, who'd been the only one without facial hair in our day, now had a full Jerry Garcia beard. Craig, who came out last, like always, and plugged in while we applauded—all four or five hundred people in the ballroom now—didn't look like the same guy at all. He looked like a businessman dressed up at Halloween to look like a rock singer.

He was a little unsteady on his feet. He was a little drunk.

"Enough of this Sixties crap!" he said. People applauded again. "Tonight, this first and last performance, we're calling ourselves *Lizard Level!*"

Then Abram hit the keyboard in the opening trill of "In-a-Gadda-da-Vida" for emphasis, then they slammed into "Proud

Mary," Creedence's version, and the place became a blur of flying bodies, drumming feet, swirling clothes. The band started a little raggedy, then got it slowly together.

They launched into the Chambers Bros.' "Time Has Come Today," always a show stopper, a hard song for everybody *including* the Chambers Bros., if you ever saw them, and the place went really crazy, especially in the slow-motion parts. Then they did one of their own tunes, "The Moon's Your Harsh Mistress, Buddy, Not Mine," which I'd heard exactly once in two decades.

We were dancing, all kinds, pogo, no-sweat, skank, it didn't matter. I saw a few of the hotel staff standing in the doorways tapping their feet. Andru hit that screaming wail in the bass that was the band's trademark, sort of like a whale dying in your bathtub. People yelled, shook their arms over their heads.

Then they started to do "Soul Kitchen." Halfway through the opening, Craig raised his hand, shook it, stopped them.

"Awwwww," we said, like when a film breaks in a theater.

Craig leaned toward the others. He was shaking his head. Morey pointed down at his playlist. They put their heads together. Craig and Abram were giving the other two chord changes or something.

"Hey! Make music!" yelled some jerk from the doorway.

Craig looked up, grabbed the mike. "Hold it right there, asshole," he said, becoming the Craig we had known twenty years ago for a second. He leaned against the mike stand in a Jim Morrison vamp pose. "You stay right here, you're going to hear the god-damnedest music you ever heard!"

They talked together for a minute more. Andru shrugged his shoulders, looked worried. Then they all nodded their heads.

Craig Beausoliel came back up front. "What we're gonna do now, what we're gonna do now, gonna do," he said in a Van Morrison post-Them chant, "is we're gonna do, gonna do, the song we were gonna do that night in Miami . . ."

"Oh, geez," said Bob, who was on the dance floor near Sharon and me.

Distressed Flag Sale had gone into seclusion early in 1970, holing up like The Band did in the *Basement Tapes* days with Dylan, or like Brian Wilson and the Beach Boys while they were working on the never-finished *Smile* album. They were supposedly working on an album (we heard through the grapevine) called either *New Music for the After People* or *A Song to Change the World*, and there were supposedly heavy scenes there, lots of drugs, paranoia, jealousy, and revenge, but also great music. We never knew, because they came out of hiding to do the Miami concert to raise money for the family of a janitor blown up by mistake when somebody drove a car-bomb into an AFEES building one four A.M.

"It was a great song, man, a great song," said Craig, "It was going to change the world we thought." We realized for the first time how drunk Craig really was about then. "We were gonna play it that night, and the world was gonna change, but instead they got us, they *got us*, man, and we were the ones that got changed, not them. Tonight we're not Distressed Flag Sale, we're Lizard Level, and just once anyway, so you'll all know, tonight we're gonna do 'Life Is Like That'."

(What changed in Miami was the next five years of their lives. The Miami cops had been holding the crowd back for three hours and looking for an excuse, anyway, and they got it, just after Distressed Flag Sale made its reeling way onstage. The crowd was already frenzied, and got up to dance when the guys started playing "Life Is Like That" and Andru took out his dong on the opening notes and started playing slide bass with it. The cops went crazy and jumped them, beat them up, planted heroin and amphetamines in their luggage in the dressing rooms, carted them off to jail and turned firehoses on the rioting fans.

Everybody knew the bust was rigged, because they charged Morey with possession of heroin, and everybody *knew* he was the speed freak.

And that was the end of Distressed Flag Sale.

It was almost literally the end of Andru, too. What the papers didn't tell you was that, as he was uncircumcised, he'd torn his frenum on the strings of the bass, and he almost lost, first, his dong, and then his life before the cops let a doctor in to see him.)

That's the history of the song we were going to hear.

Notes started from the keyboard, like it was going to be another Doors-type song, building. Then Craig moved his fingers a few times on the guitar strings, tinkling things rang up high, like birds were in the air over the stage, sort of like the opening of "Touch of Grey" by the Dead, but not like that either. Then Andru came in, and Morey, then it began to take on a shape and move on its own, like nothing else at all.

It moved. And it moved me, too. First I was swaying, then stomping my right foot. Sharon was pulling me toward the dance floor. I'd never heard anything like it. *This* was dance music. Sharon moved in large sways and swings; so did I.

The floor filled up fast. *Everybody* moved toward the music. Out of the corner of my eye I saw old Mr. Stoat asking someone to dance. Other teachers moved towards the sound.

Then I was too busy moving to notice much of anything. I was dancing, dancing not with myself but with Sharon, with Bob and Penny, with *everyone*.

All five hundred people danced. Ginny Balducci was at the corner of the floor, making her chair move in small tight graceful circles. I smiled. We all smiled.

The music got louder; not faster, but more insistent. The playing was superb, immaculate. *Lizard Level's* hands moved like they were a bar band that had been playing together every night for twenty years. They seemed oblivious to everything, too, eyes closed, feet shuffling.

Something was happening on the floor, people were moving in little groups and circles, couples breaking off and shimmying down between the lines of the others, in little waggling dance steps. It was happening all over the place. Then *I* was doing it—like Sharon and I had choreographed every move. People were clapping their hands in time to the music. It sounded like steamrollers were being thrown around in the ballroom.

Above it the music kept building and building in an impossible spiral.

Now the hotel staff joined in, busboys clapping hands, maids and waitresses turning in circles.

Then the pattern of the dance changed, magically, instantly, it split the room right down the middle, and we were in two long interlocking linked chains of people, crossing through each other, one line moving up the room, the other down it, like it was choreographed.

And the guys kept playing, and more people were coming into the ballroom. People in pajamas or naked from their rooms, the night manager and the bellboys. And as they joined in and the lines got more unwieldy, the two lines of people broke into four, and we began to move toward the doors of the ballroom, clapping our hands, stomping, dancing, making our own music, the same music, more people and more people.

At some point they walked away from the stage, joining us, left their amps, acoustic now. Morey had a single drum and was beating it, you could hear Andru and Craig on bass and guitar, Cassuth was still playing the keyboard on the batteries, his speaker held under one arm.

The street musicians had come into the hotel and joined in, people were picking up trash cans from the lobby, garbage cans from the streets, honking the horns of their stopped cars in time to the beat of the music.

We were on the streets now. Windows in buildings opened, people climbed down from second stories to join in. The whole city jumped in time to the song, like in an old Fleischer cartoon; Betty Boop, Koko, Bimbo, the buses, the buildings, the moon all swaying, the stars spinning on their centers like pinwheels.

Chains of bodies formed on every street, each block. At a certain beat they all broke and reformed into smaller ones that grew larger, interlocking helical ropes of dancers.

I was happy, happier than ever. We moved down one jumping chain of people. I saw mammoths, saber-toothed tigers, dinosaurs, salamanders, fish, insects, jellies in loops and swirls. Then came the beat and we were in the other chain, moving up the street, lost in the music, up the line of dancing people, beautiful fields, comets, nebulae, rockets and galaxies of calm light.

I smiled into Sharon's face, she smiled into mine.

Louder now the music, stronger, pulling at us like a wind. The cops joined in the dance.

Up Congress Avenue the legislators and government workers in special session came streaming out of their building like beautiful ants from a shining mound.

Louder now and happier, stronger, dancing, clapping, singing.

We will find our children or they will find us, before the dance is over, we can feel it. Or afterwards we will responsibly make more.

The chain broke again, and up the jumping streets we go, joyous now, joy all over the place, twenty, thirty thousand people, more every second.

As we swirled and grew, we would sometimes pass someone who was staring, not dancing, feet not moving; they would be crying in uncontrollable sobs and shakes, and occasionally committing suicide.

BEARS DISCOVER FIRE

Terry Bisson

"Bears Discover Fire" was purchased by Gardner Dozois, and appeared in the August 1990 issue of Asimov's, *with an illustration by Laurie Harden. It was the first of several sales that Bisson has made to* Asimov's, *and would prove to be one of the most popular stories ever published by the magazine, going on to win the Hugo Award, the Nebula Award, the Theodore Sturgeon Award, the Locus Award, and our own Readers' Award that year, an unprecedented feat. A relatively new writer, Terry Bisson is the author of a number of critically acclaimed novels such as* Fire on the Mountain, Wyrldmaker, *and the popular* Talking Man, *which was a finalist for the World Fantasy Award in 1986. His most recent book is the novel* Voyage to the Red Planet, *released in 1990. He lives in New York City.*

Here he offers us a gentle, wry, whimsical, and funny story—reminiscent to us of the best of early Lafferty—that's about exactly what it says it's about....

I was driving with my brother, the preacher, and my nephew, the preacher's son, on I-65 just north of Bowling Green when we got a flat. It was Sunday night and we had been to visit Mother at the Home. We were in my car. The flat caused what you might call knowing groans since, as the old-fashioned one in my family (so they tell me), I fix my own tires, and my brother is always telling me to get radials and quit buying old tires.

But if you know how to mount and fix tires yourself, you can pick them up for almost nothing.

Since it was a left rear tire, I pulled over left, onto the median grass. The way my Caddy stumbled to a stop, I figured the tire was ruined. "I guess there's no need asking if you have any of that *FlatFix* in the trunk," said Wallace.

"Here, son, hold the light," I said to Wallace Jr. He's old enough to want to help and not old enough (yet) to think he knows it all. If I'd married and had kids, he's the kind I'd have wanted.

An old Caddy has a big trunk that tends to fill up like a shed. Mine's a '56. Wallace was wearing his Sunday shirt, so he didn't offer to help while I pulled magazines, fishing tackle, a wooden tool box, some old clothes, a comealong wrapped in a grass sack, and a tobacco sprayer out of the way, looking for my jack. The spare looked a little soft.

The light went out. "Shake it, son," I said.

It went back on. The bumper jack was long gone, but I carry a little ¼ ton hydraulic. I finally found it under Mother's old *Southern Livings*, 1978–1986. I had been meaning to drop them at the dump. If Wallace hadn't been along, I'd have let Wallace Jr. position the jack under the axle, but I got on my knees and did it myself. There's nothing wrong with a boy learning to change a tire. Even if you're not going to fix and mount them, you're still going to have to change a few in this life. The light went off again before I had the wheel off the ground. I was surprised at how dark the night was already. It was late October and beginning to get cool. "Shake it again, son," I said.

It went back on but it was weak. Flickery.

"With radials you just don't *have* flats," Wallace explained in that voice he uses when he's talking to a number of people at once; in this case, Wallace Jr. and myself. "And even when you *do*, you just squirt them with this stuff called *FlatFix* and you just drive on. $3.95 the can."

"Uncle Bobby can fix a tire hisself," said Wallace Jr., out of loyalty I presume.

"*Him*self," I said from halfway under the car. If it was up to

Wallace, the boy would talk like what Mother used to call "a helock from the gorges of the mountains." But drive on radials.

"Shake that light again," I said. It was about gone. I spun the lugs off into the hubcap and pulled the wheel. The tire had blown out along the sidewall. "Won't be fixing this one," I said. Not that I cared. I have a pile as tall as a man out by the barn.

The light went out again, then came back better than ever as I was fitting the spare over the lugs. "Much better," I said. There was a flood of dim orange flickery light. But when I turned to find the lug nuts, I was surprised to see that the flashlight the boy was holding was dead. The light was coming from two bears at the edge of the trees, holding torches. They were big, three-hundred pounders, standing about five feet tall. Wallace Jr. and his father had seen them and were standing perfectly still. It's best not to alarm bears.

I fished the lug nuts out of the hubcap and spun them on. I usually like to put a little oil on them, but this time I let it go. I reached under the car and let the jack down and pulled it out. I was relieved to see that the spare was high enough to drive on. I put the jack and the lug wrench and the flat into the trunk. Instead of replacing the hubcap, I put it in there too. All this time, the bears never made a move. They just held the torches up, whether out of curiosity or helpfulness, there was no way of knowing. It looked like there may have been more bears behind them, in the trees.

Opening three doors at once, we got into the car and drove off. Wallace was the first to speak. "Looks like bears have discovered fire," he said.

When we first took Mother to the Home, almost four years (forty-seven months) ago, she told Wallace and me she was ready to die. "Don't worry about me, boys," she whispered, pulling us both down so the nurse wouldn't hear. "I've drove a million miles and I'm ready to pass over to the other shore. I won't have long to linger here." She drove a consolidated school bus for thirty-nine years. Later, after Wallace left, she told me about her dream. A bunch of doctors were sitting around in a circle discussing her case. One said, "We've done all we can for her, boys, let's let her go." They all turned their hands up and smiled. When she didn't die that fall, she seemed disappointed, though as spring came she forgot about it, as old people will.

In addition to taking Wallace and Wallace Jr. to see Mother on Sunday nights, I go myself on Tuesdays and Thursdays. I usually find her sitting in front of the TV, even though she doesn't watch it. The nurses keep it on all the time. They say the old folks like the flickering. It soothes them down.

"What's this I hear about bears discovering fire?" she said on Tuesday. "It's true," I told her as I combed her long white hair with the shell comb Wallace had brought her from Florida. Monday there had been a story in the Louisville *Courier-Journal*, and Tuesday one on NBC or CBS Nightly News. People were seeing bears all over the state, and in Virginia as well. They had quit hibernating, and were apparently planning to spend the winter in the medians of the interstates. There have always been bears in the mountains of Virginia, but not here in western Kentucky, not for almost a hundred years. The last one was killed when Mother was a girl. The theory in the *Courier-Journal* was that they were following I-65 down from the forests of Michigan and Canada, but one old man from Allen County (interviewed on nationwide TV) said that there had always been a few bears left back in the hills, and they had come out to join the others now that they had discovered fire.

"They don't hibernate any more," I said. "They make a fire and keep it going all winter."

"I declare," Mother said. "What'll they think of next!" The nurse came to take her tobacco away, which is the signal for bedtime.

Every October, Wallace Jr. stays with me while his parents go to camp. I realize how backward that sounds, but there it is. My brother is a minister (House of the Righteous Way, Reformed), but he makes two thirds of his living in real estate. He and Elizabeth go to a Christian Success Retreat in South Carolina, where people from all over the country practice selling things to one another. I know what it's like not because they've ever bothered to tell me, but because I've seen the Revolving Equity Success Plan ads late at night on TV.

The schoolbus let Wallace Jr. off at my house on Wednesday, the day they left. The boy doesn't have to pack much of a bag when he stays with me. He has his own room here. As the eldest of our family, I hung onto the old home place near Smiths Grove. It's getting run down, but Wallace Jr. and I don't mind. He has his own room in Bowling Green, too, but since Wallace and Elizabeth move to a different house every three months (part of the Plan), he keeps his .22 and his comics, the stuff that's important to a boy his age, in his room here at the home place. It's the room his dad and I used to share.

Wallace Jr. is twelve. I found him sitting on the back porch that overlooks the interstate when I got home from work. I sell crop insurance.

After I changed clothes, I showed him how to break the bead on a tire two ways, with a hammer and by backing a car over it. Like making sorghum, fixing tires by hand is a dying art. The boy caught on fast, though. "Tomorrow I'll show you how to mount your tire with the hammer and a tire iron," I said.

"What I wish is I could see the bears," he said. He was looking across the field to I-65, where the northbound lanes cut off the corner of our field. From the house at night, sometimes the traffic sounds like a waterfall.

"Can't see their fire in the daytime," I said. "But wait till tonight." That night CBS or NBC (I forget which is which) did a special on the bears, which were becoming a story of nationwide interest. They were seen in Kentucky, West Virginia, Missouri, Illinois (southern), and, of course, Virginia. There have always been bears in Virginia. Some characters there were even talking about hunting them. A scientist said they were heading into the states where there is some snow but not too much, and where there is enough timber in the medians for firewood. He had gone in with a video camera, but his shots were just blurry figures sitting around a fire. Another scientist said the bears were attracted by the berries on a new bush that grew only in the medians of the interstates. He claimed this berry was the first new species in recent history, brought about by the mixing of seeds along the highway. He ate one on TV, making a face, and called it a "newberry." A climatic ecologist said that the warm winters (there was no snow last winter in Nashville, and only one flurry in Louisville) had changed the bears' hibernation cycle, and now they were able to remember things from year to year. "Bears may have discovered fire centuries ago," he said, "but forgot it." Another theory was that they had discovered (or remembered) fire when Yellowstone burned, several years ago.

The TV showed more guys talking about bears than it showed bears, and Wallace Jr. and I lost interest. After the supper dishes were done I took the boy out behind the house and down to our fence. Across the interstate and through the trees, we could see the light of the bears' fire. Wallace Jr. wanted to go back to the house and get his .22 and go shoot one, and I explained why that would be wrong. "Besides," I said, "a .22 wouldn't do much more to a bear than make it mad."

"Besides," I added, "It's illegal to hunt in the medians."

The only trick to mounting a tire by hand, once you have beaten or pried it onto the rim, is setting the bead. You do this by setting the tire upright, sitting on it, and bouncing it up and down between your legs while the air goes in. When the bead sets on the rim, it makes a satisfying "pop." On Thursday, I kept Wallace Jr. home from school and showed him how to do this until he got it right. Then we climbed our fence and crossed the field to get a look at the bears.

In northern Virginia, according to "Good Morning America," the bears were keeping their fires going all day long. Here in western Kentucky, though, it was still warm for late October and they only stayed around the fires at night. Where they went and what they did in the daytime, I don't know. Maybe they were watching from the newberry bushes as Wallace Jr. and I climbed the government fence and crossed the northbound lanes. I carried an axe and Wallace Jr. brought his .22, not because he wanted to kill a bear but because a boy likes to carry some kind of a gun. The median was all tangled with brush and vines under the maples, oaks, and sycamores. Even though we were only a hundred yards from the house, I had never been there, and neither had anyone else that I knew of. It was like a created country. We found a path in the center and followed it down across a slow, short stream that flowed out of one grate and into another. The tracks in the gray mud were the first bear signs we saw. There was a musty but not really unpleasant smell. In a clearing under a big hollow beech, where the fire had been, we found nothing but ashes. Logs were drawn up in a rough circle and the smell was stronger. I stirred the ashes and found enough coals left to start a new flame, so I banked them back the way they had been left.

I cut a little firewood and stacked it to one side, just to be neighborly.

Maybe the bears were watching us from the bushes even then. There's no way to know. I tasted one of the newberries and spit it out. It was so sweet it was sour, just the sort of thing you would imagine a bear would like.

That evening after supper, I asked Wallace Jr. if he might want to go with me to visit Mother. I wasn't surprised when he said "yes." Kids have more consideration than folks give them credit for. We found her sitting on the concrete front porch of the Home, watching the cars go by on I-65. The nurse said she had been agitated all day. I wasn't surprised by that, either. Every fall as the leaves change, she gets restless, maybe the word is hopeful, again. I brought her into the dayroom and combed her long white hair. "Nothing but bears on TV anymore," the nurse complained, flipping the channels. Wallace Jr. picked up the remote after the nurse left, and we watched a CBS or NBC Special Report about some hunters in Virginia who had gotten their houses torched. The TV interviewed a hunter and his wife whose $117,500 Shenandoah Valley home had burned. She blamed the bears. He didn't blame the bears, but he was suing for compensation from the state since he had a valid hunting license. The state hunting commissioner came on and said that possession of a hunting license didn't prohibit (enjoin,

I think, was the word he used) *the hunted* from striking back. I thought that was a pretty liberal view for a state commissioner. Of course, he had a vested interest in not paying off. I'm not a hunter myself.

"Don't bother coming on Sunday," Mother told Wallace Jr. with a wink. "I've drove a million miles and I've got one hand on the gate." I'm used to her saying stuff like that, especially in the fall, but I was afraid it would upset the boy. In fact, he looked worried after we left and I asked him what was wrong.

"How could she have drove a million miles?" he asked. She had told him 48 miles a day for 39 years, and he had worked it out on his calculator to be 336,960 miles.

"Have *driven*," I said. "And it's forty-eight in the morning and forty-eight in the afternoon. Plus there were the football trips. Plus, old folks exaggerate a little." Mother was the first woman school bus driver in the state. She did it every day and raised a family, too. Dad just farmed.

I usually get off the interstate at Smiths Grove, but that night I drove north all the way to Horse Cave and doubled back so Wallace Jr. and I could see the bears' fires. There were not as many as you would think from the TV—one every six or seven miles, hidden back in a clump of trees or under a rocky ledge. Probably they look for water as well as wood. Wallace Jr. wanted to stop, but it's against the law to stop on the interstate and I was afraid the state police would run us off.

There was a card from Wallace in the mailbox. He and Elizabeth were doing fine and having a wonderful time. Not a word about Wallace Jr., but the boy didn't seem to mind. Like most kids his age, he doesn't really enjoy going places with his parents.

On Saturday afternoon, the Home called my office (Burley Belt Drought & Hail) and left word that Mother was gone. I was on the road. I work Saturdays. It's the only day a lot of part-time farmers are home. My heart literally skipped a beat when I called in and got the message, but only a beat. I had long been prepared. "It's a blessing," I said when I got the nurse on the phone.

"You don't understand," the nurse said. "Not *passed* away, gone. *Ran* away, gone. Your mother has escaped." Mother had gone through the door at the end of the corridor when no one was looking, wedging the door with her comb and taking a bedspread which belonged to the Home. What about her tobacco? I asked. It was gone. That was a sure sign she was planning to stay away. I was in Franklin, and it took me less than an hour to get to the Home on I-65. The nurse told me that Mother had been acting more and more confused lately. Of course they are going to say that. We looked around the grounds, which is only an acre with no trees between the interstate and a soybean field. Then they had me leave a message at the Sheriff's office. I would have to keep paying for her care until she was officially listed as Missing, which would be Monday.

It was dark by the time I got back to the house, and Wallace Jr. was fixing supper. This just involves opening a few cans, already selected and grouped together with a rubber band. I told him his grandmother had gone, and he nodded, saying, "She told us she would be." I called Florida and left a message. There was nothing more to be done. I sat down and tried to watch TV, but there was nothing on. Then, I looked out the back door, and saw the firelight twinkling through the trees across the northbound lane of I-65, and realized I just might know where she had gone to find her.

It was definitely getting colder, so I got my jacket. I told the boy to wait by the phone in case the Sheriff called, but when I looked back, halfway across the field, there he was behind me. He didn't have a jacket. I let him catch up. He was carrying his .22, and I made him leave it leaning against our fence. It was harder climbing the government fence in the dark, at my age, than it had been in the daylight. I am sixty-one. The highway was busy with cars heading south and trucks heading north.

Crossing the shoulder, I got my pants cuffs wet on the long grass, already wet with dew. It is actually bluegrass.

The first few feet into the trees it was pitch black and the boy grabbed my hand. Then it got lighter. At first I thought it was the moon, but it was the high beams shining like moonlight into the treetops, allowing Wallace Jr. and me to pick our way through the brush. We soon found the path and its familiar bear smell.

I was wary of approaching the bears at night. If we stayed on the path we might run into one in the dark, but if we went through the bushes we might be seen as intruders. I wondered if maybe we shouldn't have brought the gun.

We stayed on the path. The light seemed to drip down from the canopy of the woods like rain. The going was easy, especially if we didn't try to look at the path but let our feet find their own way.

Then through the trees I saw their fire.

The fire was mostly of sycamore and beech branches, the kind of fire that puts out very little heat or light and lots of smoke. The bears hadn't earned the ins and outs of wood yet. They did okay at tending it, though. A large cinnamon brown northern-looking bear was poking the fire with a stick, adding a branch now and then from a pile at his side. The others sat around in a loose circle on the logs. Most were smaller black or honey bears, one was a mother with cubs. Some were eating berries from a hubcap. Not eating, but just watching the fire, my mother sat among them with the bedspread from the Home around her shoulders.

If the bears noticed us, they didn't let on. Mother patted a spot right next to her on the log and I sat down. A bear moved over to let Wallace Jr. sit on her other side.

The bear smell is rank but not unpleasant, once you get used to it. It's not like a barn smell, but wilder. I leaned over to whisper something to Mother and she shook her head. *It would be rude to whisper around these creatures that don't possess the power of speech,* she let me know without speaking. Wallace Jr. was silent too. Mother shared the bedspread with us and we sat for what seemed hours, looking into the fire.

The big bear tended the fire, breaking up the dry branches by holding one end and stepping on them, like people do. He was good at keeping it going at the same level. Another bear poked the fire from time to time, but the others left it alone. It looked like only a few of the bears knew how to use fire, and were carrying the others along. But isn't that how it is with everything? Every once in a while, a smaller bear walked into the circle of firelight with an armload of wood and dropped it onto the pile. Median wood has a silvery cast, like driftwood.

Wallace Jr. isn't fidgety like a lot of kids. I found it pleasant to sit and stare into the fire. I took a little piece of Mother's *Red Man,* though I don't generally chew. It was no different from visiting her at the Home, only more interesting, because of the bears. There were about eight or ten of them. Inside the fire itself, things weren't so dull, either: little dramas were being played out as fiery chambers were created and then destroyed in a crashing of sparks. My imagination ran wild. I looked around the circle at the bears and wondered what *they* saw. Some had their eyes closed. Though they were gathered together, their spirits still seemed solitary, as if each bear was sitting alone in front of its own fire.

The hubcap came around and we all took some newberries. I don't know about Mother, but I just pretended to eat mine. Wallace Jr. made a face and spit his out. When he went to sleep, I wrapped the bedspread around all three of us. It was getting colder and we were not provided, like the bears, with fur. I was ready to go home, but not Mother. She pointed up toward the canopy of trees, where a light was spreading, and then pointed to herself. Did she think it was angels approaching from on high? It was only the high beams of some southbound truck, but she seemed mighty pleased. Holding her hand, I felt it grow colder and colder in mine.

Wallace Jr. woke me up by tapping on my knee. It was past dawn, and his grandmother had died sitting on the log between us. The fire was banked up and the bears were gone and someone was crashing straight through the woods, ignoring the path. It was Wallace. Two state troopers were right behind him. He was wearing a white shirt, and I realized it was Sunday morning. Underneath his sadness on learning of Mother's death, he looked peeved.

The troopers were sniffing the air and nodding. The bear smell was still strong. Wallace and I wrapped Mother in the bedspread and started with her body back out to the highway. The troopers stayed behind and scattered the bears' fire ashes and flung their firewood away into the bushes. It seemed a petty thing to do. They were like bears themselves, each one solitary in his own uniform.

There was Wallace's Olds 98 on the median, with its radial tires looking squashed on the grass. In front of it there was a police car with a trooper standing beside it, and behind it a funeral home hearse, also an Olds 98.

"First report we've had of them bothering old folks," the trooper said to Wallace. "That's not hardly what happened at all," I said, but nobody asked me to explain. They have their own procedures. Two men in suits got out of the hearse and opened the rear door. That to me was the point at which Mother departed this life. After we put her in, I put my arms around the boy. He was shivering even though it wasn't that cold. Sometimes death will do that, especially at dawn, with the police around and the grass wet, even when it comes as a friend.

We stood for a minute watching the cars pass. "It's a blessing," Wallace said. It's surprising how much traffic there is at 6:22 A.M.

That afternoon, I went back to the median and cut a little firewood to replace what the troopers had flung away. I could see the fire through the trees that night.

I went back two nights later, after the funeral. The fire was going and it was the same bunch of bears, as far as I could tell. I sat around with them a while but it seemed to make them nervous, so I went home. I had taken a handful of newberries from the hubcap, and on Sunday I went with the boy and arranged them on Mother's grave. I tried again, but it's no use, you can't eat them.

Unless you're a bear.

TWO EXCITING SERIES!
ISAAC ASIMOV'S
ROBOT CITY™

Integrating Asimov's new "Laws of Humanics" with his "Laws of Robotics," here is the dazzling world created by the grand master of robotic fiction—brought vividly to life by science fiction's finest writers!

ROBOTS AND ALIENS

Adventures covering a universe inhabited not just by robots, but by robots and aliens!

___ROBOTS AND ALIENS 1: CHANGELING Stephen Leigh
0-441-73127-9/$3.95
___ROBOTS AND ALIENS 2: RENEGADE Cordell Scotten
0-441-73128-7/$3.50

ROBOT CITY

...filled with mystery, laden with traps and marvelous adventure.

___BOOK 1: ODYSSEY Michael P. Kube-McDowell 0-441-73122-8/$3.50
___BOOK 2: SUSPICION Mike McQuay 0-441-73126-0/$3.50
___BOOK 3: CYBORG William F. Wu 0-441-37383-6/$3.95
___BOOK 4: PRODIGY Arthur Byron Cover 0-441-37384-4/$3.50
___BOOK 5: REFUGE Rob Chilson 0-441-37385-2/$3.50
___BOOK 6: PERIHELION William F. Wu 0-441-37388-7/$2.95

©Byron Preiss Visual Publications, Inc.

For Visa, MasterCard and American Express ($15 minimum) orders call: **1-800-631-8571**

FOR MAIL ORDERS: CHECK BOOK(S). FILL OUT COUPON. SEND TO:

BERKLEY PUBLISHING GROUP
390 Murray Hill Pkwy., Dept. B
East Rutherford, NJ 07073

NAME_____
ADDRESS_____
CITY_____
STATE_____ZIP_____

PLEASE ALLOW 6 WEEKS FOR DELIVERY.
PRICES ARE SUBJECT TO CHANGE WITHOUT NOTICE.

POSTAGE AND HANDLING:
$1.75 for one book, 75¢ for each additional. Do not exceed $5.50.

BOOK TOTAL	$ ____
POSTAGE & HANDLING	$ ____
APPLICABLE SALES TAX (CA, NJ, NY, PA)	$ ____
TOTAL AMOUNT DUE	$ ____

PAYABLE IN US FUNDS.
(No cash orders accepted.)

ANALOG Asimov's

YOUR SCIENCE FICTION TRAVELS ARE ONLY BEGINNING.

Enjoy powerful, provocative and penetrating stories by award-winning authors every month. **Asimov's** will keep you on the cutting edge of today's science fiction and fantasy, whereas **Analog** is the forum of the future, from the earliest and continuing visions of computers and cybernetics to our ultimate growth in space.

Subscribe today!!

- ❑ 12 issues of Asimov's for only $20.97
- ❑ 12 issues of Analog for only $20.97
- ❑ Send me both for only $38.97

Send your check or money order to:

Dell Magazines, P.O. Box 7061, Red Oak, IA 51591

Name_____

Address_____

City/St/Zip_____

Outside U.S. & Poss. 12 issues for $27.97. U.S. funds only. Canadian orders include GST. Please allow 6-8 weeks for delivery of first issue. We publish double issues two times per year. These count as two each towards your subscription.

MSCI-0

NEW YORK TIMES BESTSELLING AUTHOR

ANNE McCAFFREY

THE ROWAN

"A reason for rejoicing!" —WASHINGTON TIMES

As a little girl, the Rowan was one of the strongest Talents ever born. When her family's home was suddenly destroyed she was completely alone without family, friends—or love. Her omnipotence could not bring her happiness...but things change when she hears strange telepathic messages from an unknown Talent named Jeff Raven.

__0-441-73576-2/$5.99

DAMIA

Damia is unquestionably the most brilliant of the Rowan's children, with power equaling—if not surpassing—her mother's. As she embarks on her quest, she's stung by a vision of an impending alien invasion—an invasion of such strength that even the Rowan can't prevent it. Now, Damia must somehow use her powers to save a planet under seige.

__0-441-13556-0/$5.99

For Visa, MasterCard and American Express orders ($15 minimum) call: 1-800-631-8571

FOR MAIL ORDERS: CHECK BOOK(S). FILL OUT COUPON. SEND TO:

BERKLEY PUBLISHING GROUP
390 Murray Hill Pkwy., Dept. B
East Rutherford, NJ 07073

NAME_____

ADDRESS_____

CITY_____

STATE_____ ZIP_____

PLEASE ALLOW 6 WEEKS FOR DELIVERY.
PRICES ARE SUBJECT TO CHANGE

POSTAGE AND HANDLING:
$1.75 for one book, 75¢ for each additional. Do not exceed $5.50.

BOOK TOTAL	$ _____
POSTAGE & HANDLING	$ _____
APPLICABLE SALES TAX (CA, NJ, NY, PA)	$ _____
TOTAL AMOUNT DUE	$ _____

PAYABLE IN US FUNDS.
(No cash orders accepted.)

363